DATE			

FIREFLY COVE

Books by Davis Bunn

Miramar Bay

Firefly Cove

FIREFLY COVE

DAVIS BUNN

KENSINGTON BOOKS
http://www.kensingtonbooks.com

KENSINGTON BOOKS are published by

Kensington Publishing Corp.
119 West 40th Street
New York, NY 10018

All Kensington titles, imprints and distributed lines are available at special quantity discounts for bulk purchases for sales promotion, premiums, fund-raising, educational or institutional use.

Special book excerpts or customized printings can also be created to fit specific needs. For details, write or phone the office of the Kensington Special Sales Manager. Attn.: Special Sales Department. Kensington Publishing Corp, 119 West 40th Street, New York, NY 10018. Phone: 1-800-221-2647.

Library of Congress Card Catalogue Number: 2017951324

ISBN-13: 978-1-4967-0832-8
ISBN-10: 1-4967-0832-6
First Kensington Hardcover Edition: January 2018

eISBN-13: 978-1-4967-0834-2
eISBN-10: 1-4967-0834-2
Kensington Electronic Edition: January 2018

10 9 8 7 6 5 4 3 2 1

Printed in the United States of America

This book is dedicated to

Michelle Rapkin

For the guidance, wisdom, challenge,

And friendship most of all.

Acknowledgments

It is a rare gift indeed to enter into a publishing house that offers support and encouragement to a new author. And in many respects I am indeed very new, both to Kensington Books and to the world of romantic fiction. Even so, Kensington's entire staff has gone out of its way to make me feel included and appreciated.

I am so grateful for the amazing editorial guidance offered by Wendy McCurdy. In many houses these days, faced with the intense market pressures and need to do more with fewer hours and hands, that is usually as far as the personal connection ever goes. But Kensington has shown me a different face. The PR and marketing efforts of Vida Engstrand and her most capable team—Lauren Jernigan and Jane Nutter—have been a true delight. Jackie Dinas in sub-rights sales is an unsung hero in my book. The entire sales team has gone out of its way to forge new relationships between the book-buying public and my work. William Bauers has been a true advocate since before I even started writing the first Miramar Bay book. Lynn Cully has remained a calm and strong hand at the tiller throughout the year and a half of my relationship with Kensington. And Steven Zacharius and his son, Adam, are people I hope to one day call close personal friends.

Dr. Robert Wicks is a psychiatrist and professor of counseling at Loyola University. His assistance proved vital in shaping both the hospital scenes and the core issues.

Jeffrey Aresty is a widely respected attorney and CEO of

the Internet Bar Organization. He and his wife Ellen served crucial roles in proofing all the legal elements to this story.

As with every book I have written, my wife's support and wisdom have been essential to bringing this story to life. Thank you so much, Isabella.

FIREFLY COVE

CHAPTER 1

MAY 1, 1969

Most people said Lucius Quarterfield wore a name bigger than he deserved.

As Lucius and his sisters were passed from aunt to grandparent to cousins, family members had often said it to his face. In the forties and fifties, California's central coast was a vibrant farming region with an aggressive go-ahead attitude. Strong men tilled the earth and raised robust families. Lucius Quarterfield was a nice enough boy, quiet and watchful. But the families who took in Lucius and his sisters knew he would never amount to anything. The bullies gradually grew tired of picking on Lucius. Some even slipped into guardian roles, when it suited them. Mostly, Lucius grew up being ignored. His quiet nature made that all the more possible. He lost himself in books and schoolwork, though he was careful to hide his passions. He was a cautious fellow by nature, with a zeal for numbers.

The one thing that had come easy to Lucius was success. It did not make up for all the misery and loneliness, but it certainly made it easier to bear.

This particular doctor's office had always struck Lucius as a restful place, which was extremely odd, because most of life's problems had centered on doctors. But Nicolo Barbieri was different from those medical staff who assumed an impersonal superiority and lied to young Lucius with their smiles. Nicolo Barbieri's family was among the original Italian immigrant clans who had moved from Tuscany to till the California earth as tenant farmers. A generation later, they had scraped together enough money to buy land of their own, and planted one of the early central coast vineyards. Nico had fought against the tradition-bound family's wishes and studied medicine. Perhaps as a result, Nico Barbieri was a brusque man without a comforting bone in his body. His patients either adored him or found another doctor. "You're dying, Lucius."

"So what else is new." Lucius buttoned his shirt and pushed himself off the doctor's table. He always perspired when being examined, a leftover effect of all the pain doctors had caused him growing up. "I've been dying for twenty-two years."

"Your heart reminds me of a garbage disposal working on a spoon. I should put you in the hospital and run some tests."

"The tests will tell you what we already know."

Barbieri fished a cigarette from his shirt pocket as he slipped behind his desk. "Are you truly so cavalier about death?"

"You've been telling me I'm dying since I was seven years old," Lucius replied. "And don't light that."

"Sorry. Bad habit." Barbieri stuck the unfiltered Camel cigarette back into the pack. "This is different. Are your affairs in order?"

The room suddenly chilled enough to turn his skin clammy. "You've never asked me that before."

"Never felt the need. Are they?"

"Pretty much. I'm negotiating a new deal. Should be finished next week."

"Lucius, you don't need the stress of another deal. Your

heart can't take it. And I know for a fact you don't need the money." Barbieri opened the patient folder and began making notes. The file was almost three inches thick. "Bad ticker, weak bones, half a lung."

I have this, Lucius thought, knotting his tie and pulling it tight. *I have today.*

As though Barbieri could hear his unspoken reply, he said, "You've made the best you could of a thin life. Now go out and enjoy yourself. While you still have time."

Dr. Barbieri's waiting room always appeared half-full. The patients changed, but the setting remained the same. The adults leafed through old copies of *Life* and *Look* and *National Geographic,* while the children played with toys made sticky from hundreds of little hands. Rooms like this had been one of the few constants in Lucius's early life. He used the phone at the nurses' station to call his banker and cancel the day's meeting. The banker was a longtime acquaintance and Lucius was an important client, so he did not complain when Lucius told him to reschedule their appointment with the seller's lawyers. As he hung up the phone, Lucius caught sight of himself in the mirror behind the weight machine. He was five feet eleven inches tall, when he held himself fully erect, which seldom happened. Lucius was underweight and his posture was awful. His cheeks had become sunken during his early bout of pleurisy and never filled back in. The childhood illness had cost him his sense of taste. Smells were vague entities, like words spoken in some foreign tongue. Eating was a troublesome task. His hair was a mousy brown and limp as old noodles. His eyes . . . Lucius turned away. He rarely bothered with his appearance, even when buying clothes.

Lucius Quarterfield was twenty-eight years old.

The nurse asked, "When does the doctor want to see you again?"

"He didn't say."

Her hand hovered over the appointment book. "Are you sure, Lucius?"

"Not a peep. Maybe he thinks I'm all better."

Her smile carried all the false cheeriness of his childhood. "I'm sure that's it."

Lucius drove his brand-new Chevrolet Impala north from San Luis Obispo. He had not been back to Miramar in almost a year, though for a time he had traveled this road every week. He was not a man given to holidays and easy living. Recently his only days off had been when he was unable to rise from his bed. Otherwise his every waking hour was spent making money. When the doctor said he should take some time off and enjoy himself, this journey was the only thing that came to mind.

Lucius had never much cared for his name, which to him sounded like it was made for a guy with one lung, bad bones, and a poor heart. He had always preferred Luke. He considered Luke to be a hard name, full of the go-ahead spirit that burned with volcanic fury inside him. Three days after his sixteenth birthday, Lucius Quarterfield had taken his meager inheritance, borrowed everything his two older sisters were willing to loan him, and bought a vacant lot a block off Santa Barbara's Fifth Street. Even then his sisters recognized their brother had something most people lacked, a fire his ravaged and weakened body could scarcely contain. Lucius had strung plastic multicolored flags and buntings from the trees, paid a builder to clear the earth and lay down gravel, erected a moth-eaten army surplus tent, and put nine road-weary used cars up for sale. In the twelve years since then, Lucius had built an empire that contained eleven dealerships selling some blend of the GM lines. He also owned another four businesses that combined used cars with farm equipment. His two sisters had long since moved to Florida, as far from their father's memory as they could get, and lived in houses bought with Lucius's earnings. They sent him Christmas cards and phoned when they needed something. Lucius did not blame them for their distance. Their family situation had not been one to forge strong emotional bonds.

His life was embedded in the road. Lucius was free here. He could unleash the Impala's big V8 and let the car be strong for him. Lucius rarely indulged in past regrets. But the doctor's words cast a magnetic force over the morning, drawing in one potent memory after another. His sisters had loathed their father and revered their mother. Their father had been a stonemason and a nasty drunk. Lucius's few memories of his father had been of a burly giant, massive in every way, who had hulked over the dinner table like a bear in a graying T-shirt and suspenders. But he never laid a hand on his own family. The sisters claimed they had all remained shielded by their mother's remarkable grace, so strong it kept peace in the house long after she had died birthing Lucius. The closest he ever came to his father, at least in theory, was when they both went down with pleurisy three days after his sixth birthday. His father had died while Lucius was delirious with fever. Lucius had spent the next few years being passed around among various relatives, until his sisters had managed to find jobs and get a place of their own. Of course he took care of them now.

The drive from San Luis Obispo to Miramar took just over two hours. The road was fairly awful in places, but Lucius did not mind. The authorities were always talking about building a proper county route, linking Miramar to the new highway. State Route 1, also known as the Pacific Coast Highway, had officially been opened the previous year, but the steep hills surrounding Miramar had forced the coastal thoroughfare inland, isolating this little oceanfront haven. Most of the locals were of two minds over building a better link to the outside world.

Some wanted growth, while others feared all the bad things they remained sheltered from. And in 1969, there was certainly a lot of bad to avoid.

At the top of the hour Lucius turned on the radio to catch the news. It was more out of habit than anything. Virtually none of what he heard had any bearing on his very constricted world. The launch of Apollo 10 was approaching, and this final run before man landed on the moon was the only bright spot in a series of grim tidings. The Basques in Spain had earlier set up a new guerrilla army called, of all things, ETA, and their outlaw government were demanding the right to form a nation of their own. British troops arrived in Northern Ireland to reinforce the local constabulary, and the Catholics referred to them as invaders. Harvard's administration building was taken over by Students for a Democratic Society. A ferocious battle had erupted in Vietnam at someplace called Hamburger Hill. The news ended and the announcer introduced a song by Sly and the Family Stone off their new album, *Stand.* Lucius liked the music well enough, though it made him feel more isolated than ever from the sweep of current events and all the good things other people his age were enjoying. He wasn't sorry when the hills closed in and the signal faded.

At the final approach to Miramar, Lucius pulled off the road and parked where a cluster of California pines offered a masking shadow. He peered across the street at the smallest of his dealerships, a Buick-Chevy-Olds he had acquired two years and eleven months ago. Nowadays his banker was pressing him to sell the place and put his money in a region with stronger growth. But Miramar held a special place in his poorly functioning heart.

During Lucius's first visit there, the old man who sold him the dealership had regaled him with legends dating back to the Wild West heyday of abalone fishing and Mexican banditos and the occasional gold prospector. Back then, the rough and frigid waters had earned the town its original name, Castaway Cove.

Around that same period Miramar had latched onto a very odd claim to fame. Stay there for a while, so the tales went, and you might be given a second chance. Second chance at what, Lucius had asked. He had instantly regretted his question, for the old man had taken on the smug look of someone offering a secret of supposedly great worth, but which Lucius already knew was bogus. The old man had then replied, "Whatever it is that you most want to try your hand at again."

Lucius had smiled over the fable, signed the purchase papers, handed the old man his check, and two hours later had fallen head over heels in love.

Whatever else he might think about the town and the lady, Lucius had known it had nothing whatsoever to do with Miramar's fable. For the event was singular. As in, the one time in his short, hard life he had ever known for himself what love actually meant.

Lucius liked to spend a few days loitering around every new acquisition. He called it "kicking the tires." Everyone was on his best behavior, at least at first. But Lucius fit so naturally into quiet corners that gradually the employees relaxed and slipped back into their routines. Lucius learned a great deal in those early days, mostly about money. As in, where the most revenue was generated. Where changes were needed. Where potential profits were being missed. Over his solitary evening meals, Lucius made notes in a script so precise his aging secretary described it as human lithotype. With each new dealership, Lucius brought in the employee he had come to trust the most, named him president of that particular location, and gave him a ten percent share, with an option to purchase another ten percent. Loyalty among his employees was fierce, turnover almost nil. Putting his plans down on paper gave spice to his otherwise tasteless dinner.

One of the first things Lucius noticed about the Miramar dealership was how the salesmen mostly ignored the new vehicles. They clearly made higher commissions pushing used cars. This suggested they were bilking the former owner out of part of his share. On that fateful day Lucius took up station at an empty salesman's desk, blocked from view by a gleaming new Buick Riviera. It was a car he especially liked, with the newly redesigned GM engine and a luxury velvet finish to corners that before had sharp and dangerous edges. Vent windows were a thing of the past, replaced by air-conditioning made standard on all Buicks. It was altogether a beautiful machine, as far as Lucius was concerned. This made the way the salesmen clustered together in the used-car lot all the more irritating. Quiet, silent Lucius Quarterfield was mostly ignored.

Which was when the young woman planted herself directly in front of him and declared, "I hate cars, don't you?"

"Excuse me?"

"Positively despise them." She was far too lovely to be spending time with the likes of him. Tall and willowy, she had a face that was filled with an electric fire that sparked through her wavy, auburn hair. Her eyes were alight with a mischievous emerald gleam as she went on. "Great humping metal beasts just looking for an excuse to bellow."

"That bellow is why I'm here," Lucius replied. "I consider it the finest music on earth."

She pulled over a chair and seated herself so close, their knees almost touched. "How positively dreadful."

Normally, he was so shy around women his own age that he could scarcely speak. Today, however, he heard himself reply with ease, "For years I've wanted to own a Jaguar, simply because I love the way their engine sounds."

"Then why on earth don't you buy one?"

Her matter-of-fact tone surprised him. "How do you know I can afford it?"

"Don't be silly. Everybody knows you just bought this business and paid cash."

"Who is everybody?"

"*All* of Miramar, of course." The way she spoke made it sound like, *All the known universe and beyond.* "Why do you think I'm talking to you?"

"I have no idea."

"Because you're fabulously rich and ever so mysterious, of course. I'm Jessica Waverly, by the way."

"Lucius Quarterfield."

"Are you really? I've never met a Lucius before, much less a Quarterfield. You haven't just stepped out of a Charlotte Brontë novel, by any chance."

"I don't know who she is."

"You can't be serious."

"I haven't read a novel since my sixteenth birthday. I left school and went to work. Since then I've hardly had time to read everything I need for my business."

She gave a cheery shrug. "In that case, I shall just have to educate you. Your name should obviously belong to some great strapping stable lad who goes around tossing cows for a living. You don't, I suppose."

"I can state with absolute certainty that I have never tossed a cow in my entire life."

"What a pity. What with owning your own business, and being stinking rich and loving to make these awful motors bellow, if you also tossed cows, I fear my father would marry me off in a flash. That's him over there, by the way, trying to convince my dear mother that he needs a new car more than his next breath."

"Then I'll just have to go out and toss my first cow this very afternoon," Lucius replied. And just like that, his heart was lost to the woman whose fire was as merry as his own was morose.

Lucius relied constantly on his objectivity and his logic. Both of which he lost completely whenever in the company of Miss Jessica Waverly. She referred to their relationship as *Pride and Prejudice,* the title of her favorite novel. Jessica refused to say which aspect referred to him. She remained stubbornly blind to his many frailties. She insisted that her parents positively adored Lucius, when he could see they were growing ever more alarmed by his calls and visits.

Jessica's father was Miramar's only dentist. Jessica had served as his assistant ever since her mother had developed problems with her joints. Her father had pressured Jessica to attend dental school and take over his practice, but Jessica was incredibly stubborn in her capricious manner. She claimed to have no intention of ever working that hard, not in school and certainly not for the rest of her professional life.

Their disapproval of Jessica's lack of ambition and their love of cars were the only two items that Lucius and Jessica's father agreed on.

Jessica confessed in their next time alone that it was neither dentistry nor working alongside her beloved father that made her so passionate about her job. Jessica was, in her own words, born to touch hearts. She saw the fear and discomfort the patients carried as opportunities to share with them her special brand of happy comfort. When she had spoken the words, Lucius had the distinct impression that Jessica expected him to scorn her for aiming too low. She sat there with her chin angled up, defiant and already hurting from what she thought he might say. In truth, Lucius was so moved by her willingness to share the illogicality of her beautiful heart, he needed several minutes to speak at all. When he did, it was to confess the impossible words of love for the very first time.

When her father finally demanded that Jessica address what he called "the Quarterfield situation," Jessica stubbornly insisted to Lucius that it didn't matter, none of it did. Even when Lucius knew full well that Jessica's father had issued an ultimatum to his only child. And in the process had broken her heart.

But when they next met, Jessica did not want to talk about that. She wanted to discuss what color his Jaguar should be. Lucius replied, "I will never buy such a car. But Jessica—"

"Then I just suppose you'll have to sweep me away on your yacht."

"I don't own a rowboat and I can't swim. About your father—"

"Oh, never mind him. I think fifty feet is a nice round number for a boat, don't you?"

"I won't buy a yacht for the same reason I will never own a Jag. I don't like to draw attention to myself."

For a brief instant she sobered. "I understand that."

"Do you really?"

"Actually, I've spent much of my life perfecting the ability to hide in plain sight."

"But why? You're . . ." He started to say "healthy," which sounded like he was sizing up a prize steer. So he said what he really thought, which was "beautiful."

She tilted her head. "Do you really think so?"

"You are quite simply stunning," he replied. "You take what little breath I have completely away."

"See? Why should I let Daddy pester me when a fabulously wealthy man with a lifetime of secrets, and who thinks I'm lovely, is going to buy me a fifty-foot yacht?"

"I will not do any such thing."

"Oh, well, never mind." She waved it aside. "As if beauty ever mattered. All the beautiful ladies in Jane Austen's novels die of the pestilence, alone and ravaged by cruel fate."

Her sudden changes in direction left him dizzy. "Really?"

"Well, no. But they should have."

"Jessica, why do you want to spend time with me?"

She cocked her head and showed him an expression of utter amazement. "Why, because you need me, silly."

It was only later, as he drove back to his lonely house outside Santa Barbara, that he realized she had succeeded in doing precisely what she had intended all along. Which was to tell him about the situation with her father, then avoid talking about it an instant longer than necessary. She was, Lucius decided, the most adroit negotiator he had ever met.

Three days later, Lucius journeyed to Miramar once more. Jessica had made a picnic, her determined method to ignore the fact that he had come with a very definite purpose in mind. He allowed her to take off his socks and shoes and roll up the trouser legs over his pale shins. They set up the picnic by the southern cliffs. The sea was calm, the sunlight fierce for early May. A trio of beachfront eucalyptus offered a perfumed shade. They walked, hand in hand, down the beach, as far as Lucius felt comfortable. Half a mile north, they stopped and watched two young girls and a spaniel race joyfully along the shore, chasing gulls. Jessica released his hand so as to slip her arm around his waist. She settled her head upon his shoulder. Lucius felt the warmth and strength and life in her vibrant form, and was grateful when the breeze tossed her hair into his face and blocked his tears from view.

After the picnic all he wanted was to stretch out beside her and have her rest her face upon his chest. Her every smile almost broke his resolve. But he had to be strong. For her.

"Jessica. Sweetheart."

"You've never called me that before." She rose to a seated position and tucked her knees under her dress and wrapped her arms around her shins. "Is this to be a serious discussion?"

"I fear it must." He shaped the words, very slowly, allowing it to linger on his tongue. And in his heart. "I love you so much."

Her eyes grew huge. "You're saying good-bye." Her breath caught on the last word, like a hook's barb had become lodged in her throat. "Aren't you."

"I love you . . ." He needed a hard breath to dislodge his own barb. "Too much—"

"There's no such thing as 'too much,' " she whispered.

"—to make you my widow."

"Silly you." She tried to laugh. But her tears refused to give her enough air. "We're all dying. Every day is just one more step toward the final end."

"Not this soon," Lucius replied. "You have years left to live."

"You don't know that."

"I have weeks. A few months. Perhaps only days."

"You don't know that, either," she said, but the words were mangled now. She refused to stop talking, not even when her every word was forced around sobs that convulsed her entire frame. "Shall I tell you why I love you, Lucius? Because you are the loneliest man on God's green earth."

It was true. The truest thing he had ever heard. So true he was silenced. His reasons for doing as he did vanished in the flood of her sorrow. But not his resolve. All he could do was sit there, the distance between them impossibly wide. Even when she pleaded desperately for him to reach over and offer the comfort that only his arms could give.

When he did not speak, Jessica went on talking. "You need me to give you what you will never have without me. And that, my dearest beloved, is joy."

That is true as well, he wanted to tell her. He could not even have named the flavor of ecstasy until their first conversation. Even now, when he was filled with bitter regret, he knew he was saying not just farewell to her, but to any shred of happiness. Any hope of bliss.

His silence defeated her. She started crying too hard to help him gather up their belongings. When the car was packed, he came back to where she sat, staring blindly at the Pacific, helped her to stand, and supported her weight back to the parking lot. One cripple helping another.

The first comforting sign that he had done the right thing came when he pulled up in front of her parents' home. Jessica had recently taken an apartment in town. But Lucius did not want to take her back there, both because he did not want her to be alone just then, and because he did not want to test his broken resolve. As he rounded the final corner, he saw Jessica's mother standing on the front walk, waiting for them. There was no way the older woman could have known what had just taken place, yet there she was, watching worriedly as Lucius pulled up. When he cut the motor, Jessica fumbled blindly for the latch. Finally her mother opened the door and enfolded Jessica in a comforting embrace.

Lucius watched the two women climb the steps and enter the house and seal him out. Only then did he rise from the car and open the trunk and lift the remnants of their last day together. He started up the drive, carrying the blanket and the hamper and her shoes. The garage door opened, and Jessica's father emerged. Jessica's father set the burdens on a shelf by the door leading into the house. Then he unbent enough to take Lucius in a strong embrace. Lucius was so shocked he did not know how to react. He stood there, frozen in place. He had only shaken the man's hand twice, and one of those was the day he had sold the man his new Buick. Then Jessica's father released him and stepped back and shut the garage door. All without saying a word.

That had taken place eleven months ago. Today was the first time since then that Lucius had returned to Miramar.

Anywhere else along the Pacific coast, a place as beautiful as Miramar would have been swept up in the boom that had dominated California throughout the sixties. But Miramar was too isolated and too small and too hemmed in by steep hills and too far from the new highway system. Many of the local residents would have it no other way.

For a brief period Lucius had imagined himself pulling up stakes and moving north. Settling here and establishing his office in this haven. But then the breakup had come, and logic had dominated, and he had remained in Santa Barbara, the town of his birth.

Yet even now, when heartache filled his car with a force strong as the daylight, he wished that it had somehow been possible to call this charming refuge his home.

He pulled into the broad parking area for the town's seafront playground. It was named after some long-forgotten mayor, but all the locals knew it as Bent Pine Park. A stand of wind-twisted cypress and California pine anchored the southern edge and clambered up the cliffside beyond. His first visit, Jessica had brought him here, of course. From the moment of his arrival, Lucius knew he had found a new favorite place.

The Pacific mist was spiced by eucalyptus hidden among the hillside grove. The beach was half a mile wide and over two miles long. Cliffs anchored both ends, forming a natural refuge strong enough to keep out even the beast of time. A few fireflies wandered about, a rarity for the California coast. But obviously they found this place as wondrous as he did. And best of all, there had been a beautiful young woman who was thrilled to see how much he loved her hometown.

The car was empty now, but Jessica felt close as his rasping breath. Which was why it had been almost a year since his last visit.

Lucius took off his shoes and socks and rolled up his trousers. He rose from the car, and in that instant he noticed the difference.

Most days Lucius operated with some level of discomfort. His pain boundaries had been pushed and stretched over the years. He knew he could tolerate far more aches than most people, and do so without medication. He disliked anything that had a dulling effect on his mental faculties.

But he had also developed an acute sensitivity to his body's erratic rhythms.

He tried to tell himself that he was merely responding to being back here, in the place where he and Jessica had said their last farewells. No doubt he resonated at the level of heart and bone and sinew to Jessica's absence. Not to mention possible aftereffects arising from the doctor's worrisome comments.

But Lucius knew there was something more at work.

He walked down the path to the beach by sheer strength of will. His limbs felt disjointed, as though his body was severely irritated with him for insisting they carry his meager weight. When he finally reached the lapping waves, he turned and looked up the gentle rise that connected the shore to Miramar. There in the clutch of rooftops was Jessica's home.

He ached with an uncommon force for what he could not have. Defeated by the futility of another lonely day, he started down the beach.

His stance was crooked, even by his own lopsided standards. He felt as though his body had adopted a new pose, intended to protect his aching heart.

A pair of fireflies floated around him. Some claimed there were no fireflies along all of California's central coast. Yet here they were, two wandering flecks of light that danced and weaved about his face, as though seeking to illuminate this loneliest of hours.

There was a bitter majesty to his solitude. The beach was entirely his. No one remarked on his unbalanced walk. Nobody was there to notice his tears.

Why had he been pressed into this wretched body and this lonely life? Was it so much to ask, a healthy tomorrow shared with a woman he loved? Was he such a wretch that this forlorn day was all he deserved?

Why had he returned to Miramar? His physical pain was dwarfed by a regret so profound his frail body could scarcely hold it in. Why relive all the sorrow he had caused by forcing Jessica away? Repeatedly telling himself he had done the right thing changed nothing.

It was then he heard the sound above the crashing waves.

Lucius realized he had heard it for some time, but had dismissed it as the cry of a passing gull. Now his heart leapt with the joy of knowing he had been wrong.

He turned and saw Jessica running toward him. Her bare feet spurted sand up behind her, like a galloping horse. Her hair was an auburn mane, a rainbow of glory in the daylight. Her impatient energy sang through her entire being, from the hands that clutched at the distance between them to the taut force that pulled back her features. Lucius saw the liquid sparkle on her cheeks, and realized she was crying, too.

She stopped an arm's breadth away from him, and fought to shape words that came with wretched difficulty. "You came. You came. I knew you would. Why ever did you make me wait this long?"

Lucius reached for her. Or tried to.

It was then that he realized the doctor had been right all along.

Having so few moments left that he could actually count them gave him the strength to open his arms.

It was a terribly selfish act. Jessica flung herself at him with a heat as famished as his own. "Lucius, Lucius, my darling man!"

He released the words that had resonated through his mind, his heart, his lung, from the first instant of their first meeting. "I love you, Jessica."

The attack struck like a Pacific wave, a great beast of agony that wrenched him from her arms and sent him crashing to the sand.

Jessica cried his name, over and over, as she knelt in the sand and clutched at him. The sweet bliss of her embrace was stronger than his heart's final pain. The frigid waves lapped over them both, as though all the world's tears had gathered to bid him farewell. He lay there, her beautiful face filling his vision, until he saw no more.

CHAPTER 2

TODAY

Wednesday started quite poorly for Asha Meisel and grew stranger with every passing hour. She was woken at nine minutes past five by a call from her supervisor. Dino Barbieri lectured at Cal Poly, where Asha was completing her graduate studies in marriage, family, and crisis therapy. He had also helped her obtain an internship with the hospital where he served as chief therapist in the mental-health wing. Asha had read his textbook on crisis management as an undergraduate and had chosen Cal Poly so that she could study under him. After her father, Dino Barbieri was quite possibly the most important man in her life.

Of course there was also that other minor matter. One she had not shared with anyone. Asha had been halfway in love with Dino Barbieri since the first day she had walked into his office.

But Dino was a complete and utter professional. If he was even aware that virtually all of his female students were utterly infatuated with him, he gave no sign. So Asha counted herself fortunate to also consider Dino a friend, and pretended that was as much as she ever wanted, because it was all that she would ever gain.

Asha Meisel was a slow starter. She needed a good half hour and three cups of coffee just to get her brain functioning. What was worse, the phone call had interrupted a dream about her former fiancé. Jeffrey was still down in Los Angeles, as far as Asha knew. But in the dream he had shown up at her doorstep, pleading to give him one more chance. They had split and reunited three times. Eighteen months earlier, Asha had finally accepted that the relationship was broken and could not be fixed. Such nightmares came less often these days, but they still carried a seismic jolt. When the phone rang, she almost didn't answer, fearing that it was Jeffrey, that he had somehow managed to obtain her new unlisted number and was invading her life. Again.

Thankfully, her boss was well aware of Asha's morning routine. "I need you to get up and put on a pot of coffee and then call me back."

"Oh . . . Okay."

"Don't go back to sleep, Asha. And hurry. I need you fully alert."

Fifteen minutes later, Asha was at least partly connected to the unfinished dawn. "What's going on?"

"Luke Benoit." There was the sound of a car's motor in the background. "You've been acting as his therapist, correct?"

"For the past two months." As part of her final term, Asha was assigned several patients. Her sessions were carefully monitored, and she was going through counseling herself with the university's senior therapist. The intention was to help her learn through direct experience what it meant to separate her own issues, life, emotions, and perspective from those of her patients. "What's happened?"

"Last night he committed suicide."

"Oh, no." Asha was glad to be standing by the kitchen counter. It gave her something to grab hold of. "That's terrible."

"This is not his first go at it, correct?"

"His third." She found herself leaking tears. It was a thoroughly unprofessional response to the news, but she couldn't help herself. "The poor kid."

"The file shows his age as twenty-one, correct?"

"Luke turned twenty-two the day before yesterday. He dreaded the birthday. He said it marked another wasted year of a totally futile life." She cleared her face with the hand not holding the phone. "But there was something utterly childlike about him. I found it easier to reach him if I spoke like I would to a nine-year-old. That's how I came to see him. I thought we were making progress."

Dino gave Asha a moment to regain control, then asked, "Are you able to drive?"

"Yes, I'm fine. Well, not fine, but . . ."

"He has no living next of kin. Which means you will need to identify the body. The hospital is sending it to the coroner's. An autopsy is required in all suspect-death cases. You know where that is?"

She swallowed hard. "No."

He gave her the address, then did so a second time. "I'll meet you there and we'll start prepping."

"Prepping for what?" Asha felt her body go cold. Now she understood the real reason for his urgency. "The peer review."

"The hospital board has a session scheduled for this morning. They'll want to take up this case."

She had already played a secondary role in one such review, where the hospital's senior medical staff examined every crisis or failed surgery. It had been one of the most harrowing experiences of her entire life. "No, Dino, I can't."

His voice was as gentle as it was firm. "You don't have any choice."

* * *

Asha considered her name to be the one truly Persian aspect of herself.

Most people, upon seeing her striking dark looks for the first time, assumed Asha was South American. She spoke excellent Spanish and sometimes enjoyed stringing strangers along. That, too, was part of her Persian heritage, Asha knew, this love of secrets and the subtle power of deception.

Asha was a name that dated back to the Parthian Empire, the eastern kingdom that Rome had considered its most dangerous foe. Two thousand years ago, the Parthians had threatened Roman legions from Damascus to the southern seas. Her name's origins were woven into the empire's fire-worshipping heritage. The name Asha meant Truth-Bearer, or Keeper of the Flame, titles once used by the Zoroaster high priestess. All this Asha had learned from her grandmother Sonya, who had emigrated to the United States and married into one of California's oldest Jewish clans. When the family in Tehran had learned of the marriage, they had spoken prayers of the dead over an open grave.

A storm had apparently passed through earlier, for the streets glistened in her headlights. As she turned onto the main thoroughfare rimming the town's southern boundary, her phone chimed. Dino's voice rang from the car's speakers. "Where are you?"

"About a mile out."

"Turn around. I need you to meet me at the hospital." Dino now clipped off the edges of his words. Terseness was a sign of rare tension. When stressed, Dino applied a surgical precision to everything he said. "Your patient has just woken up."

Asha swung through a U-turn on the empty street, her tires hissing in the wet. "Dino . . . You said he was dead."

"I know I did. Hang on, I've got the ER doctor on the other line, let me patch him in." There followed a series of clicks, then, "Dr. Emeka, can you hear me?"

A deep and distinctly African voice replied, "Loud and clear."

"I have Asha Meisel, the patient's counselor, on the phone. Please repeat for her what you just told me."

"EMV delivered Luke Benoit at three thirty-one this morning." The doctor's voice was as resonant as a church organ. "His pulse was unsteady, his breathing almost nil. He had been discovered, wait, let me check . . . Yes, here it is. Eleven minutes before three, his flatmate found Benoit unconscious on the bathroom floor. An open bottle of triazolam was by his side. Did you prescribe the medication, Dr. Meisel?"

Dino responded for her. "It is Ms. Meisel, and she is a therapist in training. She recently replaced Dr. Weathers."

"Ah." Three months earlier, Alice Weathers had been forced into early retirement, after four failed peer reviews in a row. Of course, no one actually used the word "failed." Just as no one stated outright that Asha had been granted the internship because Dino wanted her to become Alice Weathers's replacement. The ER doctor said, "It is clear to me now. I thought I had heard the name before. This is not Benoit's first suicide attempt, yes?"

Asha spoke for the first time. "His third."

"Right. The hospital computer system is down. I could not access . . . Never mind. That can wait. Back to this morning. The medics inserted a saline drip en route. We were ready with a gastric evac as soon as the patient arrived. When this was completed, we left him in the ER wing because no other bed was available. Or if there was one, we couldn't find it with the computers not functioning. Benoit was listed as stable but critical."

When the ER doctor went silent, Dino pressed, "And then he died."

"At four forty-one this morning his heart stopped. Our attempts to restart were unsuccessful. He was declared dead by me, personally, at four fifty-seven." Dr. Emeka's words became cautious, measured. As though he, too, saw himself facing his own peer review. "We were quite busy this morning. EMV said it would be a few hours before they could transport the body to the coroner's. So it was decided to shift the body downstairs. The orderly was just pushing the gurney into the hospital morgue when the patient . . ."

Dino supplied, "He woke up."

"In an extremely loud and agitated fashion," Emeka confirmed. "It required a very large orderly and two cleaners to hold him down. I was next on scene, and eventually managed to sedate him."

"Where is Benoit now?"

"In the critical care unit. His vitals show him as stable. CCU needs his bed. I have agreed he should be moved into a ward for non-crisis patients."

Dino asked, "Benoit remains strapped in?"

"Oh, most certainly. I saw to the restraints myself."

"Asha, where are you now?"

To her surprise, she realized she had covered almost the entire distance to the hospital, as though the car had found its way all by itself. "I'm just turning into the lot."

"I'm five minutes out." Dino lived in Morro Bay, half an hour west of San Luis Obispo. "Wait for me in the parking area. Dr. Emeka, how can we connect with you?"

"Have the receptionist ring me when you arrive. We'll go see the patient together."

CHAPTER 3

Asha knew very little of Dino Barbieri's personal background. As was the case with many senior medical personnel, Dino kept what little private life he had distinctly separate from his professional responsibilities. Asha knew he had studied medicine in San Francisco and completed his residency in psychiatry at Boston University. Dino was thirty-eight years old, twelve years older than herself. She knew he had married a woman from San Luis Obispo, but they had divorced some four years back. She knew he now lived in Morro Bay. Little else.

Of course she also knew he was exceedingly handsome.

Dino Barbieri had saturnine features, dark and virile and carved from some rich Mediterranean stone. His eyes were an astonishing blue, so dark as to appear almost black in some lights. The photograph on the cover of his textbook showed a younger man with film-star looks and a smile to match. Asha considered it a shame that he revealed his smile so seldom. Instead, Dino met most days with a look of weary surprise, as though the world continued to both astonish and demand more than he had to give. But what endeared him the most to Asha was how children responded to Dino with an instantaneous trust. Asha had observed an almost comatose young girl come alive the moment he ambled into a room. She reached out her arms and begged him to offer a comfort all his own.

Asha pulled into the hospital lot, cut her motor, and rolled down all four windows. She settled back and listened to the predawn world. The streets remained mostly silent. An ambulance halted by the ER entrance, its lights flashing, but the siren off. The hospital doors slid open, and a male nurse emerged to help pull the gurney from the back. The voices were softly professional. The gurney rattled over the entry and the doors slid shut. A mockingbird started up from one of the neighboring trees, its song as loud as a full-throated bellow. The air was sweet from the rain.

It was good to be alive.

Ten minutes later, Dino's Jeep Cherokee pulled into the spot next to hers. Asha rolled up her windows, took her white hospital coat from the seat beside her, and rose from the car.

Dino greeted her, "Ready?"

"Yes," she replied. And now she was.

They entered the hospital together. Dino asked the duty officer to let Dr. Emeka know they had arrived. He returned to where Asha stood by the front windows and said, "You've had five sessions with the patient, correct?"

"Six. Today would have been seven. Unless . . ."

"What?"

"Should I withdraw?"

"Why on earth would you do that?"

"Come on, Dino. My patient almost succeeded in killing himself."

"Luke Benoit is a repeat offender. Plus, he's been in and out of counseling for how long?"

"Nineteen months."

"With how many different therapists?"

"Three. I'm number four."

"Do you get along with the patient?"

"I sensed a growing rapport."

Dino crossed his arms. "Summarize his case."

"Two years ago, his parents were killed in an automobile accident. Benoit was in his fifth semester at Cal Poly. Business and finance, but he had difficulty maintaining his grades long before that incident. He had previously been in and out of two community colleges, his records show barely passing grades. He has taken two leaves of absence from Cal Poly since the accident."

"So the incident devastated him," Dino said. "Benoit is an only child?"

"There was a sister, sixteen months younger. In our last session he confided something that is not mentioned anywhere in his records. Luke's sister died when he was seven. He blames himself. They were playing in a tree house. She fell."

"Did he cause the accident?"

"He says no. I believe him."

"So. Benoit has carried an unjustified guilt his entire adult life. His most recent decline was set off by yet another traumatic incident. He has no close living relatives. Compounding the initial shock is the fact that he is now effectively an orphan."

"He was in counseling after his sister's death," Asha added. "He mentioned that in our last session. Since that took place in Canada our own records make no mention of it."

"So Benoit has a history of depression stretching back to childhood. A clearly definable pattern, leading up to multiple suicide attempts. The state's guidelines on institutionalization have been met."

Asha wanted to say there was still hope for him, though she knew it was the same dogged stubbornness that she carried into so many of her own personal issues. She struggled to find a foundation for protest, but came up blank.

Dino seemed to find her silence utterly acceptable. "To answer your question, I absolutely want you to remain this patient's therapist." He unwound his arms so as to point behind her. "Here comes the ER doctor."

CHAPTER 4

Lucius was so drugged that waking and sleep were simply two sides of the same coin. It spun in the air, he woke and felt his body held by padded restraints, and then he slipped away again without opening his eyes. Sometime later, he returned once more. The light beyond his closed eyelids had strengthened. He loathed hospitals, but at least he was no longer in that dismal chamber filled with the vile odors and the white-shrouded bodies. The memory of that first horrifying instant, waking with a sheet over his face inside that icy realm of death . . . He had feared the eternal worst.

"Luke? Can you hear me?"

He shifted slightly, or tried to. But his arms and legs and waist were all bound. He could feel the padded straps anchoring him to the bed. Hardly a surprise, given his terror-stricken return to life.

Life.

"Luke, can you hear me?"

He could not fathom how he had possibly survived. The

heart attack had been massive. The darkness that followed had carried an overwhelming sense of finality . . .

Jessica.

He opened his eyes, blinked, and saw . . .

A dark-haired angel.

Asha stood with the two doctors opposite the patient's bed. Dino said, "Perhaps we should reduce his meds."

Luke Benoit only stayed with them a few moments. Long enough to whisper a woman's name. "Jessica." Then he asked for water. He spoke again, more strongly this time, asking where Jessica was. A third time, and then he slipped away.

"I agree." Emeka walked over, took Benoit's pulse, then touched the machine's controls. From the deeply resonant voice she had heard on the phone, Asha had expected Dr. Emeka to be massively built. Instead, he was almost elfish, an inch or so shorter than her own five-nine, and with delicate birdlike features. His voice was the only large component about him. "Let us see how he responds to a reduction of fifty percent, and a doubling of the interval between doses."

Dino turned to Asha. "Who is Jessica?"

"I have no idea. I've never heard him mention her before," she replied.

"Did you bring his file with you?"

"It's in the car."

"Why don't you take a moment and review—"

"I don't need to. There isn't any mention of a Jessica."

Dino and Emeka both observed her. "You have memorized the patient's entire file?"

"I have studied it enough to know all of the major characters and most of the minor."

Dino frowned at the patient. "So. No Jessica."

"Did you see how he said it?" Asha studied the slumbering young man. "Like he was expecting her to be here in the room."

Emeka said, "I have seen and heard many remarkable occurrences tied to near-death experiences."

Asha hesitated, then decided she should say it. "Something about him is completely different."

Dino said, "What do you mean?"

Now Asha wished she had not spoken. "It's hard to put into words."

"Try."

"In our sessions he rarely meets my gaze. At first I thought perhaps he had a trace of Asperger's. When I asked him about it, he said sometimes it hurt to be inspected. Like others are seeing things about him that he is afraid to see himself."

Dino's attention was fully on her now. "When did he say that?"

"Our last session."

"You are definitely staying on this case," Dino said.

"But did you see how intent he was when he woke up? He focused on each of us. Directly."

"Same response," Emeka said. "Near-death experiences represent an extreme level of emotional and mental trauma."

Asha shook her head. "This did not strike me as a response to trauma."

"He was heavily sedated," Dino said. "This following an incident so violent the patient needed to be forcibly restrained."

Emeka pointed to the wall monitor, then stepped back over to where Dino and Asha stood. "He is returning."

CHAPTER 5

Lucius put it down to the drugs and the shock, how it took him so long to realize they were referring to him as Luke.

The drugs were unlike anything he had experienced. There was a small blue machine attached to the IV. Twice he heard it beep, and almost instantly an icy veil fell upon his mind. Fifteen seconds later, he departed. Neither his frantic worry over Jessica nor his strength of will made any difference whatsoever. The machine's contents pulled him down like an anchor to the bottom of the ocean.

When he resumed consciousness, the lovely dark-haired woman asked once more, "Luke, how are you feeling?"

"Please don't inject me with any further medication."

His words clearly surprised them. The tall, handsome man motioned to the smaller, dark-skinned doctor, who checked something on the portable electronic apparatus. The woman kept her gaze directed at him. She asked again, "How are you?"

"Ready to be untethered," he replied. He debated a moment, then added, "Please."

"Do you understand why you are here, Luke?"

The woman's exotic beauty and her apparent concern had temporarily disarmed him. But the drug continued to release his mental capabilities. He had learned early and well that with most of the medical profession, the safest answer was also the shortest. He replied, "Yes."

"So you also understand why you are currently restrained."

"I do. Yes."

"Will you tell me, Luke?"

"I was frightened. I overreacted." He gestured with his chin at the blue machine. "I must assume this apparatus is set on a timer. Can you please stop it before more drugs are injected?"

The woman clearly liked having a lever. "What scared you, Luke?"

In reply he turned his head and stared at the machine. He allowed the silence to linger, then repeated, "Please."

The small man placed two fingers upon his neck. Lucius had the distinct impression the doctor did so as a test. Lucius studied him. The doctor held himself with an intelligent poise, like an aging dancer. There was something distinctly foreign about him. Lucius tried to recall if he had ever encountered a foreign, dark-skinned doctor at any point before. The doctor shifted his gaze to an electronic panel on Luke's opposite side, and said, "All signs remain stable."

The taller doctor spoke for the first time. "So let's give it a try."

The small man touched the blue machine, then walked back over and joined the other two. The woman asked, "What scared you, Luke?"

"If I answer that, will you respond to a question of my own?"

The trio shared a look. Something about his response left them . . . Lucius searched for the proper word.

Disoriented.

Well, that made four of them.

The woman replied, "I am happy to answer any question you might have, Luke."

"Another lie. One of many."

"I'm sorry, what did you say?"

"I should not have spoken. Don't inject me with any more of that brain-numbing drug."

"There is no need, so long as you remain calm," the woman said.

He opened the hands tethered to either side of his body. "Observe. This is me at my calmest."

It was then that Lucius noticed the first difference.

Not to his surroundings.

About himself.

His eyesight had always been adequate. As in, he could drive, he could see his surroundings, he could read a ledger or a newspaper. But his eyesight was no stronger than the rest of him. Spectacles only gave him headaches.

Not now.

The trio stood at the opposite side of the room from where he lay strapped to his bed. Attached to the wall to their right, almost grazing the ceiling, was a flat black panel. Along its lower edge was a silver word he knew vaguely, SONY. What he found remarkable was how he could read it at all. What was more, he could also read the name tags attached to their white coats. From across the room.

The woman asked, "Do you remember me, Luke?"

He read, "Meisel."

Again his response surprised them. The woman said, "Why don't you use my first name, Luke?"

Lucius needed to orient himself. In private. He needed a temporary respite from this woman's softly penetrating questions. He needed . . .

He said, "I need to go to the bathroom. Please."

The birdlike doctor left the room and returned with two orderlies, massive brutes who appeared almost comical in their hospital blues. Five people plus Lucius made the hospital room very cramped. But the doctors showed no interest in vacating the premises. Instead, the trio shifted over beside the window. They stood shoulder to shoulder while the interns positioned themselves to the left of his bed. Both of the men had swarthy complexions and grim expressions and cautious gazes. The larger man took a firm grip on Lucius's left forearm and shoulder, then demanded, "Are you gonna give me any trouble?"

"No trouble at all," Lucius replied. He found it mildly interesting how few Caucasians were in the room. He studied the three doctors and their intent manners. Like they were a set piece. A quorum. But for what purpose, he had no idea. What could he have possibly said or done upon awakening that would invite this manner of investigation?

The orderly who had spoken nodded to his associate, who began the process of unstrapping him.

"Come on up," the orderly told him. "Slow and easy."

The second orderly gripped his right arm as Lucius rose from the bed. Lucius did not protest, both because he knew it would do no good and because he was not sorry for the support. He felt overwhelmed by a sense of disconnection from his own limbs.

"Steady, now."

It was completely different from how he had felt upon the beach. But it took Lucius a few steps before he could identify the change. Lucius was utterly pain-free. What was more, he seemed to be breathing more easily. And yet his legs functioned with reluctance. He had to concentrate on planting each step. There was a tingling down his legs, all the way to his bare feet.

When they reached the bathroom, the first orderly asked, "You going to be able to handle it from here?"

"Yes, thank you."

"Polite, that's real good. Now look here." He pulled a set of keys from his pocket, attached to a metal chain that unwound as he reached for the bathroom door. "I'm setting the lock so you can't seal the door. Don't complain because that's how it's gonna be."

"I understand."

"This works two ways. You need something, you give me a shout." He nodded to his companion, who released Lucius. He did the same, then repeated, "No trouble, now."

"None whatsoever," Lucius assured them. He stepped inside and gripped a tubular support rod screwed into the wall by the door frame. He waited until the door shut, then shuffled forward.

Then he stepped in front of the sink, and his reflection came into view.

Lucius Quarterfield stared at a face that was not his own.

CHAPTER 6

Dr. Emeka was paged just as Lucius entered the washroom. He said, "I must go and check on an incoming patient."

"I think we're good here," Dino said. "Asha?"

She asked, "Do you think the restraints are necessary? The patient has no history of violent behavior."

Dino and Emeka exchanged glances. The diminutive doctor said, "I have no objections."

"Let's give him some space when he comes back," Dino decided. "See how he responds."

Emeka said to the orderlies, "Could we ask you gentlemen to remain close by, but hands off?"

"Fine by us," the first orderly replied. "This one is a kitty cat."

Emeka nodded to Dino and Asha. "See you in a few moments."

Asha had almost managed to forget the peer review. She waited until the orderlies resumed their soft conversation to ask Dino, "Do we still have to go before the board?"

"You know the rules. A patient's attempted suicide is considered grounds for review." He offered a professional smile. "You'll do fine."

She swallowed her queasiness. Her one experience with a peer review had been as a witness. The experience had branded her.

"What do . . ." Dino was halted by the chirp of his phone. He checked the readout, then said, "I have to take this." He stepped into the hall.

The two orderlies were deep into a conversation about the chances of some LA team in the play-offs. Asha assumed they were talking about basketball, but she did not care enough to ask. As a result she was the only one who was watching when Luke Benoit opened the door.

Because the orderly had fastened the latch open, the door made no sound. For one brief instant Luke Benoit revealed a deep state of shock. His features were drawn into an almost rictus snarl, as though he struggled against some internal tempest, or very deep pain.

Asha was about to demand what was the matter, when Luke underwent a drastic shift. The instant the orderlies turned toward him, Luke's face went blank. In the time it took for him to shuffle one step forward, he smothered his emotions completely.

Asha had seen professional gamblers do this, wear a mask that remained utterly disconnected to their thoughts and emotions.

Yet in her six sessions with Benoit, the patient had revealed an utter inability to control his feelings. It was one of the traits noted by all of his former therapists. The man was an open book when it came to his internal state.

She remained where she was, intently focused as the orderlies shepherded the patient back into bed. His limbs shook, the tremors so intense he could not seem to lift his feet off the floor.

And yet he held to his bland disguise. Asha was certain that was actually what she observed. A camouflage.

Dino reentered the room just as Luke settled into his bed. He said into his phone, "Hold on just a minute." He informed Asha, "We need to get downstairs."

Asha was so intent upon the patient, the pending review could not impact her. "Luke, do we need to restrain you?"

"Absolutely not." He met her gaze for the first time, revealing nothing. "I am quite capable of remaining tranquil, I assure you."

Dino said, "Mr. Benoit, if you show any further aggression, there is every risk you will be confined to a room in the mental ward. Tell me you understand."

"Completely. The previous incident will not be repeated. You have my word."

Dino's attention was clearly elsewhere. He said to the orderlies, "We'll be back in a couple of hours. In the meantime . . ."

"We got your back, Docs," he assured them.

"Fine. Let's go, Asha. They're starting."

Once everyone had left, Lucius felt his thoughts spread out and crowd every inch of the otherwise empty room. He allowed himself to drift upon the tempest, all the images sweeping about, illuminated by lightning flashes and the thunderous impact of seeing his own reflection.

He reviewed numerous items that he had discounted upon first awakening. The blue machine was now disengaged but remained stationed beside his bed. Next to that was the monitor that blinked softly with each of his heartbeats. He studied the electric patterns that clearly represented his breathing and pulse and blood pressure. The bed itself was unlike anything he had seen before, with illuminated controls upon a cable that lay on the sheet beside his right hand. He used them to raise his head. He started to shift from the bed so as to peer out the window.

The orderly chose that moment to open the door leading to the hallway. "You need to go again?"

"No, I just . . ."

"They want you planted right there in that bed until they get back." He must have seen a hint of rebellion in Lucius's expression, for he went on. "Listen up, man. You're standing on the brink. One false step, and they'll lock you up in a padded cell. You hear what I'm saying?"

"Why on earth would they want to confine me like that?"

"On account of you trying to do yourself in, what do you think?"

"I . . . What?"

"That's why they're watching, see if you're gonna bug out again." The orderly used his considerable strength to press Lucius firmly into the mattress, then gave the bedsheets a military tuck. Sealing him in. "You're lucky this is California. They got a strict set of rules about locking people up. The problem is, once you're in, there's a world of trouble getting *out.*" The orderly turned for the door. "You best think good and hard on what I'm telling you."

Lucius was stunned to immobility by what he had just heard. He had only caught that one glimpse of himself in the mirror. But what he had seen, what he felt now, was that he was encased within a body that was completely, entirely healthy. He had a collection of professionals that appeared to be genuinely concerned about his well-being. The questions filled the white walls of his room with the script of mystery.

What on earth could this young man have been facing that had brought him to preferring death?

Who was this Luke Benoit?

Where was he?

When was he?

Why was he *here*?

Most important of all, where was Jessica?

CHAPTER 7

The peer review was fairly awful, but nowhere near as bad as Asha had feared.

The term had two very different meanings. Peer review also referred to the process that every scientific article underwent before publication. Normally, a research team would alert the journal they hoped might publish their work long in advance. This early notification was a declaration that their study was producing results. Hopefully, the journal would then agree to consider their work for publication. The article was written and submitted. It went before an editorial board. If found acceptable, it was sent out for peer review, a critical analysis by one or more experts in the field.

The process Asha faced was the same, only different.

The hospital's review board met at least twice each month. Cases involving serious legal or ethical issues, particularly where the hospital might be found liable, were held in the director's conference room. All others took place in the hospital's basement auditorium. Partly because it was located on the same level as the morgue, but mostly because of these reviews, the auditorium was known among the hospital staff as the boneyard.

Asha's case was the fourth, and last, to be taken up that morning. She and Dino found seats by the right-hand aisle, midway up the rising bank of rows. Dino left soon after, drawn away by the same crisis that had called him from the hospital room. Dr. Emeka was seated three aisles farther up, with colleagues from the ER wing. Asha found she did not mind the solitude. She faced a collection of unanswered questions regarding Luke Benoit and his behavior. She pulled a pad and pen from her purse and began making a design of her thoughts, almost like a Christmas tree with a growing collection of ornaments. To the right of her diagram she drew a massive question mark, and reinforced it every few minutes. She was increasingly certain she was not seeing something. A clue, a sign, a shift at some core level in Benoit's behavior . . .

The director's voice drew Asha from her reverie. "Our last case, patient Luke Benoit."

Asha followed Dino down the sloping aisle and climbed onto the stage. The last time she'd endured this, she had been so terrified it had felt as though she'd pushed through a vat of invisible glue. Now she felt . . . nothing. In fact, she was impatient to get through this so she could return to her patient. As she seated herself between the two men, she wondered if this was what it meant to become a professional clinician.

Their three chairs were positioned so they faced both the audience and the officials, always a senior doctor and a hospital administrator. Today it was the hospital's general manager, a courtly gentleman known to pour oil on the most troubled of waters, and a female pediatrician whom Asha did not know. They were seated together behind a cloth-covered table on Asha's right.

The auditorium was about one-third full. Attending peer reviews was not required. But most hospital doctors and many senior staff participated whenever possible. There was an element of learning involved, but Asha suspected the real reason was more salacious in nature. There was nothing the hospital staff appreciated more than having a doctor they disliked be caught out and officially censured for making a mistake.

The review board's preliminary questions were handled by Emeka, who accepted the microphone and addressed the gathering without rising from his seat. Then Dino took the mike and gave a concise coverage of Benoit's patient history.

The hospital administrator said, "We will now hear from the clinician responsible for the patient."

Dino said, "Actually, Ms. Meisel has only been involved for a very brief period. I can . . ."

Asha turned so as to face him. "I'd like to do this."

"You sure?"

"Yes." She decided to stand at the podium. She wanted to remove herself from these two more senior staffers. Asha was grateful for their concern. But it was time she was identified as, well, the professional she intended to become. And something more.

She was still hunting for the missing item.

Asha summarized her previous six sessions, then laid out today's sequence of events, starting from her entry into the patient's room. She made her comments as complete as possible, hoping this public recollection would help in her search.

She could hear her words slow as she arrived at the point when Luke emerged from the bathroom. She described how she was the only one to see the abrupt change. She dwelled on how Benoit slipped on the gambler's mask, then related how totally unlike his previous behavior this was.

Then it hit her. The simplicity was so astonishing, she could not believe it had taken her this long to realize . . .

"Ms. Meisel, are you done?"

She turned to the panel at the table. "He's lost his accent."

"Pardon me?"

"Luke Benoit spent his early years in Quebec, then relocated to Vancouver five and a half years ago, when a new job took his family there."

Behind her, Dino spoke into the wireless mike. "Of course."

Asha went on. "His English carried a very distinct French-Canadian accent."

Dino said, "How could I have missed that? It's mentioned by all of his therapists."

The administrator and the pediatrician exchanged a glance. "What are you suggesting?"

Asha looked out over the auditorium filled with medical staff. "I have no idea."

CHAPTER 8

After a time Lucius rose from his bed and inspected himself in the bathroom mirror. The image remained branded inside his brain. The man he saw looked remarkably like who he knew himself to be, and yet was also completely different. He touched the unshaven cheek with fingers that did not belong to him, and saw the flesh move in response. It was a handsome face, in many regards. The hair was longer than he cared for and somewhat unkempt. The skin was pallid, but perhaps that was due to the drugs he could still feel. He was also heavier by a good thirty or forty pounds. And the blue-gray eyes looked terrified. When he reached a point where he feared the questions would overwhelm him, Lucius staggered back to the bed.

By the time the orderly brought his first meal, he had arrived at three basic conclusions. It was not much, but they formed a foundation to resolving all the other mysteries. What was more, they anchored him. They kept the fears partially at bay.

He had to assume, first and foremost, he was alive. Impossible, but true nonetheless. Of course he might be caught in some bizarre paradox or cosmic mistake, or perhaps even purgatory.

But evidence suggested otherwise. He breathed, he thought, he felt, he . . . lived.

Second, he occupied the body of a suicide victim named Luke. He needed desperately to know more about this stranger. What was more, he needed to know *when*. The *why* could wait. He had spent his entire existence being unable to answer that one. Lucius corrected himself. His *former* existence.

And third, unless he was very careful, the powers that ruled his small corner of this hospital were going to lock him up.

A certain dark temptation lurked here. Lucius knew it would be easy to take shelter inside a padded room from this confusion.

But Lucius was a fighter by nature. He had always made the most of what little had been his to claim.

He stared at the sunlit window. The prospect of entering the world with all its menacing unknowns was terrifying. But over the clamor of doubts, one word resonated at the level of his bones. One name.

If Jessica existed within this baffling realm, he had to find her.

When the orderly returned, Lucius was ready. But the aromas that rose from his meal tray assaulted him so powerfully, he almost forgot his strategy. "What is *that*?"

"Meat loaf and glazed carrots. I know, it ain't much. But we've both had worse, right?"

He had not even realized how hungry he was until that moment. Lucius had known little of food's fragrance and none of its taste since his childhood illnesses. Even so, he did his best to ignore the tray. The orderly was the one who had addressed him earlier. The opportunity was too good to pass up. "Am I permitted to use the phone?"

"I'll have to check on that one."

"And something else."

The orderly was confident enough in his strength to smile briefly. "Don't go pushing your luck, man."

"Is there any chance you might bring me a phone book?"

"Man, I doubt there's one anywhere in this place. Besides, what do you need one for? Ordering a pizza's definitely out. You didn't have any ID on you when they brought you in, much less cash."

"A phone then. Please. This is important."

"Lemme have a word with the duty nurse. You eat up."

Lucius could not control the tremble to his hand. He was so hungry, his entire body felt hollow. The first attempt to lift the fork spilled everything off. He used his left hand to pile on the carrots, then kept the fingers in place and crammed the food into his mouth. He groaned out loud. The vegetables had been boiled until they were almost mash. The gravy was slightly congealed. The two slices of processed meat were only a degree or so off cold.

He had never imagined anything could bring such pleasure. He finished his plate and started on a cup of Jell-O with fruit, astonished over how each squishy bite exploded into flavors. The power of tasting what he ate was so exquisite, his eyes filmed over.

When the orderly came back, he surveyed the empty plates. "You done good, man."

"May I ask your name?"

"Jorge."

"Thank you, Jorge. If you have an extra meal, could I perhaps trouble you for seconds?"

Jorge's dark eyes showed a grim wisdom. "Being that close to the final door changes things, I expect."

"You have no idea."

"I'll check on another tray. And the nurse says only the docs can make a decision on the phone call."

"But . . ."

"No good arguing, man. Least, not with me. My advice is, show the doc you're done with, you know, trying to off yourself. Give them what they want, maybe they'll let you connect with the outside world." He lifted the tray. "Lemme go see if there's anything left on the trolley."

But when Jorge returned, Lucius told him, "I will give you a hundred dollars for that phone call."

Jorge set down the tray. "I already told you, man. You don't have a dime to your name."

"Not with me. But out there. They can't keep me here forever."

"You'd be surprised." But Jorge's movements were slowed by the prospect. "Hundred won't do it. Maybe five."

"For five hundred dollars I could buy a car!"

"Not any car I'd want to be seen in. And keep your voice down."

"All right, Jorge. Five hundred."

"How do I know you're good for it?"

"I am a man of my word." Lucius reached out a stranger's hand. "Five hundred dollars for the phone book and one call."

"No phone book, no way. Even if there was one around here somewhere, I can't let the nurses know what's going down." He must have seen Lucius's dismay, for he said, "Who's so important you got to call now?"

"I want to hire an attorney."

"Yeah, I guess that makes sense." This time Jorge revealed a single gold molar. "I might be able to help you out on that score."

CHAPTER 9

Asha and Dino did not emerge from the peer review until after two. She had not had anything to eat or drink since her predawn coffee, so they stopped by the hospital cafeteria. She used the wall phone to check on Luke Benoit. Dino waited until they were seated at a table by themselves to ask, "Anything?"

"Benoit ate two complete meals. He remains calm. The shift has changed, and one of the incoming orderlies has called in sick. The duty nurse wants to withdraw the constant monitoring of our patient. She says the staff is needed elsewhere and she'll check on Luke when she has time."

"What did you tell her?"

"I don't have the authority to object," Asha reminded him. "But even if I did, I didn't see a reason to do so."

"I agree." Dino smiled "By the way, you handled the review like a seasoned pro."

Asha waited to respond until she finished her salad and peeled an orange. Dino used the time to check his messages and shoot off a half-dozen e-mails. Their relationship had undergone a subtle shift, she knew. She was no longer merely a student, nor he a mentor. They were colleagues. Asha ate a slice of orange, another, and waited until Dino stopped texting and set his phone aside. Then she said, "You've told me a dozen times that part of being a good clinician is learning how to correctly interpret the unspoken."

"Hundreds of times," Dino agreed.

"Everything we're observing about Luke Benoit leads me to one conclusion." She took a breath and said, "We're not dealing with the same man."

It was a thoroughly unprofessional way of describing her patient. With more time she would find some way to couch it in clinical terms. But that was precisely how she felt.

But all Dino said was "The accent."

"That and everything else. Up until this morning Luke's behavior has maintained an established pattern that has not changed through four therapists. He uses his counseling sessions as a dumping ground. He lashes out at fate, events, other people. Everything that happens in his life is someone or something else's fault. Blame is his shield. It is his method of coping. Every time a therapist has tried to probe beyond his venting, or tries to have him accept at least partial responsibility, he stops therapy."

Dino leaned back and crossed his arms. The cafeteria's muted din faded into insignificance. "How did you get through to him?"

"I took a different course. I agreed with him that life has been horribly unfair. I tried to show him I care. And I do. Truly. Maybe too much." Asha gave Dino a chance to warn, object, something. When he remained silent, she continued. "I tried to show him that our sessions were his haven from life. Here he was protected, sheltered. He could reveal the bruised and battered little boy. Come to know himself a little better. In utter safety. Without risk of being judged or found wanting."

She feared she had said too much. It was a risk, revealing her offbeat strategy to the man responsible for her professional career. But Dino merely nodded and said, "Tell me about the differences you detect in him."

"Take what the nurse just reported about Luke devouring two meals. Luke Benoit is a fast-food addict. He loathes most vegetables. And now he finishes everything on his hospital tray and asks for another?" Asha thought back to the moment her patient had emerged from the bathroom. "The Luke we met in there is different. He is hiding something. And doing so with a remarkable level of self-control."

Dino's phone buzzed. He picked it up, studied the readout, and said, "Give me a moment."

As he texted, Asha resumed her internal struggle. Only now did she truly feel the review's aftereffects. The panel had not found her at fault in any way. There had been almost no response from the doctors in the audience. The patient had survived. Proper protocol had been followed. The issue of confinement was not a matter for the peer review to decide. California's laws on confining mental patients were the nation's strictest. The doctors were only too happy to leave that in her and Dino's hands.

Dino set down his phone. "Do we hold Benoit for observation?"

Asha nodded. That was the issue. She was immensely glad she did not possess the authority to make that decision. Because she had no idea what was best. When she realized Dino was going to wait as long as required for her response, she replied, "I'm conflicted."

Dino might as well have been reading from the text. "Patients may only be confined if they pose a risk to themselves or the general public. We are talking about an individual who has attempted suicide on three different occasions. We have grounds. But is this truly in the patient's best interests? I'm inclined to say yes."

Asha wanted to object. She felt a real aversion to confining Luke against his will. And yet there was every possible textbook reason for doing so. She followed Dino from the cafeteria, wishing there were some way to phrase her objections in clinical terms. Not liking the idea simply wasn't good enough.

Plus, there was the distinct possibility that Dino was right.

Despite the issues that swirled about them, Asha found a distinct pleasure in simply walking the hospital corridor alongside Dino. Most of the female staff who passed eyed him, then glanced at her. Envy, curiosity, an occasional knowing smirk. Not even the argument she was having with herself could erase that spice.

When they arrived at the hall, Dino greeted the duty nurse and asked, "Anything to report with Benoit?"

"He's been the perfect little lamb since I came on," she replied. "I checked on him four times. Then his visitor showed up."

Dino frowned. "I distinctly recall issuing a 'no visitors' policy for this patient."

"I saw it in the records. But it didn't make any difference."

"What are you saying?"

She pointed at Benoit's door. "The patient's lawyer is in there."

CHAPTER 10

Asha could see the news of a lawyer's presence rocked her boss. And she understood why. It threatened Dino's authority. His decisions were now subject to legal challenge. What was worse, as soon as the hospital administration heard, they would insert an attorney of their own.

"Who authorized the patient to make a phone call?" Dino demanded.

The nurse bridled. She was a senior warhorse, well accustomed to holding her ground in hospital politics. "I certainly didn't. And to answer your next question, the room does not have a phone."

"Then it must have been one of the orderlies," Dino decided. "Where are they?"

"The only ones your patient had contact with have gone off duty."

Dino's scowl creased his features from neck to hairline. The nurse responded by rising to her feet. Two seasoned veterans ready for battle.

"Dino." Asha gripped his arm and pulled him back a step.

He continued to address the nurse. "I need the names and contact numbers for all orderlies who were on duty—"

Asha broke in with, "It's happened. It's over and done. It's too late to be talking to the orderlies or anyone else." Asha gave him a chance to object, then said, "We're going about this all wrong. We need to rethink our strategy."

Dino turned slowly. The ponderous motion of a man withdrawing from an unlit fuse.

"We're treating Benoit as a *victim.* Like we *know* him. Like we *understand.*" Talking it out helped solidify Asha's swirling thoughts. Gradually her idea took concrete form. "Our assumptions are clearly wrong. We need to accept that we have no idea who we're dealing with."

There were a hundred reasons for Dino to shoot her down. Starting with how the student was lecturing the professor. In public. In a potential crisis situation. Not to mention how she was leaping to conclusions based on a meager few moments of observation.

Instead, Dino merely nodded once and said, "Benoit is your patient. You take the lead."

CHAPTER 11

Asha knocked on Luke's door. When there was no response, she waited for a time, then knocked again. When a voice finally spoke from within, Asha opened the door a fraction and asked, "May we come in?"

Clearly, Luke and the man seated on the bed's opposite side were expecting a confrontation, not a request. Asha's polite approach caught them off guard. As she had expected.

Finally Luke turned to the man and nodded. Only then did the newcomer say, "Of course."

"Thank you." There was only one other chair. Asha indicated that Dino should sit down, while she remained standing just inside the closed door. "My name is Asha Meisel. I am the patient's therapist."

"You have been his therapist up to this point," the lawyer countered. "Your future role is yet to be determined."

"Thank you very much." It was a distinctly Persian sort of response, using polite formality to mask any number of emotions. Inwardly Asha fed off the room's tension. It clarified her vision to a remarkable degree. She felt as though she could parse each of her rapid heartbeats. Observe the patient and the man seated beside him down to the level of bones and secret thoughts. "May I ask your name?"

"Sol Feinnes. I am the patient's attorney of record."

She kept her gaze on Feinnes, but her real focus was on Luke. In her secret non-therapist thoughts, Asha had always considered Luke Benoit to have wasted a substantial portion of good looks. His face had formerly remained creased like an infant about ready to wail. He denied ever using controlled substances, but Asha had often smelled the treacly-sweet odor of marijuana or hash on his clothes. His eyes were usually red-rimmed and weepy. She had found it very easy to treat him as a wounded child hiding inside an adult's body.

No longer.

Luke had the bed angled up as far as it would go, so his head was almost level with her own. He studied her with an intently focused gaze. Silent. Still as a forest animal. Cautious.

In control.

Asha continued to address the attorney. "Do you practice family law, Mr. Feinnes?"

"No. I am a litigator. As your director knows, to his regret. I have successfully brought suit against this hospital on two previous occasions."

"May I ask why the patient feels your presence is necessary?"

"To ensure my *client* is released. Now. Today."

"Of course. If you think that is best for our *patient.* Mr. Benoit is hereby released."

Behind her, Dino's chair creaked loudly as he shifted his weight. Asha held her breath until she was certain her boss was not going to object.

Feinnes was in his fifties, with thinning silver-gray hair and the air of an intelligent, thoughtful gentleman. He wore his gray pin-striped suit like a uniform of office. His voice was deeply resonant. Asha thought he would probably charm a jury with ease. He demanded, "My client is free to go?"

"I just said that. We can complete the paperwork in a few hours. Perhaps less." She watched the attorney and patient exchange another glance and took a distinct pleasure in knowing she had disarmed them both. "Am I permitted to address your client?"

"I . . . We have no objections to a few questions. Within strict limits."

Asha bowed slightly from the waist, the act of a servant. Her demeanor remained utterly calm, which did nothing to ease Luke's evident tension. The patient's jaw muscles were so clenched he looked like he held a pair of walnuts in his cheeks. "Luke, why don't you trust me?"

The question caught both patient and attorney off guard. Luke struggled for a moment, then demanded, "Why should I?"

"During our six sessions together, have I ever lied to you? Have I ever done anything that did not keep your best interests at the forefront?"

He hesitated, then asked, "Were you going to lock me up?"

"Dino and I discussed that issue for over an hour." She indicated the man seated behind her. "Dr. Dino Barbieri is the hospital's chief clinician. He was inclined to hold you for observation. The reasons for confinement are straightforward. You have attempted suicide three times. On this occasion you were actually declared dead by the medical staff. Clearly, you are a threat to yourself. Even so, I was not so sure."

Each of her declarations had caused the patient to wince. "Why?"

"Excuse me?"

"Why didn't you want me locked up?"

"I already told you, Luke. Every action I have taken, every moment we have been together, has been with one goal in mind. To do the best for you that I possibly can. And I simply was not sure that holding you over was the proper course of action. For you. We had returned here so that I might ask you that very question. Which you have now answered." She gave that a moment, then asked, "Will you tell me one thing about your current state, Luke? Please."

The distress in his eyes carried an animal-like intensity. "I don't remember anything about . . . who I was."

Asha took an involuntary step forward. "Who you *were.*"

"I remember waking up beneath the shroud. Before that . . . nothing."

"So you don't know where you live, what happened to your family?"

"Nothing." The word cost him terribly.

Feinnes protested, "An admission of amnesia is not grounds for imprisonment."

"I told you. I have no intention of confining the patient." Asha's gaze remained on the man in the bed. "Luke, would you like me to drive you home?"

CHAPTER 12

They left the hospital two hours later. Five minutes into the drive Lucius was certain that Asha Meisel knew.

She might not know *what* she knew. But it was only a question of whether he trusted her with the missing fragments. Because one thing was certain. With every mile they drove farther from the hospital and its known boundaries, the more he needed an ally.

But the uncertainties could not dispel the wonder he felt. Asha's car was a relatively modest design, yet everything about it suggested a sophistication he had never seen before. The ride was incredibly smooth, the engine quiet as a whisper. Beyond the sunlit windscreen was a half-familiar world. The traffic was certainly unlike anything he had ever known, and the cars were nothing short of astounding. The buildings they passed and the streets they drove were a mix of the recognizable and the alien.

His sense of smell was very acute. He registered a multitude of sensations with every puff of air through his open window. It reinforced the shocking changes he had known. Gone were the frigid, salty flavors of the Miramar beach. Gone, too, the hospital. Now that he was outside, he recognized the vast differences between the infirmary he had just left and all the others he had known. The biting scent of carbolic acid and astringent cleaners, the faint shadow of pain and open wounds, all had been absent.

Instead, the hospital where he had awoken had smelled like . . . nothing.

He took another deep breath, reveling in the thrills and the fears, and asked, "Did it rain recently?"

"Did it . . ." She glanced over. "Just before dawn."

Lucius wanted to ask why his question caused her to frown so. But just then he was enveloped in a wave of eucalyptus. The tall trees bordered the street now, a gentle bond that reconnected him to everything he had lost. He was still recovering, when a pleasant woman's voice came over the radio, "In one quarter of a mile, take a right on Monterey Street."

Lucius asked, "What was that?"

Another glance. "GPS. Does it disturb you? I can probably find your house without it."

He repeated slowly, "GPS."

"Global positioning satellites. Or system. I can't remember which." Each word was carefully positioned, the calm statement drawn from a turbulent mind. "Why? Don't you remember that, either?"

She was probing. And she had every reason to do so. What was more, he wanted to tell her. Desperately. Despite every reason his past granted him to maintain a distance from any member of the medical establishment, he felt that here was a woman he could genuinely trust. "What is your heritage?"

The question was enough for Asha to put on her blinker and pull into a parking spot. She turned in her seat, not quite facing him, and said, "My father's mother is Persian."

"I thought perhaps one of the regional Indian tribes."

"Native American," she corrected, watching him.

"Interesting."

"What is, Luke?"

"Everything." She was an astonishingly lovely young woman. Her dark hair was pulled back into a French twist, drawn high to reveal a sharply defined neck and jawline. Her lips were full, her skin an olive blend that suggested a permanent need for sunlight. Her eyes were her most remarkable feature, dark and slightly slanted and flecked with honeyed gold. "What kind of car is this?"

He saw the confusion crease her features once more. But before she could speak, the car was filled with the sound of a ringing phone coming through a number of hidden speakers. Asha lifted a small device and grimaced at what she saw on its illuminated screen. "Oh, no."

"What is it?"

"Nothing." She turned off the radio, then hit a button on the side of the phone. Instantly the small electronic apparatus went quiet. She remained where she was, studying the blank screen. Ten seconds later, it flashed on again and emitted a softer ringtone. Asha said, "Today of all days."

"Is something wrong?"

She pressed the button, then turned so as to face the front windscreen. When it rang a third time, she touched the screen, then answered with, "I asked you never to call me again. No, Jeffrey, as it happens, now is a terrible . . . I am with a patient. No. I will not call you back. I don't care to hear about any new crisis . . . No. I don't care that my mother . . . There is nothing more to be said. Good-bye."

Asha lowered the phone slowly. She took a very hard breath. Another. "That was extremely unprofessional."

"And very human." Despite all the reasons for caution, Lucius felt drawn to this young woman. "That was your former . . ."

She stared at the phone she held in both hands. "It was. Yes. He does that when he is upset, calling repeatedly in hopes he can break into whatever I am doing. His needs are always paramount."

"I'm so sorry for whatever it is you're going through." Lucius watched her attempt to repress a tight shudder. "Would it help to talk about it?"

" 'Would it help?' You're asking me that?"

"You are being very kind to me. It is only natural—"

"Only *natural*?" Slowly she set the phone in the cubbyhole between their seats. "Luke, whenever something interrupts one of our sessions, you take it personally. You become upset to the point of ourtrage."

"That man," Lucius said, "sounds like a young fool."

"*What* man?"

Lucius looked down at his hands. *His hands.*

When he did not reply, she demanded, "Why won't you trust me?"

He nodded slowly. There was no question but that he needed an ally. Lucius could hear the genuine concern in her voice, see it in her fractured gaze. "I will tell you whatever you want to know," Lucius decided. "If you will please do two things for me."

"What things?"

"Stop treating me as a patient. I don't need a doctor. I positively loathe most members of the medical tradition. I need an ally."

" 'The medical tradition,' " she repeated.

"Second, I need your help finding someone."

"Who?"

"Her name was Jessica Waverly."

"*Was?*"

"Yes. In 1969." He resisted the urge to ask what date this was. He would find that out soon enough. "Whatever you can tell me about her. Where is she? How is she? Is she . . ." He swallowed against the upswelling of his own impossible burden. "I need to know. Desperately."

CHAPTER 13

Asha pulled up in front of Luke's home and cut the motor. Jeffrey's call had left her feeling extremely vulnerable. The professional distance between therapist and patient had been shattered. And yet, the conversation with Luke had added a new fragment of evidence to her sense of a very real change. She watched Luke rise unsteadily from the car and asked, "Are you all right?"

"Very weak." Luke studied the house with a worried expression. "I live here?"

Luke Benoit's residence was a modest two-story affair in a neighborhood of sixties-era homes, situated between Old Town and Cal Poly. There was an unkempt front yard and a fine view of Bishop Peak. Various trees sheltered much of the street, and there was the sound of children laughing somewhere out of sight. Traffic rumbled along a major thoroughfare two blocks over, but this street had a remarkable calm.

Asha replied, "You inherited this from your aunt, who had no children of her own. Your parents helped make the upstairs into an apartment. The downstairs is rented by four graduate students." Asha studied him across the car's hood. "You don't remember anything? Really?"

"No." He did not move. "One of the tenants found . . . my body?"

"Water was dripping through the ceiling of his bedroom. He went up to investigate."

He shuddered. "Let's get this over with."

Thankfully, no one was at home. Asha watched as Luke slowly climbed the stairs. When he reached the landing he gripped the rail and swayed slightly, his eyes clenched against the sudden weakness. Asha waited and observed. His strength of will was clearly evident, and this defied everything she thought she knew about him.

They entered the ratty sitting room that Luke had often described as his haven against the world. Only now, Asha thought, Luke Benoit appeared dismayed by everything he saw. He stood in the center of the parlor and made a slow circle, taking in the dishes that covered every flat space in his kitchenette, the dirty clothes piled by the washer-dryer, the stained sofa and chairs, the massive flat screen and mountainous stereo speakers that formed the only nice elements to the otherwise bleak room. He walked over and threw open the dusty French doors leading to his narrow balcony. He asked no one in particular, "Who lives like this?"

Asha nodded in silent agreement. The answer was, Luke Benoit was a young man in utter and wretched despair, who had given up hope that life would ever offer him anything of value. She watched Luke inspect the place with very real dismay and asked, "Will you tell me what you're thinking?"

"I will tell you everything." He hesitated, then amended, "Everything you are willing to hear. But first . . ."

"You want me to locate this missing woman," Asha offered.

"I don't know if she's missing or not. Just try. Please."

She took another step into the parlor and closed the door leading to the stairway. "Does this mean you are refusing future therapy?"

He pondered that for a time, staring at the threadbare carpet by his feet. "First I will tell you what you want to know, then we will discuss the therapy issue."

"If you wish."

"I'd like to ask your help with something else." Luke lifted his gaze. "I know you are an extremely busy professional. I've taken far too much of your time. You must tell me if you need to be elsewhere. I will understand."

Once more, what would have been a normal statement from most people was utterly unlike anything she had ever heard Luke speak before. "All of my day's other appointments were rescheduled because of your . . . incident. What do you need?"

"Does . . . Do I have any money?"

"Your parents left you a small trust." Asha knew the answer because her bills were sent to the law firm that handled Luke's inheritance. "You own this home. The rents are also managed by your trustees. What do you need the money for, Luke?"

He cast another bleak glance about the room. "Will you help me find another place to stay?"

Asha insisted that Luke change and pack some belongings. He clearly did not want to spend an instant longer in the apartment, but did as she said. When he entered his bedroom, Asha started to put her purse down on the kitchen counter, then thought better of it. The grout between the cracked tiles was grayish brown with old dirt. Every surface she could see needed to be boiled and sterilized. Asha crossed the living room and stepped onto the narrow balcony. The folding aluminum chairs with their frayed straps looked as unappealing as the rest of the apartment. Asha leaned against the iron banister and used her phone to book Luke into a B and B her grandmother had once used. Then she decided to try and see what she could find about the woman Luke had mentioned.

Jessica Waverly was a remarkable name, something from a Victorian novel. Asha actually wondered if the person existed at all. But then the search engine flashed a series of pages linked to the name.

Two hundred thirty-nine thousand pages, to be exact.

Asha stared at the search results, then scrolled down to the Wikipedia link. The online encyclopedia often contained a wealth of incomplete or utterly false data. But Asha had used their overviews on a number of occasions as a basis for further research.

This time, however, she searched no further. She couldn't. What she found on the Wikipedia site left her more confused and alarmed than ever.

CHAPTER 14

Asha had set aside Thursday to do a final proof of her master's thesis. It had been a lot of work, but in many respects it had gone more smoothly than she had expected. That left her worried that she might have neglected some crucial element, or gotten it completely wrong. Just the same, she decided late that afternoon that the work was ready for review, and sent it off as an attachment to Dino, her supervisor.

Her thoughts returned constantly to Luke Benoit. Over the course of the day Asha phoned him three times. She had no idea what was the norm in such cases. But she decided to err on the side of caution. Twice they spoke briefly. Luke sounded tired, subdued. But his answers were clear, his responses good. The third time the guesthouse receptionist said he had gone out for a walk.

At noon on Friday, Asha's grandmother arrived in San Luis Obispo for one of her regular visits. Sonya Meisel liked getting away from Los Angeles for a night. Their visits followed a routine, sort of. Her grandmother disliked the idea of adding to

Asha's burdens. Instead, Sonya's aim was to be a useful friend. She arrived in the late morning, made herself a cup of jasmine tea, and napped. By the time Asha finished with the day's patients and studies, her grandmother would already have made her way through the fresh markets and purchased what was necessary for their evening meal. Asha's primary responsibility was to decide upon their dinner menu, leave Sonya a shopping list, and clean the apartment for her grandmother's arrival. Sonya was a stickler for neatness. Asha was the exact opposite. Without this regular goad her home would have resembled a hurricane's aftermath.

They met as usual in a café midway between the hospital and the town's main market area. Theirs had always been an easy relationship. It was not Sonya's way to pry, neither about Asha's demolished love life nor her patients. Instead, Sonya allowed Asha to choose the topic; then she handed down her opinions in the manner of a queen giving directions. Most of the time Asha smiled and dropped her grandmother's advice in the great circular file of life. Her grandmother did not mind. In fact, she seemed to enjoy Asha's ability to absorb whatever opinion Sonya cared to give, and then make her own decisions. She was genuinely proud of Asha and her intelligence and her determination.

But fifteen minutes into their meeting, Sonya noted, "You are not with me today."

"No, I suppose not."

Her grandmother was a woman isolated by mannerisms drawn from a different epoch. She was as lofty and opinionated as a Persian countess. She belonged in a world of palaces and servants, where supplicants approached on bended knee. Today she was dressed in a Chanel suit of black-and-white herringbone checks, with a woven gold chain around her neck. Her dark hair was laced with silver, and her cheeks were creased with age. Sonya Meisel remained a striking figure, regal and intent. If she even noticed the looks she garnered from men and women alike, she gave no sign. She never did. "You should have said something if you did not want me to travel up."

"It's not that." Asha reached across the table. "I can't tell you how much these visits mean."

"Even today?"

Asha withdrew her hand. "Today especially."

Sonya surprised her then. For the first time ever, she asked, "Is it a patient?"

"Yes. I'm scheduled to meet with him at four. Only he doesn't want to be a patient. He wants to be my friend."

"As in, romance?"

Asha had considered that very seriously. "No. I am fairly certain he does not see me in that light."

"Then what . . ." Sonya stopped talking because another shadow had fallen over their table.

Asha looked up, then said, "Dino!"

"I was passing by and saw you through the window. Am I disturbing?"

"Not at all. Dino, this is my grandmother. Nana, this is—"

"Dr. Barbieri. What a distinct pleasure. My granddaughter speaks so very highly of you."

"I am pleased to hear it, madame. Your granddaughter is a credit to our profession."

"Please, good sir. Do us the honor of joining us." Sonya was in her element now. "I fear there is no table service in this establishment."

"No matter. I'll be right back."

When the doctor stepped to the counter, Sonya said, "You never mentioned that your superior is so extremely handsome."

"I . . . Nana, he's twelve years older than me."

Sonya sniffed her disagreement. "You young people. You see the shell. The clothes, the hair, the skin, the age. *Bah.*"

In truth, her grandmother's words left her feeling almost

giddy. She had never spoken to anyone about her infatuation. Asha felt her face flame as she whispered, "Nana, that man is my boss and my supervisor. And do you see the way he dresses?"

"My darling Asha, for some reason you fail to notice the true man. Dino Barbieri has suffered some great blow. He has lost his ability to see himself. He takes poor care of his appearance. He lives alone, yes?"

"I . . . He went through a bad divorce a little over four years ago."

"There. It is as I said. What you do not see is the man's potential. He is more than handsome. He is arresting."

Asha repressed a sudden urge to confess how much she secretly thought of Dino Barbieri. "I've never heard you describe anyone like that."

"Because there are very few of them, I assure you. Your grandfather was such a man. To the outside world, a grave and difficult figure. But inwardly he was as striking as this gentleman."

Asha felt so unsettled she changed the subject. "Let's not forget the fact that I'm still getting over Jeffrey."

"Ah. Jeffrey. Him." Sonya sniffed. "Los Angeles is filled with too many of his ilk. Which was why I was so pleased when you moved here."

Asha was still trying to come up with a response, when Dino returned to the table and asked, "You're sure I'm not disturbing?"

"You would do us great honor," Sonya replied. "My granddaughter has been poor company, I fear."

"Nana," Asha protested.

"I am simply sharing the truth with your trusted adviser, no?" To Dino, she continued, "My Asha has a patient who is troubling her such that he has invaded our time together. She mentioned it was a patient because he was already present at the table. But she has told me nothing else, I assure you."

"I know this patient. I'm not surprised to hear she's troubled."

It felt to Asha as though the café gradually slipped away, leaving their table isolated from the noise and the people. The three of them were captured by a very unique stillness, one that emanated from the look shared between Asha's grandmother and her boss. When Sonya turned back, she said, "Perhaps you should repeat for Dr. Barbieri what you just told me."

"Call me Dino, please."

"You do me great honor, sir. And I am Sonya."

Asha knew her mouth was ajar. She knew something had just happened. She should be able to identify it. She was, after all, a highly trained clinician. But she was still searching for an answer when Dino turned to her and said, " 'I'm listening.' "

It was one of their little insider jokes, Dino using the line made famous by the sitcom character Frasier Crane, star of a radio talk-show. Asha told him, "The patient no longer wants me as his therapist."

Dino shifted back in his seat. "He wants a different analyst? Again?"

"He doesn't want *any* therapy. He wants me to be his friend."

Dino's words slowed drastically. " 'His friend.' "

"Right. And no, I don't think he means anything romantic by this."

"You're sure?"

"A beauty like my granddaughter learns early and well to sense when a man is contemplating the forbidden step," Sonya said. "If she says this gentleman is not romantically inclined, I would accept it."

Dino nodded slowly. "Tell me what happened."

Asha gestured at her grandmother. "Is that proper?"

"You are no longer his therapist. We have an issue. Your grandmother strikes me as a remarkable woman." Dino turned to Sonya and then explained, "Wednesday I woke Asha with the news that one of her patients had attempted suicide."

"Oh, my darling girl. Are you all right?"

"Yes, Nana. I'm fine. Truly."

"She handled herself with a professionalism that would have been a credit to a seasoned therapist," Dino assured her, then turned to Asha. "Will you tell us what happened?"

Asha found it a relief to recount her Wednesday afternoon and the previous day's conversations. Sonya was a great listener, with her flashing dark eyes and her natural poise. As Asha described the drive to Luke Benoit's home, Dino crossed one arm over his chest, propped his elbow on his arm, and fitted his hand around the lower half of his face. The result was an intensity that left her certain he saw nothing, *thought* of nothing, except her.

She related how Luke had entered the house and surveyed it with the look of a complete and utter stranger. He had to be directed upstairs to the studio apartment where he lived.

Sonya asked, "The home is his?"

"His mother was born in San Luis Obispo and met her husband at Cal Poly. The home was left to Luke by his aunt, who died childless. His parents placed it in the same trust that now also handles all his inheritance."

Dino explained, "The patient was orphaned a year and a half ago. Traffic accident."

"Former patient," Sonya corrected.

For some reason that comment was enough to draw a smile from Asha's boss. "I stand corrected." Dino glanced from one woman to the other. "What are you planning for later?"

"I'm scheduled to meet with Luke Benoit in an hour and a half," Asha replied. "He refused to come to my office. I told him I would stop by the guesthouse."

Dino's easy banter was replaced by an expression of sharp concern. "So he's serious about halting therapy."

"Apparently so."

"And afterward?"

"My granddaughter is making me dinner," Sonya replied. "She is a remarkably good cook."

"I am certain you are the cause of that," Dino said.

"Well, perhaps, a little." Sonya's gaze rested on her granddaughter. "Mostly in the manner of herbs and spices and the freshness of produce. But she has an artist's sensibility when it comes to the actual preparations."

Dino's expression was almost solemn, but his midnight-blue eyes flashed with a smile that did not quite touch his lips. "An artist," he said. "My family would adopt her on sight."

Sonya asked, "You are native to this land?"

"Five generations and counting. My forebears emigrated from Tuscany. They worked as tenant farmers, saved every dime, and bought hill country that was considered too angled for proper farming. They established a vineyard that is still run by my relatives."

"You broke with that tradition?"

"My grandfather was the first to attend college," Dino replied. "There was an almighty battle, one they still talk about at family gatherings. My father teaches internal medicine at UC Irvine. By the time I left for school, it had almost become a second custom."

"That is the way with families, no?" Sonya flashed a smile at her granddaughter. "What was once an arena of conflict becomes the lore of Sunday gatherings."

"And good-natured arguments," Dino said. "And excuses for behavior and habits that hold no logic whatsoever."

"What possible role does logic play in human behavior?" Sonya demanded.

"Madame, I think you would have made an excellent clinician."

She gave a regal gesture, sweeping that aside. "I am quite content to take pride in my granddaughter's accomplishments."

The two of them shared a smile. Then Dino said, "Might I suggest a change of venue? Allow me to make you dinner at my home. Call Benoit and see if he'll join us. I'd like another opportunity to inspect this young man and his altered personality."

"But Sonya . . ."

"If your grandmother would not mind assisting us, it might actually prove useful to meet him in such a setting. We want Benoit to see us as his allies in whatever he is going through, and get him back into regular care."

Asha glanced at her grandmother, who nodded approval. "Thank you, Dino. We're happy to accept."

CHAPTER 15

Lucius found himself scarcely mobile on Thursday. He spent much of the day planted in the chairs by the fountain. His limbs were leaden, his thoughts slow and disjointed. He could not make sense of the television. Reading a newspaper was impossible. He did his best to avoid looking in the mirror.

When Asha Meisel called, she seemed unfazed by his complaints. She offered a soothing response and spoke about the body's need to cleanse itself. She urged him to take it easy. Rest. Sleep as much as possible. Lucius took his meals in the inn's restaurant and only ventured outside once, when he managed a walk around the block.

Thursday night Lucius dreamed of a grave. He stood before the lumpish rectangle of recently tilled earth. A new headstone gleamed at the far end. Leaves rattled across the ground, whispering to him in a cold, dark tongue. A lone woman stood beneath the shrouded sky. He could not see her face. He did not need to. When he woke, his heart pounded and his body was drenched in sweat. And yet he felt no fear. He left his little room and seated himself on a stone bench. Moonlight sparked through the fountain. Gradually the water's music replaced the unnerving sound of lonely leaves.

Lucius woke early on Friday, as if it was just another day. The change was as astonishing as it was welcome. He felt utterly renewed. He dressed in jeans and an unironed shirt and old sneakers, the only clean clothes he had found in that young man's wardrobe. He entered the sunlit restaurant and ordered coffee, then took his time over the lovely breakfast buffet. He forced himself to eat slowly, and did his best to set aside the barrage of questions until he was done. Then he wandered through to the front room, where he found a forgotten *LA Times.* He bundled it up and carried it back to his room. There was a little rectangular table set beside the front window. He pulled over the desk chair, seated himself, then spread out the paper.

The shock was far less than he might have expected. The cars, the buildings, the speech, the rainbow variety of races, everything he had seen the previous two afternoons, had readied him for this. Lucius traced his finger over the date.

The reality of what he saw there on the paper's front page actually helped anchor him. There was no escaping the simple facts. He had died in May of 1969 and had awoken forty-nine years later.

Abruptly the room felt too confining, so he carried the paper out to the bench beside the fountain. He took his time and read the entire paper. The advertisements were an astonishment. Especially those for cars . . .

So many cars.

Then he spotted one advertisement, and his breath locked in his throat.

The sky clouded over while he sat there by the fountain. He might have remained there all day, had the receptionist not come out and informed him that he had a phone call. Lucius followed her inside, his brain still captured by the implications of that advertisement. He was directed to the guest phone, and heard himself answer in a voice not really his, "This is . . ."

"Luke?"

"Asha. Good morning."

"How are you?"

He looked down at the newspaper in his other hand. "Surprised by so much."

"Do you want to talk about it?"

He heard the hint of clinical detachment, the professional seeking answers of her own. "Not just yet."

"But you are feeling better than yesterday?"

"So much. You were right, of course. Your calls have been most reassuring."

"I'm glad to hear it." She hesitated, but then continued. "You met Dr. Barbieri at the hospital."

"The doctor who was there with you, but did not speak," Lucius recalled. At the time, the name had not registered. With so much else to take in, Lucius had failed to recognize the name of his previous doctor. He stared at the sunlit world beyond the inn's front window. So many mysteries beyond his comprehension.

Asha said, "Dr. Barbieri is as concerned as I am about your desire to halt therapy. He has invited us to his home this evening for dinner. My grandmother is in town and has agreed to join us. Will you come?"

Lucius halted his immediate response before it was uttered. That no dinner would change his mind regarding future therapy sessions. That he disliked intensely the idea of being manipulated by the medical establishment. The fact was, he faced a universe of mysteries, and he needed allies. Something told him he could trust this young woman with his secret. He took a long breath, then decided, "I would be honored to accept."

* * *

Lucius returned to his room for the wallet he had found in the upstairs apartment. He knew Asha was addressing a young man who was not there. If he was to seek Asha's help, he would have to tell her the truth. The inescapability of this fact actually helped seal him into the here and now.

He returned to the lobby, asked directions from the receptionist, took a card with the guesthouse's address in case he got lost, then started walking.

Some street names were familiar, of course. He had visited San Luis Obispo on a number of occasions. But many intersections were not as he recalled, which unsettled him. He wondered if he might have passed through some unseen juncture, and entered an imperfect mirror image of the world he had left behind. He took a left off Pacific Street onto Broad, crossed Marsh, and then turned right on Monterey. He passed the Museum of Art, circled around the old Mission, then took Chorro back to Higuera. He entered a men's shop and selected a pair of khaki trousers and a white knit shirt. The prices were shocking, but he was going to dinner with Asha and her associate that evening, and he wanted to wear something nice. Everything he had taken from the stranger's apartment was unironed and slovenly. Lucius added a woven leather belt and dock shoes and socks and underwear to the pile, then handed over the credit card in his wallet and waited for the plastic to melt. But the salesperson merely smiled and asked him to sign. The amount of money he had just spent caused his eyes to water.

He walked back to McLintock's for the finest burger of his life. When he was done and the waitress had removed his empty plate, Lucius took the folded sheet of paper from his rear pocket. Slowly he displayed the advertisement he had torn from the *LA Times.*

There across the top was his own name.

Quarterfield Motors was apparently having its annual spring

bash. New and used cars. Employee pricing on most models. Seventy-two hours only.

The advertisement covered two entire pages. Lucius hated to think how much that must have cost. The page was split into distinct segments, each advertising a different line. Two were German, Mercedes and Porsche, neither of which he had carried. Two were British, Land Rover and Jaguar. More newcomers. Then the familiar Cadillac and Buick logos, but minus the Oldsmobile and Pontiac lines that Lucius had always joined with the two other high-end GM models. And Lexus, whatever that was. And, apparently, Chrysler and Jeep were now sold as one line.

Slowly and deliberately he refolded the advertisement and put it back in his pocket. He paid for his meal and rejoined the pedestrian flow. He retraced his steps to the guesthouse, where he unpacked his purchases. He took a shower, then lay down on the bed. His limbs felt leaden and his head ached. Lucius wondered if this was some lingering aftereffect from the overdose he had supposedly taken.

He slept and dreamed of an empire that was no longer his to claim.

CHAPTER 16

It was five o'clock on Friday afternoon, and Asha was late. Lucius stood on the guesthouse's shaded veranda and took pleasure in the swallows cutting swaths from the cloudless sky. Then he heard the sound of a racing engine, followed by Asha flying into the guesthouse's circular drive. She signaled urgently for him to climb in. Asha had the car in motion the instant Lucius shut his door. She told him, "I got held up with a patient."

He gripped the door handle as she took a curve at high speed. "I'm so sorry."

"For what?"

"For damaging your schedule. Interrupting other appointments you no doubt had scheduled by . . . this incident."

Asha cast him a hard look, but did not speak.

"I am grateful that you would invite me for dinner—"

"I didn't. Dino did." She halted at an intersection and drummed the steering wheel. "This light takes forever."

"In any case I apologize for the disruption I have no doubt caused."

At that moment the light turned green. She powered through the intersection, then said, "I had planned to go home, change, pick up my grandmother, then come by and fetch you. But I'm late, this is the first time I've ever been to Dino's home, and my place is twenty minutes closer to Morro Bay. So now . . ."

It was clear enough what disturbed her. "You dislike having me know where you live."

"It breaks several dozen different protocols," Asha agreed.

Lucius decided it was not the time to point out how he was about to reveal rule-breaking secrets of his own. "I will respect your privacy. And I am grateful for this gift of trust."

Asha looked like she was about to speak, but shook her head and remained silent. Twelve harrowing minutes later, they pulled up in front of an attractive apartment block, red bricks and stone, four stories, and set back in a well-kept lawn. Asha cut the motor and leapt out. "I won't be long. Will you stay here?"

"Of course. I am absolutely . . ." He stopped because she was already gone.

Ten minutes later, perhaps less, Asha returned wearing a pleated khaki linen skirt and white blouse that set off her hair, now braided in a long raven rope that nestled on her right shoulder. With her walked a queen.

Asha was a most attractive young lady. This older woman was something else entirely. She was stately without effort, and beautiful in a timeless manner. All the foreign elements hinted at in Asha's demeanor were on full display here. The impenetrable gaze, the high cheekbones, the impossibly erect carriage. She wore a simple off-white frock with a gold medallion at the throat of her high collar. The woman was understated, elegant, and completely in control.

Lucius rose from the car and walked forward to meet them. Asha said, "May I present Sonya Meisel, my grandmother. She is . . ." Asha's gaze tracked behind them, and her expression melted. "Oh, no, no, no."

Lucius turned in time to observe a gleaming red sports car rush toward them. The horn beeped, as rich a sound as the engine. Lucius recognized the Ferrari's prancing horse on the hood and door pancl.

The older woman demanded, "How does this one come to be here?"

"I have no idea. I never told him where I lived. I'm not the owner of register, I went through a lawyer just like you said."

"Your mother," Sonya Meisel said. "It has to be."

"No, no, no."

"Go deal with this one. I will remain with our guest." She turned to Lucius. "Be so good as to walk with me."

The driver raced the engine once, twice, then cut the motor. He emerged and smiled and called, "There you are! Good afternoon, Sonya! Lovely as ever!"

Lucius thought the newcomer was movie-star handsome. A man with utter confidence in his looks and his wealth and the magnetic power of his flashing smile. Lucius allowed himself to be turned away and asked, "That is Jeffrey?"

"My granddaughter told you his name, did she?"

"Only because he called while she drove me home yesterday," Lucius replied. "Three times. No, four."

"Some people think Jeffrey has everything to make the two of them a perfect match. At least on the surface." She walked in slow cadence, and spoke softly enough for them both to hear the clamor of rising voices behind them. "Asha's mother is among them. But I must respect my granddaughter's privacy and speak no more, you understand?"

"Of course."

"She will be extremely distressed that you, her patient, witnessed this exchange."

"Former patient," Lucius corrected. "I am an expert at remaining blind to things I should not see."

Sonya rearranged the edges of her eyes and mouth, whether in humor or approval, Lucius could not tell. Behind them the car's engine roared back to life. Sonya said, "Perhaps we are safe to return."

Asha declared, "This is terrible. Terrible."

Jeffrey offered a disappointed sincerity. "You certainly know how to make a guy feel welcome."

"But you're not welcome, Jeffrey. As you would have known, if you had called to ask if you could come."

As always she was pulled in two conflicting directions. Which characterized her attitude to their relationship. Jeffrey was truly remarkable, and in so many different ways. Intelligent, handsome, a great listener, and so much fun. Asha said, "I suppose my mother put you up to this."

"She didn't put me up to anything, Asha. She said—"

"She had no right to say anything at all." Asha turned her back to the street and her grandmother and her patient. Her *patient.* "Did it ever occur to you that if I wanted to have contact, I would have told you myself where I lived?"

"Your mother said I should come and try to make things right. She said . . ." Jeffrey stepped off the sidewalk and onto the lawn, drawing himself into her field of vision. "Never mind. You're upset."

"Of course I'm upset. You're *here.*"

"You might try to be a little grateful, Asha." He had a most expressive face. And he knew it. Jeffrey could do wounded and sincere better than any man she had ever known. Perfect hair, perfect tan, great car, beautiful clothes sense, a wonderful lover. As so many women knew. "I'm in the middle of a hugely important—"

"Stop, just stop. I don't want—"

"I left a five-million-dollar deal on the table. So I could drive up and apologize. And you won't let me finish one sentence?"

The pull on her heart was so strong. Even now, after eighteen months since their last meeting, and all the reasons Asha had for breaking things off. "That's exactly what is happening."

"I told your mother you'd be like this."

"And for once you were right." She wrapped her arms around her middle, gripping herself tightly enough to keep from reaching out and embracing him. She spoke the words as much to herself as to Jeffrey, "This isn't about you. It never will be again."

"You've said all that before." Jeffrey was an attorney, making his mark within the viciously competitive LA film world. He had learned early and well that "no" was simply another door he had to barge through. "You were wrong then. You're wrong now."

Asha felt the niggling thread of doubt weave its way into the tapestry of yet another shattered dusk. Jeffrey was ideal in so many ways. He had introduced her into the rarified world of parties high in the Bel Air hills, where they had danced and laughed and stared down at the flickering earthbound stars of Los Angeles. She had enjoyed the heady atmosphere more than she had thought possible. But Jeffrey had broken her heart and shattered her trust three times. Twice she had accepted his apologies and his promises. Twice she had forced herself to believe that he sincerely wanted to change. That he was going to change. That . . .

"Asha, we're meant to be together."

Even now, after so many fractured hours, she wanted to be with him. Breaking up remained the hardest thing she had ever done. There was a component of her life that only felt complete with him. If only he had not hurt her so badly. If only . . .

Asha forced herself to say, "I thought that was true. I was wrong."

"Your mother disagrees."

Asha felt her internal conflict drain away, leaving her utterly depleted. A great void opened where her heart should have resided. She tightened her hold on her middle.

"Asha, say something. You know we deserve one more—"

"What happened with Tiffany?"

He shrank back a fraction, then caught himself. "That was finished months ago. You need to let it go. One mistake—"

"But it wasn't just one mistake, was it." Her voice sounded dull to her own ears. Empty. Defeated. A narrow, bitter thought rose unbidden. This was her fate. She would never be free of this man or this argument or this futile hour. "Don't lie, Jeffrey. We both know what makes her unique. She was the only one who told me to my face."

"I love you, Asha."

"But you haven't loved *just* me. As we both know all too well."

"I can . . ."

"Change? Stay true to your lover? Good. I'm glad. Now go find somebody and make it your reality from your very first day together."

The realization that she meant what she said tightened his features. Asha glimpsed beneath the polished exterior, and saw the other side of this wonderful man. Because he was just that, in so many ways. And she had spent two and a half years trying to convince herself that she could live with this *other* Jeffrey. The man for whom success meant always getting his own way.

She remained where she was, her arms fastened around her middle, as he slammed the door and the engine roared to life.

CHAPTER 17

Lucius and Sonya returned to find Asha standing at the sidewalk, staring at the empty space where Jeffrey's car had been parked.

The Ferrari bellowed down the small street, burned rubber, turned the corner, and vanished.

Asha stared bleakly at the empty road. Sonya's poise remained intact, even when witnessing her granddaughter's distress. Lucius took his lead from the older woman and kept quiet.

Finally Asha sighed and blinked and wiped her face. Her voice was a low and broken murmur. "We should be going."

Dino Barbieri's home was notable only because it faced directly onto Morro Bay. The west-facing wall was entirely glass. The cottage was one room wide, scarcely broader than a mobile home. It had been built in the late fifties, and everything possible had been done to make it more suitable to the modern age. But scarcely ten feet separated the residence from its neighbors to either side. The living room was floored in ship's teak and the ceiling had been opened and fitted with mock rafters. A new kitchen anchored the parlor's back wall and was fitted out as precisely as a ship's galley.

The public rooms were cluttered as only a bachelor could make them. Asha saw evidence of hurried cleaning everywhere. Shelves along the sidewall were jammed with books and journals and papers and computers, no doubt cleared away for his guests' arrival. The furniture was expensive and worn. Nothing Asha saw suggested that she was in the home of a distinguished professor and clinician.

Asha felt as though the argument with Jeffrey cast a pall over the meal. She had spent the entire day hoping that this might mark a genuine shift. Transforming her relationship with Dino from supervisor and student into . . .

She might as well admit it. *Lovers.*

Instead, she could not shake the fact that the ghost of her past mistakes had joined them at the meal. Making it impossible for her to step into a new relationship.

That is, if the potential for one actually existed.

Dino was a most gracious host. If he noticed Asha's distance, he gave no sign. In fact, the evening was dominated by pleasant chatter between Dino and Asha's grandmother. They talked with the gay ease of lifelong friends. Asha smiled when she thought it was appropriate, but she heard almost nothing of what was said.

They dined on Dino's rear deck, by far the nicest part of his home. Dusk painted a golden hue over the shoreline and the sea. A few brave gulls passed close by, hoping for scraps. Otherwise the evening was theirs. Luke spoke only when a comment was directed his way. Otherwise he sat and ate and followed the conversation with the intent focus of a professional listener. When Dino cleared away the plates, Asha watched as Luke straightened in his chair, his expression solemn. Dino returned to his seat, and looked at her. The entire table waited.

Asha said quietly, "It's time."

* * *

"I was born Lucius Quarterfield in 1941, and my mother died while birthing me. My father was a stonemason who injured his foot as an apprentice, so he could not go off to war. I don't know if it was losing his wife or remaining out of America's great battle that caused him to carry such a load of bitterness. But he was. Bitter and angry and, by all accounts, a brawler and a nasty drunk. He died when I was six. I do not recall my sisters ever speaking his name after his death."

The evening possessed a rare inland bite. An arid wind blew off the land, carrying desert flavors of creosote and sorrel. Asha found herself breathing deeply, as though needing to anchor herself.

"I don't remember much of my childhood before the illness struck me at six," Luke went on. "I recall being fairly happy. My sisters served as surrogate mothers and did their best to shelter me when my father endured his dark hours. I do remember that much. Then the pleurisy struck, and my world was permanently altered for the worse."

They were seated on the deck, shielded from Dino's neighbors by exterior slat walls. Asha's grandmother and Dino were both angled so as to watch the sunset, as if they found a need to offer Luke this gift of privacy. Sonya shifted in her chair and said, "Please forgive me, I do not know this illness."

"Pleurisy," Dino said. "You don't see it so much nowadays, but it was once a killer. Especially among children and the very old. It refers to an inflammation of the pleurae, the membranes of the tissue surrounding the lungs. The pain can be very intense."

"'Intense,'" Luke agreed. "That is the word."

"Basically, the word 'pleurisy' refers to the symptoms," Dino went on. "But the potential causes are numerous. Aortic dissections, autoimmune disorders, erythematosus, hepatitis, lymphoma. But the two issues of greatest concern among the young are viral infections or bacteria for which there is no known cure. Thoracentesis, extraction of fluid from the pleural cavity, is the standard treatment for the symptoms."

When the deck went silent, Asha said quietly, "Go on."

"My father and I entered the hospital within days of each other," Luke said. "I was interned for three and a half months. When I emerged, I had lost my father and a lung. I lived my entire life in the shadow of that ailment. Bones, lung, heart, all forged in that awful period. As well as my dislike for hospitals and doctors."

For the first time that evening Asha focused completely upon the evening. Luke's story was absurd, of course. His claims represented a number of very serious mental and emotional issues. She could see that Dino was completely unimpressed. Her grandmother, however, appeared utterly engrossed. Asha could understand why. Sonya had always been comfortable with elements so timeless in their power that man could not fathom the questions, much less determine the answers.

Luke interrupted himself then and asked, "Do you want me to go on?"

"Of course I do," Asha said.

"I only asked because you seem very distracted."

"You tell me you were born almost fifty years ago. You sketch out a tragic yet perfectly reasonable existence for yourself." She responded as though it was just the two of them. "How am I supposed to seem?"

This time Luke's smile came more easily. "Exactly as you do now, I guess."

"Go on. Finish your story."

So he did. The final visit to his doctor, the drive to Miramar, the walk, and his tragic departure from Jessica Waverly.

When he was done, Luke turned his face toward the darkening sea. The pain of retelling was etched in his features. He looked almost craven, a grim mask of lonely sorrow. Luke Benoit had aged a thousand years in the telling.

It was her grandmother who broke the silence. "So you died in the arms of this woman."

"Jessica. Yes."

"You recall the experience clearly, I take it."

"The feel of her embrace. The cry of gulls. The crashing waves. The frigid water. I remember it all vividly."

"The darkness."

"The end," Luke agreed. "It is with me still."

Dino asked Sonya, "Are you accepting that this literally happened?"

"Your patient has described an experience with utter clarity, one that defies all logic. I neither believe nor disbelieve. I am simply listening."

"Ex-patient," Luke corrected softly.

CHAPTER 18

There followed a dense silence. Dino offered coffee, but no one seemed inclined to linger. Asha felt a sudden urge to excuse herself and walk the moonlit sands, listen to the ocean, try and fathom some logic to an evening of impossible events. But she merely waited with the others until Sonya finally said, "It has been a lovely evening."

"I am glad you could come." Dino's warmth was absent now. In its place was a professional formality that chilled the home's atmosphere.

Asha asked Luke to see her grandmother to the car. Dino waited until Luke and Sonya had entered the night shadows to ask, "So what was your response to Luke Benoit's revelations?"

She said what she knew he expected. "New delusion, same problem."

"That's good to hear, Asha." Dino leaned against the doorjamb. "I was concerned that your patient might be drawing you into his version of reality."

"He spun a very compelling tale," she said.

Dino shrugged. "No matter how much he might try to believe it and persuade others, it's still just a reflection of your patient's internal state."

"Is Luke still my patient?"

"He needs to be. Desperately." Dino stared at the shadows lining his drive. "You understand what role the factor of organicity plays here?"

"Sure."

Dino explained himself anyway. "Luke Benoit exhibits a new delusional state. We need to assume that it is derived from a shift in his brain's biological functions."

Asha felt a faint disquiet, but she stifled it and responded. "From the drug overdose related to his third suicide attempt."

"And near-death experience. Correct. His current level of environmental stress has basically pushed Luke over the edge."

"Luke's natural reservoir of coping abilities were never very high," Asha said. "You're suggesting his tenuous hold on reality has basically evaporated."

"I am indeed. Which means . . ."

"It raises the likelihood of a fourth suicide attempt. One that has every chance of being successful."

Dino nodded approval. "We need to up his dosage of meds."

"My guess is, he'll resist that."

"Then he'll die." Dino crossed his arms, sealing out the trauma of losing a patient. "You need to prepare yourself for that possible outcome, Asha. You can't see yourself as responsible for what could well be just around the corner. Sooner or later, he's going to come face-to-face with undeniable evidence that his supposed recollection of this past existence is just another delusion. When that happens . . ."

Asha let the sentence remain unfinished. "There's something I need to tell you."

His smile rearranged his features. "I'm not sure I'm able to absorb another shock tonight."

"I've identified Jessica Waverly, the woman Luke claims to be searching for."

"You did? And?"

"Waverly is her maiden name. Nowadays she's known as Jessica Wright."

The news pushed him down the steps and into the street. "Not *the* Jessica Wright."

"None other."

Dino turned and stared down the empty lane. "Tomorrow is Saturday."

"Last I checked."

"I suppose you were going to do something with your grandmother."

"I can put her off. She'll understand."

"I hate leaving this until Monday. Luke might seek to make some further step, which could be disastrous."

"It took me all of thirty seconds to make the discovery online," Asha agreed.

"Could we meet with Luke together at ten o'clock? At my private office."

"Ten o'clock is fine." Asha did her best to ignore her final wish that the evening had turned out differently. "Thank you for a lovely evening."

CHAPTER 19

Lucius allowed Asha's grandmother to set the pace down the unlit lane. He asked, "May I offer you my arm?"

"How gallant." Sonya moved in close enough for a hint of lilacs to enter the salt-laden air. "You are a most interesting gentleman. Shall I call you Luke or Lucius?"

"I suppose . . . Luke would be fitting."

"Then Luke it is. Do you like stories, young man?"

"Very much."

"My own grandfather, of blessed memory, was a senior official in the Shah's government. He even once served as Iran's ambassador to France. I rarely speak of such matters. But tonight we are revealing secrets. When my grandfather first detected signs of the revolution, he began pestering my father, who was a very . . . How should I say this?"

Lucius found no need to speak. The pavement was cracked and uneven. The alley was made even tighter by the cars parked along one side. Their only illumination came from the windows they passed and the silver moon. Revealing his own secrets had left Lucius strangely replete. As though he had scaled some great peak, rising through clouds of emotions so thick he did not even realize what he had climbed. He looked up at the moon and took long breaths of the shadowed night.

"Decisive," Sonya went on. "Yes. And confrontational. He was Tehran's senior prosecutor and very political. When my grandfather insisted the family flee Iran, my father refused. For eight months they argued over this. And then, finally, my father relented and sent me and my brother to America. I was eighteen. Alas, Selim, my brother, was never in good health, and died of kidney failure the year after we arrived. I was very much alone, and very much broke, because all of the funds we had brought were devoured by his medical bills." Sonya was silent for a time, then, "I dreamed of Selim recently. After all these years, he is with me still."

Lucius asked, "What of your family in Iran?"

"Lost. All of them. Asha and her parents are my family now. There was a doctor who treated my brother. A young resident, a man who deeply cared about my poor brother and, eventually, for me. For myself, I seem to have been head over heels in love with this young doctor from the very first meeting. With a Jew. Me, a Muslim and a Persian. And so eventually I accepted the invitation of marriage from an American Jew."

They emerged from the narrow lane into a well-lit street. A car passed them on whispering tires. Somewhere in the distance a dog barked. Otherwise the night and the avenue were theirs. "When word of my wedding reached Tehran, my family disowned me. More than that, young man. They spoke the service for the recently deceased over an open grave. My father commanded that my name never again be uttered."

Lucius halted beneath a streetlight. He had no idea what to say, so remained silent. The woman's features were turned craven by the yellow shadows. She appeared a figure drawn with such power that the meager events of any modern era were rendered insignificant.

"I heard the news from a neighbor, my mother's dearest

friend, who wrote in secret," Sonya continued. "The letter arrived the same day I learned I was pregnant with Asha's father. And I knew in that first horrid moment that I faced a choice. One that would shape the remainder of all my days. Either I turned away from the tragic events that had shaped one reality, or it would consume me. Blind me. Seal my fate. Ruin any hope I might have of being the mother and wife that I yearned to be. But there was a very grave problem. The past is the dominant force in my culture. It is very difficult for an outsider to comprehend the power that the past holds over every act, every decision, every spoken word. The past is now. Understand that and you begin to understand the Persian mind. And yet for me to succeed in this new life, I had to turn away from my past and my heritage."

"The past is now," Lucius murmured.

"And so for the sake of my new family, I turned away from the impossibles. Not once, but every time the unbearable elements of life threatened to overwhelm me. My brother's funeral. A wedding in an empty office of the justice of the peace, with two strangers for witnesses. News of the Iranian revolution and the Shah's downfall. The disappearance of my family in Tehran. I continued to turn away. I built a life with what I was given. With what brought me and my husband joy."

Lucius felt his being resonate at some deep and invisible level to the power of her words. "Could I see you again?"

Sonya took her time inspecting him, then replied, "You strike me as an intensely lonely young man."

"Jessica said very much the same thing."

"Jessica is your lady friend from . . ."

"Before. Yes. Jessica Waverly."

Her dark eyes glittered as she examined him. Luke waited patiently. She had not dismissed his impossible tale out of hand. She had offered him a companionship worthy of the night. Sonya could look as long as she liked.

She said, "Asha considers it part of her professional duties to create a safe haven for her patients."

"I am not one of those," Lucius replied, his voice as soft as her own.

"She does not see that."

"Yet," Lucius corrected. "Sooner or later, that must change."

"But for now, she thinks she has failed you tonight. That is what has left her so troubled, far more than anything that Jeffrey might have told her. Asha wants her patients to know that when they are with her, they are safe, they are cared for, they are shielded, and they can reveal their innermost selves."

"Her patients are very fortunate indeed," Lucius said.

Lucius stood there, enduring her penetrating gaze and listening to the passing traffic, until Sonya said, "I think it would be very nice to speak with you again. But perhaps it would be best if you allow me to discuss this with my granddaughter when I feel the time has arrived."

"I understand."

But Sonya felt a need to explain. "Asha is a skilled professional. But she is also a product of her culture and her generation. My Asha sees the world as black or white, left or right. I, on the other hand, am gifted with the flexibility of the East."

"You believe me?"

Sonya lifted her chin, a polite negation. "That is not for me to decide this night. What I *do* believe is this. You need a friend."

Then Asha came rushing around the corner. "Sorry to make you wait."

"It was a pleasure," Lucius said. And meant it.

CHAPTER 20

The next morning Asha sat in Dino's outer office and listened to the muffled voices from next door. Saturday morning was often a clinician's busiest appointment period. The weekend's woes collected into a crisis that could not wait. She winced as a strident voice shrieked through the wall, "I'm at my *wit's end*!" Her eyes felt grainy and her limbs partially disconnected. Her sleep had been repeatedly shattered by impressions of two men. One of them had shouted with the voice of a Ferrari, the other spoke calmly about events from the previous century. Both seemed amazed that she would question their ability to spin truth from lies. Which they had been doing, of course. In the harsh morning light it seemed abundantly clear that Luke Benoit was fashioning a new reality that suited only him, one as false as his previous state of perpetual victimhood.

Which was what she was reflecting upon as the door opened and the couple stormed past, and Dino waved her inside.

Dino's inner sanctum looked more like a leather-lined library than a clinician's office. All the medical journals and books were hidden in antique mahogany cabinets. Instead of a desk, Dino used an oval table of some blond wood, probably maple. There was no large computer screen, no phone, not even drawers. A trio of Swedish recliners encircled a coffee table by the side window. The walls held paintings by local artists, mostly seascapes, including one Asha had always been drawn to by the late Miramar Bay painter, Gareth Cassick. The result was a gentle invitation to rest easy and talk freely with a friend and confidant.

Dino greeted her with, "Coffee?"

"I'm good, thanks."

Dino walked to the rear corner and opened a sliding wooden screen to reveal a full kitchenette. "When is Luke due?"

"Now. He's late."

"Then I'll come straight to the point. Asha, I had the distinct impression that last night you faced some issue unrelated to Luke." He refilled his mug and carried it back to the chair behind his table. "I just wanted to be certain it wasn't that you were troubled over meeting in my home."

"No, not at all. Last night . . ." Asha hated talking about her own problems, but there was no alternative. She described the emergency that had caused her to be an hour late. Rushing back to the apartment, revealing to Luke where she lived, her grandmother waiting at the door, and Jeffrey. And the argument. In public. In front of a patient.

Dino's response surprised her. He rose from his desk and walked to the window, then returned and picked up his mug and stepped back over to where he could watch the passing traffic. His office was across the broad thoroughfare from the university's main entrance. Over half of his patients came through the university's medical center. He wanted them to understand that this was a place both separate and private. And yet close enough to show a clear sense of understanding to the world and pressures they currently faced. "I suppose you heard about my divorce."

"I knew it had happened, but very little more."

"She ran away with my childhood friend, the best man at our wedding. Apparently, it had been going on for several years." He kept his face close enough to the window to fog the pane with his breath. "At such times, Asha, it is almost impossible to keep your private world from crowding into your professional life."

She swallowed hard. "I try so hard."

"And I want you to know that as far as I can see, you are doing an excellent job." He returned to his chair. "I'm also very sorry that you've had to endure this ongoing trial with your former boyfriend."

Asha managed, "Thank you."

"As for Luke, the patient trusts you. You need to forge an even closer relationship. In some respects, seeing you at your weakest may actually help us save his life. I think . . ." He was interrupted by a soft chime. Dino swung his chair around, checked the security cam wired to his tablet, and said, "Your patient has arrived."

CHAPTER 21

Lucius was seventeen minutes late arriving at Dr. Barbieri's office because he had been taking his first lesson in computers.

He would have been much later, had it not been for how his instructor's mother had become anxious.

His teacher was a nine-year-old lad named Matt. Lucius had met him while seated by the fountain, reading another astonishing newspaper after another splendid breakfast. Over the water's music he had heard the faint sound of tapping, and found a serious young boy typing furiously into what Lucius learned was called a "laptop." Lucius had apologized for interrupting, introduced himself, then asked Matt what he was doing. Matt had responded with questions of his own, until Lucius found himself dancing around an explanation of why he had no idea how to operate a computer. But, apparently, Matt had experience in asking questions for which adults supplied no decent answer. And Matt clearly relished the chance to share his passion. So Matt began explaining the rudiments of computing to a complete and utter neophyte. Forty-five minutes later, Matt's mother emerged, and Lucius found it necessary to retreat from her far more strident questions. Only then did he realize he was already late.

Asha's directions were clear enough. The office building was only half a mile from the guesthouse, a four-story block of offices built to resemble the older structures along the avenue. Lucius pressed the button by the name BARBIERI and pushed the door open. He reveled in the strength to climb two flights of stairs. The outer door was ajar, but Lucius knocked anyway, and Dino called for him to enter.

Dino's office was entirely different from the barely controlled chaos of his small home. The doctor's professional persona was revealed here. Everything was precisely laid out, a theater set intended to relax the patient. Lucius felt the old tension return in a rush, his instantaneous response to all the half-truths so many doctors used to control, to dominate, to reduce the patient to measurable components.

Asha's greeting was the only genuine element in the entire place. "Thank you for coming, Luke."

Dino shook his hand. "Or should we call you Lucius?"

He saw the same tight analysis behind Dino's smile. So similar to Dino's grandfather, and so different. "Whichever you prefer."

"In that case, let's stay with Luke." He pointed to a chair on the empty table's opposite side. "Is that suitable? Or would you be more comfortable on the sofa?"

"Most definitely not."

Asha said, "You seem tense, Luke."

He looked from one face to the other, and knew a mild dismay over the fact that Asha had joined forces with the other doctor. "Evidently neither of you accept my account as true."

"I haven't said that."

"No lies. Please. We've been honest up to this point. Let's hold on to that at least."

Asha nodded slowly. "All right, Luke. You are correct. The clinical evidence suggests that you have entered into a delusional state. One that could very well endanger your life."

"Then we don't have anything further to discuss."

But as he rose from the chair, Dino said, "If you leave my office now, I will be compelled to alert the police."

Lucius found it something of a relief to have the man's hostility out in the open. "Then I will have no choice but to revert to legal action."

This time Dino did not back down. "You can take whatever action you like. But recent court decisions are on my side. Given what you stated last night, in front of multiple witnesses, the court may very well decide that you pose a distinct threat to yourself and to others."

Asha now sided with her associate. "Are you willing to take that risk, Luke?"

"I don't see that either of you are offering me a choice."

"Of course you have a choice." Dino responded with the sort of superior distance that Lucius had known and despised his entire life. "You can continue regular counseling sessions with Ms. Meisel."

Asha tried for a more placating tone. "We need to ensure that you remain safe, Luke. It is our professional responsibility—"

"Very well. I agree."

Dino went on talking. "And you will begin a regimen of medicines that are intended—"

"No drugs. Not now, not ever."

"Luke, be reasonable. You can't expect us—"

"I will not allow you to cloud my mental capacities. I will take you to court over that if I must."

Asha asked gently, "Instead, you will continue to self-medicate with marijuana and alcohol?"

Lucius shook his head over the revelation. He felt disgust, and yet could not help but feel pity as well. What a total disaster that poor young man's life must have been.

"Luke?"

"I will agree to weekly blood tests to ensure that I remain free of all such nonsense," Lucius replied. "If I fail to do so, then I agree to take your medicines."

It was their turn to hesitate. Lucius realized he had entered into familiar terrain. He was putting together a deal. He was negotiating terms.

Dino's chair creaked softly as he leaned back. "What you told us last night, Luke, was a mental and emotional fabrication, one that I think you sincerely believe to be true. Do you see where I'm coming from?"

Lucius was tempted to simply depart. Accept counseling, leave it at that. Nothing he said was going to change this doctor's opinion. Lucius had endured the iron-hard superiority of the medical profession for most of his previous existence. They spent years learning the discipline of medicine. They were so tightly focused on what they had been forced to endure in their training that they refused to even consider the variants beyond those boundaries.

Asha pleaded, "Please, Luke. Please let us help you."

Lucius knew it was probably futile, but the young woman's genuine concern pushed him to try once more. He asked Dino, "You have a relative named Nico Barbieri?" When Lucius saw Dino was not going to respond, he went on. "You must be related. There is so much of that man in you. And so much that is absent, I'm sorry to say. Check his records. I was his patient for almost twenty years. Lucius Quarterfield. Died in May of 1969 . . ."

Lucius stopped talking because he saw the walls descend over Dino's gaze. Dino's expression turned hard, angry. And in that instant Lucius knew there was no hope for him here in this room. Whatever Asha might have felt about his claims no longer mattered. Dino would force her to choose between her professional future and the outlandish claims of a former patient. Lucius was glad now he had not shown them the advertisement torn from that morning's paper, the one folded and stuck in his back pocket. Four pages this time, all color, all promoting Quarterfield Motors. They did not need to know what this possibly meant about his Jessica.

Lucius rose from his chair and said to Asha, "I agree to counseling. And blood tests. But no drugs. I wish you both a good day."

CHAPTER 22

Asha had never before seen her supervisor so angry.

"I am utterly baffled," Dino said. He rose from his chair as though drawn by threads of rage. "How did he get his hands on information about my grandfather? Did you say something?"

"No, Dino. Of course not. But your grandfather was a physician, I recall you telling Sonya."

"Internal medicine, with a focus on the long-term effect of childhood diseases." Dino's gaze remained tightly focused upon the empty chair across from where he stood. "Your patient obtained information that could be used to manipulate the situation. It is worse than wrong. It is *dangerous.*"

Asha realized what upset him so much. Dino had lost control of the session.

"I am utterly flummoxed. How he could possibly have accessed my grandfather's medical records is beyond me." Dino pointed at the door leading to his outer office. "That man is a menace to himself and everyone around him. He needs to be locked up. For his own good." Dino's chest rose and fell like he was coming off a marathon run. "I am going to call the police and demand that he be placed in the secure wing. *Today.*"

Asha spoke as calmly as she could manage. "You think he structured his story around information he gleaned about your grandfather. The claim of having suffered from pleurisy was merely a means of tying the two of them together."

"I had not thought . . ." His gaze locked on her. "You don't actually *believe* him."

"Of course not," Asha replied slowly. "But I also think there is more at work than Luke simply weaving a series of lies around your past."

"Whatever his motivations, Benoit has trampled over the boundaries that maintain safe limits within the patient-doctor relationship. He has created a potentially dangerous situation."

"I agree," Asha said quietly. "What I do not agree with is your response."

Dino stared at her, still standing behind his desk. Blinking slowly.

"We need to decide what is best for the *patient.* And the only way this can be determined is if you calm yourself." Asha gave that a beat. "I suggest you start by *sitting down.*"

After a long moment he fumbled his way into his chair.

Asha hated taking the step. But she saw no alternative.

She reversed their roles.

"The symptoms of dissociative identity are hotly disputed," she said. Her voice was unemotional, like a clinician lecturing to a student. "But one trait is certain, because it is shared with other delusional states. The patient seeks to convince others that his reality is the *true* reality."

Dino did not respond. He did not even blink.

"The correct response is clinically established," Asha went on. "The *only* response that has been proven to work. A high level of trust must be built between patient and clinician. Only then is the patient willing to reveal whatever internal crisis fuels his delusion."

Dino remained silent.

"You do not *challenge.* You do not *provoke.* You do not *arrest.* That only invites further conflict. And violence."

Dino's voice was cold. "And I say he is a menace."

Asha pointed at the phone. "So make your call. Tonight he's locked up. Tomorrow he appears in court with his attorney. You tell the judge Luke Benoit has researched your family's past. The judge then sees a young man who is utterly calm. Completely in control. Responding to every question the court might place before him with intelligence and restraint. What happens then, Dino?"

Her boss did not reply.

"The court will have no choice but to let him go. Only now we have lost contact. So when he *does* lose control, when his delusion *is* fractured, what then? Because we both know it's coming. And we also know we need to be there to keep Luke from exploding and harming others."

CHAPTER 23

Lucius carried a heavy sense of isolation with him during the four and a half blocks back to his guesthouse. The walk was long enough for him to accept the simple fact that Dino and Asha were not on his side, and probably never would be. Of course he had expected nothing less. Few people would believe such a wild tale as his. Given half a chance, the hospital's chief clinician would lock him up. Lucius made a mental note to phone the attorney. He had to get plans . . .

He stopped there at the entrance and turned so that he faced straight into the sunlight. The notion was so self-evident, now that it had occurred to him. He had to do things. He had to take control. He was here, this was happening, and he needed to . . .

Lucius stopped by the front desk and asked for a pad and pen. He entered the central courtyard and sat at one of the iron tables between the restaurant and the fountain. He had always been good at making lists and putting ideas into motion. This had been the foundation for much of his former success.

The young computer genius passed by, his mother in tow. The boy waved at Lucius, the mother frowned. Lucius smiled and returned to his writing. He found a singular comfort in watching the precise script take form.

There had never been a time when planning things out was more important than now.

There was an established pattern to Sonya's departures. Asha escorted her grandmother down the front walk and carried Sonya's overnight satchel, a vintage Hermès that Asha had found in a local flea market. The gold plating had long since worn off the hinges and the leather corners were scuffed. Asha had accused the seller of dealing in fakes and paid next to nothing. But Sonya was certain that it was an original prewar Hermès, and treated it as a prized possession. Asha set the valise in Sonya's trunk, kissed her grandmother on both cheeks, and said, "Thank you so much for coming. I'm just so very, very sorry—"

"Hush, my darling child. If I am to involve myself in your life, I must accept the imperfections. Which are few and far between, I assure you."

Asha found herself staring at the sunlit space where Jeffrey's Ferrari had been parked the previous afternoon. "Shame we can't say the same about the men in my life."

"But that one is *not* in your life any longer," Sonya corrected. "And you handled yourself extremely well, I must say. Both with that Jeffrey, and during the evening that followed." Sonya hesitated, then said, "I find Luke to be a most intriguing gentleman."

"Don't tell me you believe his story."

"What I believe . . ." Sonya stopped when Asha's phone rang.

Asha checked the readout because she had been waiting hours for this call. "It's Dino. I need to take this."

"Please thank him again for the lovely evening. And one thing more."

She answered the phone, told Dino to wait a moment, then said to Sonya, "Yes?"

"You must phone your mother."

Asha sighed. "You're right."

"Of course I am." Sonya gave her granddaughter a swift hug. "I will be somewhat delayed getting home. I'll call you when I arrive."

Asha wanted to ask where Sonya was going, and why it made her smile to be headed there. But her boss was still waiting on the phone. So once Sonya had shut the driver's door, Asha said, "Yes, Dino."

"I owe you an apology."

Asha waved as her grandmother pulled away from the curb. "For what?"

"That is twice your patient has gotten under my skin. And twice you saved me from a potentially serious mistake."

Asha played at an overly casual tone. "What mistake is that?"

He sighed. "Taking action where the hospital's attorneys might become involved would open an enormous can of worms."

Asha waited.

Dino finished, "And do our patient no good whatsoever."

She nodded to the sunlight. That was what she had been waiting to hear. "We also failed to address the Jessica Wright issue."

Dino was silent, then confessed, "I totally forgot."

"I know."

"What have you done?"

"So far, nothing."

"He's bound to find out. That is, if he didn't base his fable upon knowing who this woman is."

"I agree."

"When are you going to see him again?"

"I had planned to phone tomorrow afternoon and set up appointments for next week."

"He *must* come in for therapy."

"Yes, Dino. I won't threaten. But I will make clear he understands his options are limited."

"Asha . . ."

"Yes?"

"Have dinner with me tomorrow night."

The air around her condensed. She was about to beg off, but her grandmother's statement in the café whispered in the tree limbs overhead. "Are you asking me out on a date?"

It was Dino's turn to hesitate. "I have not been on many dates since the divorce. I don't even know what the proper protocol might be."

"Don't call it 'protocol' for a start," Asha replied. "It's too clinical."

"Yes, Asha. I am asking you out on a date. Will you accept?"

It felt as though the sunlight drew the smile from her. "It would be my pleasure."

CHAPTER 24

The inn's receptionist was an attractive young woman with an intelligent can-do attitude. Lucius had always sought out such people for his top positions. He had hired three women as managers specifically for this reason, though it had created no end of hostility with some of the men. One of the elements he most liked about this new world was how women and people of all races appeared to be coming into their own.

A new world it most certainly was.

"Can I help you?"

"I would like to hire some hourly workers to help renovate a home that I . . . have inherited."

"You mean, students?"

"That would be splendid. They need to be self-motivated. I want to give them certain tasks and leave them to work out the details."

"No problem. The university runs an online notice board. You can post your request, but I suspect you'll find all the workers you need, just scrolling through the page."

The woman's words were perfectly clear. The problem was, Lucius had no idea what they meant.

He was trying to reframe his question when a voice behind him said, "Perhaps I can help."

As he led Sonya into the sunlit courtyard, she said, "From the rather grim cast to your features, am I to assume things did not go well at your meeting this morning?"

"Things," Lucius confirmed, "were fairly awful. Dino patronized me. I became somewhat confrontational. He demanded evidence. I responded by describing my contact with my previous doctor, who happened to be Dino's grandfather. He was not amused. I left."

"And Asha?"

"She is firmly in her boss's corner, I'm sorry to say."

"Perhaps not. That is, if she didn't actually come out and say as much."

"There was no need. It was in her face, her voice, her . . ." Lucius waved it aside. "You've said it yourself. She's a professional. What I've told her does not exactly fit inside the professional box."

Sonya had retrieved her own laptop from her car. She selected a metal table beneath the restaurant awning. The manager emerged, most likely to inform them the restaurant was closed. But he was unable to resist Sonya's imperious charm. Their table was soon crammed with a formal tea service and a tray of sandwiches.

Sonya proved an excellent teacher. She powered up her computer and showed him how to go online. Then she made Lucius do it all himself. Everything from then on was accomplished by his own hand.

She did not lecture him on how to use her laptop. Instead, she translated. "Each of these phrases written in blue represents a portal. You select the ones that might help you access your end goal. As you search, you need to maintain a balance between your stated destination and the somewhat convoluted path the Internet might take you on. Remember your end goal. That is crucial. Otherwise you will become sidetracked and wind down trails that lead nowhere, as I know all too well."

She patiently walked him through a Google search, then showed him how to scroll through the Cal Poly's online notice board. When he identified the students he wanted to hire, Sonya gave him her cell phone and instructed him on how to use it.

With that accomplished, they moved on to the real search.

"Jessica Waverly," Lucius said.

"Your young woman," Sonya said. "From before."

The older woman spoke with a honeyed calm. There was a roughish burr to her low voice, a gift of intimacy and understanding with every spoken word. It suggested to Lucius that beside him sat a lady he could perhaps surprise, but never shock. He asked again, "Do you believe me?"

"You *intrigue* me," she replied. Her gaze was as fathomless as it was dark. "And I have not yet found a reason to *disbelieve* you."

"I have perhaps discovered evidence that might change everything."

"What do you mean by that?"

"It would be easier if I showed you." Lucius closed the laptop, then extracted the newspaper from his back pocket. He unfolded it on the table between them.

Sonya's eyes widened. "You don't mean to tell me . . ."

"In the months following our breakup, I rewrote my will, leaving all my dealerships to Jessica."

She traced her hand over the corporate name emblazoned across the top of both pages. "Quarterfield Motors."

"I asked that ten percent of all profits be sent each year to my sisters in Florida. Otherwise Quarterfield Motors was hers to do with as she wished." Lucius ran his hands over the newsprint, flattening the surface. "By the looks of things, Jessica might be a very wealthy woman. Which will make my approach all the more difficult."

Very carefully Sonya lifted the double-page ad and refolded it. She set it on the chair to her left, then opened the laptop. "Let's have a look, shall we?"

CHAPTER 25

For Lucius, returning to Luke Benoit's home was as awful as he had feared. He endured the tenants' sickly dread, their false smiles and expressions of relief, because he had no choice.

Lucius thanked the young man who had supposedly saved his life. He assured them the so-called episode was behind him now. He claimed the shock had done him a world of good, and now he was determined to turn his life around. Starting with this house, which was in desperate need of renovation. Lucius then shifted their attention by asking for a list of repairs that needed doing. Starting, of course, with the water-stained ceiling in the back bedroom.

Luke Benoit's car turned out to be a late-model Kia, whatever that was. The color was probably green, but the car was so filthy it was hard to tell. Both front and rear bumpers were dented. A gouge ran down the passenger side, so deep Lucius doubted he could open the rear door. The right-hand exterior mirror was held in place with electrician's tape. The interior was a repository for fast-food containers, cups, and wilted fries. The smell was appalling. When his six student workers arrived,

Lucius directed one of them to give the car a thorough cleaning. He dreaded the thought of driving it anywhere.

By four that afternoon every stick of furniture had been carried downstairs and loaded into the pickups driven by two of his students. The carpets went next. Lucius was tempted to tear out the bathroom and kitchen as well, but reluctantly decided he would make do with a thorough cleansing and a new fridge. While packing up his supposed belongings, most of which was headed for a charity shop, Lucius came upon a second set of car keys. He returned downstairs and circled around the garage. Beyond a stand of eucalyptus he found a car hidden beneath a bird-stained cover. He swept off several seasons of leaves, untied the cover, and smiled for the first time that day.

The car was a 1968 Jaguar 420G, an upgraded version of the venerable Mark X and one of the finest automobiles ever made. Lucius had been present for the car's debut at the Los Angeles auto show. The vehicle was equipped with massive disk brakes on all four wheels, Borg Warner automatic transmission, triple SU carburetors, and a Thornton Powr-Lok limited-slip differential. The exterior color was Jaguar's trademark version of British racing green.

Lucius fitted the key in the lock, opened the door, and slipped behind the wheel. The interior leather was saddle brown and the smell, even with the overlay of dust and age, was exquisite. The mileage counter showed the car had been driven less than four thousand miles. He opened the glove box with its embossed burl-wood finish, and extracted a leather billfold stamped with the Jaguar emblem. Inside were papers declaring that one Denton Benoit had owned this car since new. Lucius shut the papers back in the glove box, rose to his feet, gave the car a careful once-over. All the while, he asked himself how a young man might prefer to hide away such an incredible machine, and instead drive a vehicle he had reduced to a trash heap on wheels.

One of the students was only too happy to put down his

tools and drive Lucius to the local shopping center. Lucius did not explain why he was not driving himself, and the student did not ask. From how the young man refused to meet his gaze, Lucius assumed one of his tenants had been talking. Either that or news of his near-demise had already spread around the university.

Lucius bought the same laptop and phone as Sonya had used. The prices were shocking. The two items cost almost as much as his last car. But the salesclerk ran the items onto his credit card, and wished him a good day.

Next they visited a hardware store that to Lucius appeared like a massive concrete cave. The ceiling was lost to shadows beyond the stalactites of illumination. The student seemed to find nothing odd about the place, so Lucius did his best to ignore the alienness. He ordered paint and brushes and rollers and more cleaning implements and a fridge. He arranged for the store's carpet expert to come out the next day and take measurements. As he waited in line to pay, he found himself examining this incredible body. He had been on the move for an entire day. His joints did not hurt. His body was both weary and hungry, but pleasantly so.

As he left the hardware shop, he spotted the next store's name and said, "I'll meet you at the truck."

Lucius entered a shop called Running Free and told the salesclerk, "I want everything. I'm recovering from a long illness, you see. I need to equip myself for the first exercise I'll be having in a very long while."

"Then you've come to the right place," the young lady replied. "Because that's exactly what we sell. Everything."

As soon as Lucius reentered the upstairs apartment, he knew something was terribly wrong. The students all now showed him the same sense of false cheeriness as his tenants. He was about to ask what was the matter, when their elected spokesman asked, "What do we do with your stash?"

"I'm sorry, what?"

He pointed at the bedroom door. "We found it when we were cleaning out your closet."

"Found what?" Lucius entered the bedroom to discover a trio of glass pipes and a carved wooden box stationed by the closet door. Lucius saw a rear panel had been set to one side, revealing a secret cupboard. He opened the box and heaved a long sigh. Plastic bags held various tablets and powder. The largest held some pungent herb, Lucius assumed it was marijuana.

He carried the paraphernalia through the silent parlor, down the stairs, and dumped it in the growing pile of rubbish. For the first time that day, climbing his stairs did not come easy.

Lucius entered the living room and said, "I think that about does it for today."

CHAPTER 26

When Sonya phoned to say she had arrived home safely, Asha was preparing her solitary meal. The call had become a favorite ritual for them both. Her visits with Sonya always carried aftereffects. Asha's mental dialogue continued long after Sonya's car disappeared into the sunlit distance. When Asha answered, Sonya's first words were "Have you phoned your mother?"

The vague disquiet she had been feeling all day congealed into a dense ball that filled her middle. "Not yet."

"Jeffrey will have called her as soon as he departed. You need to express your concerns."

"I know. It's just . . ."

"My darling, if Jeffrey is the only voice your mother hears, things will only grow worse. The two of them will continue to scheme behind your back."

"You're right." Asha pushed her half-completed salad to one side. "I hate arguing with Mom."

"Even the most experienced of counselors must concede

when their efforts are not bearing fruit. You must call her, Asha."

"I will." She pressed the hand not holding the phone into her middle. "How was your trip?"

"Disturbing."

"In what way?"

"Asha, my strongest impression of last night is that Lucius is very much alone."

"Luke."

"I'm sorry, what?"

"His name is Luke."

Sonya went silent. Asha found this very surprising. Her grandmother came from a long line of Middle Eastern diplomats. She rarely criticized when a significant pause would do. But what Sonya could possibly find wrong in Asha referring to the patient by his actual name was beyond her.

Sonya finally said, "I speak to you now both as your grandmother and as a woman with much hard-earned wisdom. That young man desperately needs a friend. Far more than he needs a therapist. And because of that, I decided to meet him for coffee before returning to Los Angeles."

Asha pulled up a stool and seated herself. "Why am I only hearing about this now?"

"I started to tell you as I was leaving. But your Dino phoned, and I decided it could wait. Was I wrong to do this?"

Asha resisted the urge to say that Dino was not *her* anything. "I'll have to come back to you on that."

"Thank you for even considering it." There was a long silence, then, "I also think you should contemplate the possibility that Luke Benoit is telling you the truth."

Asha was very glad she was seated. "You do not mean, accept that he is telling what he *believes* to be the truth."

"No, my darling." Sonya described the man's initial lack of comprehension when studying her laptop computer.

"He said in the hospital he did not remember anything from before his latest attempt," Asha recalled. "That's why I drove him home."

"And yet you think he has somehow fabricated this entire story? Really?"

"Nana . . . Luke could have been working on this for weeks. Longer." Asha related what she had discovered about Jessica Wright. "This suggests a new level of calculated subterfuge."

Sonya again responded with silence.

Asha said, "You might as well go ahead and tell me what you're thinking."

"You are suggesting that after he spent so much time developing this new concept, he then tried to commit suicide?"

"What else could it be?"

"Asha, you are the expert, not me. I am simply suggesting that you consider *all* options."

Asha's response was halted by the memory of how Luke had dressed for dinner at Dino's. Luke's wardrobe was mostly limited to jeans and T-shirts with provocative statements. Yet for dinner that evening Luke had worn chinos and a white button-down shirt and Topsiders and dark socks. Asha tried to recall ever having seen him in anything ironed before.

"Asha? Are you there?"

She refocused on the conversation. "You know who Jessica Wright is?"

"My darling, I live in Los Angeles, not the other side of the moon. One of the wealthiest women in California? Of course I know."

"Then you also know that to have him contact Jessica Wright for any reason, much less with this outlandish tale, could lead to a multitude of disasters."

Sonya's response was slow in coming. "Which is why it may be crucial for Luke to have a friend he trusts."

"That makes no sense at all, Nana."

"Think on it for a moment, please. Luke Benoit is going to contact Jessica Wright. It will happen. You cannot stop it. And the more you object, the more you will drive a wedge between this young man and yourself."

CHAPTER 27

Lucius returned to the guesthouse burdened by far more than the cardboard box of records he carried. He wished it were simply possible to dismiss Luke Benoit's previous existence. But this was not some suit of clothes he had been given on loan. He was not simply wearing the man's skin. The stash of illegal drugs was only the most troubling of any number of issues. *His* issues. *His* history. It shadowed him throughout dinner. For once, he found no joy in eating. As he pushed the food around his plate, it occurred to him that he had come across no personal correspondence. Perhaps it was all on the man's laptop or phone, but he had not located a password for either. The tenants had not been able to help him. He made a mental note to ask Asha.

After dinner he began sorting the bundles of bank statements and legal documents. But the vague tendrils of dismay continued to pester him. He put it down to unaccustomed physical fatigue and decided to call an early night.

He was packing away the documents when the tsunami struck.

A huge black wave crashed down on him, an assault of woe and remorse. In his weakest moments, struggling against a rapidly failing body and missing Jessica with every fiber of his being, Lucius had never known anything so bleak. Not even that final walk along the empty beach could compare.

Lucius collapsed to the floor by the foot of his bed. The papers from the overturned soapbox were strewn across the carpet. He was incapable of moving. Every breath was a futile effort. One thought surfaced, strong as an echo resounding through his dismal cave. Even death would be better than this.

"Sonya? It's Lucius. I hope I'm not calling too late."

"No, of course not. Wait and let me turn on the light."

"I woke you. I'm so sorry. I'll call back—"

"Don't be silly. It's scarcely gone eleven. I've just lain down. All right. Tell me what's the matter."

"Did I say something was wrong?"

"You didn't need to. You call an hour before midnight and your voice sounds like the grave. What is it?"

"That's just the problem. I have no idea. I came back from . . ." Luke felt as though every word had to be dredged from the bottom of an abyss. "I should never have called."

"Luke. Lucius. Stop. I am here. I gave you my number because I feared you might find yourself facing just such an hour as this. Now start at the beginning and tell me what has happened."

As he spoke, Lucius feared he was making a terrible mistake, trusting this woman with such dark confessions. Lucius recalled sitting on Dino's porch, telling the three of them who he was, who he had been. What he had revealed to Dino and Sonya and her granddaughter was impossible. It could not have happened. It could not be believed. Impossible, too, was his need to speak with this stranger in his moment of abject helplessness. He had spent his entire life getting by, and doing so alone. There was no need for this call, none at all. To all these doubts he only had one answer. He trusted this woman.

When Lucius finished describing his day, he sat there on the carpet, his back against the wall next to the bedside table. He had no problem whatsoever with Sonya's silence.

When she finally spoke, it was to ask, "You will take advice?"

"Of course."

"There is no 'of course' here. Sometimes just speaking is enough. Just having a listening ear you can turn to."

For some reason the words caused his eyes to burn. "I would appreciate anything you have to say."

"Very well. First you must begin to watch your diet. Your complexion did not look healthy to me. I suspect you eat far too much junk food. Do you exercise?"

He recalled the detritus in the car and the box of drug paraphernalia. "Probably not."

"Eat vegetarian and organic. Have smoothies at least one meal each day."

"A smoothie is what exactly?"

There followed another of those silences Lucius was coming to recognize. Part surprise at his question, part accepting further evidence that he was who he said, and *what* he said. Sonya replied, "Smoothies are fruit, vegetables, natural additives, all blended into a drink. Ask at the front desk for the nearest juice bar."

"Tomorrow," he promised.

"Next, call my Asha. Tomorrow. See her regularly. She will no doubt advise you to take medicines—"

"No drugs," Lucius declared. When Sonya did not respond, he continued, saying, "My mind was the only portion of my previous existence that worked properly. Even in the worst moments, I took nothing stronger than aspirin."

Sonya's words slowed. "And yet you yourself say that this is a new existence. A new era."

Lucius had no idea what to say, other than "I loathe the idea of taking drugs."

She sighed. "Shall I go on?"

"Please."

"Very well. Here is the most important advice of all. Be gentle with yourself. Forgiveness begins in the mirror. Do one thing simply to take pleasure from each day. Make a list of what brings you joy."

"I'm good at lists," Lucius said. "But this one might well defeat me."

"Make a list," she repeated. "Whatever you choose to do that day, see it as a reward."

"For what?"

"Exactly. That is the question you must ask. What have you done to deserve this glimpse of joy." She gave that a beat, then added, "Now I want you to do something for me."

"Anything."

"Careful, Luke or Lucius or whatever name you wish to claim tonight. It is very dangerous to offer yourself so freely to a woman of the East."

"I trust you."

"Do you?"

He smiled for the first time that night and repeated, "Anything."

"I want you to come to church with me next Sunday."

He drew the phone out so as to stare at the device. Then, "Church? Really? Where?"

"Los Angeles. Now, do you see how dangerous it can be to agree before you hear the request? You will need to travel down the day before, ask my granddaughter for details. She must agree to allow you to come. And you, my young man, must make her do just that."

CHAPTER 28

Since breaking up with Jeffrey, Asha had only been out on two dates, both of which had been awful. She knew it was silly to look forward to this evening as much as she did. She tried to tell herself that the invitation was simply Dino's way of paving over a difficult moment and resuming their harmonious relationship. Their *professional* relationship.

Even so, she spent over half an hour trying on different outfits before finally selecting a black Versace she had last worn to a reception celebrating her father's promotion to head of surgery. She avoided even looking at the frocks Jeffrey had given her. She wanted no hint of that man along this evening.

Dino suggested they meet at the restaurant, as he would be coming straight from the hospital. Asha was mildly disappointed, but at the same time glad for a sort of boundary to their time together. There were so many ways this evening could go wrong. And yet she felt an adolescent flurry of nerves the closer she came to Novo, a restaurant in Old Town that Asha had never visited. As she pulled up, Dino rose from a patio table. Which meant he had been looking for her, and which Asha thought was just so totally great. Dino smiled at her approach, the dark features and the strength and the natural goodness were highlighted by the patio's soft lighting. She returned the smile, thinking that candlelight was made for the glow in Dino's eyes.

Dino kissed her cheek and insisted upon holding her chair. When he resumed his seat, Dino asked the waiter to give them a moment, then said, "Thank you so much for agreeing to this. I know it must seem like a disaster waiting to happen."

Asha realized aloud, "You're nervous."

"Oh, no. I left nervous behind several hours ago." Up close his smile looked strained. "Borderline terrified, more like."

Asha found herself calming down. "I almost called and canceled."

"Why didn't you?"

"I have no idea."

"Am I allowed to say you look lovely?"

"Thank you, Dino."

"Would you like something to drink?"

"A glass of wine would be very nice, thank you." Asha was a professional observer. So much of her training centered upon seeing what others assumed remained hidden. Asha found herself retreating inside the same serenity that had helped her through countless therapy sessions. She did not like or dislike her internal state. It simply was. Dino radiated a tension that had no concrete foundation in logic. He was so worked up his hands trembled. He started to speak, then caught himself and swallowed whatever was on his mind. It was the sort of anxiety she would expect from a first-time patient, one who held an enormous secret that they both wanted to share and were terrified . . .

Dino endured her silence for as long as he could, then nervously asked, "Is something wrong?"

"No. Not at all. It's just . . . I know you said this was a date."

"Isn't that what you want? Because we could just—"

"No, Dino. I want this very much."

"You do?"

"I'm delighted to be here with you." She spoke slowly, choosing her words with great care. "But I also want our professional world to remain a part of this evening. And every evening we might have together in the future. It's who we both are."

She could actually see it happen. Dino's nervousness simply evaporated. His posture improved. He smiled, and this time he meant it. "I like that, Asha."

"Do you?"

"Yes, Asha. I like that very much. We're passionate about our work. Being on a date shouldn't change that."

What she wanted to say was that she loved how he spoke her name just then. But now was not the time. So she filed that away for a later moment, almost giddy from the prospect of more such moments coming her way. "I'm so glad."

From that point the dinner took on a rhythm and course all its own. Like a melody Asha had hummed for years, a favorite tune that rose from her heart whenever she was happy. As she was right now.

They talked about Dino's life since the divorce, only this evening the pain did not crease his features. "I retreated from the town and the world we had known as a couple. I had no choice. Anywhere I went in this town, I ran the risk of running into the two of them. My best friend and my ex. Time I spent with friends seemed stained by everything they weren't saying to me."

"So you moved to Morro Bay."

"A friend's mother was selling the place. It needed a huge amount of work. The renovations gave me an outlet." He smiled at passersby he did not actually see. "In a strange sort of way I found the constricted nature of the place very comforting. I walk down the alley and enter my home, and it's just me. None of the troubles I knew before can follow me. Even the commute has helped."

"I'm glad it was there for you," she said. And she was. Really. But she found herself thinking that she would never, not in a million years, ever consider moving into that cluttered bachelor's pad, especially when he'd moved there to recover from a divorce. That meant their relationship would require yet another transition . . .

Asha froze in the process of lifting her glass. Her face flamed at the realization of where her thoughts had taken her.

Thankfully, Dino was too lost in his own revelations to notice. "The best thing I can say about that former relationship is I'm just so glad we didn't have children."

She started to ask if he ever wanted a family. But the course of her revelations kept the words unspoken. Instead, she smiled brightly and said, "Should we have a look at the dessert menu?"

Over a shared slice of key lime pie, conversation flowed naturally to her own recent relationships. Asha replied, "There is no *recent* anything, I'm afraid."

"I'm so glad to hear it," Dino said. Then caught himself. His face turned so red, not even the candlelight could hide the flush. "That was a terrible thing to say."

"Horrid," Asha agreed. "And utterly unprofessional."

They shared a smile. Dino said, "Pretend I didn't utter a word."

"I suppose I can do that."

Over coffee Dino turned very serious indeed. "Can I ask what you intend to do with your future?"

The question caught her completely by surprise. "Assuming my thesis is accepted and I pass my exams?"

Dino held up both hands. His fingers were surprisingly long and seemed to move in the flickering light, as though he was playing a melody upon the night. "Asha, I have reviewed the preliminary draft of your thesis. It would be speaking out of turn to say anything. But I don't care. Your work is first-rate."

Her voice rose a full octave. "Really?"

"Yes, really. You have some minor issues to cover. Do that, and you will be graduating with honors."

"What about my exams?"

"Exams. Hah! You know the material. You are an outstanding therapist."

"Not, I 'will become' one."

"No, Asha. You have already arrived."

"And here I thought the evening couldn't get any better. Thank you, Dino."

"You are welcome. Now back to my question."

"I haven't thought further than finishing the course." She tasted her wine. "I suppose I could go on for my doctorate."

"You could. Or . . ."

"What?"

"Asha, I think you should consider going for a degree in medicine and becoming a psychiatrist."

She took very great care in setting down her glass.

"There are serious advantages to this approach," Dino went on. "It would position you at the top of the hospital department's totem pole. You could continue counseling and social work, but added to this would be your ability to prescribe both drugs and examinations. Psychology has changed, Asha."

"I know," she said quietly.

"Treatments have become increasingly medicinal. Psychotropic drugs have completely shifted the landscape. And this is only the beginning." He gave her a chance to respond, then continued. "The true holistic approach requires a medical degree. Not to mention how it would open up an entirely different world. And put you in a position to write and teach and research anywhere you choose to go."

What she thought was *My father would be thrilled beyond words.* Asha said, "What about getting accepted somewhere?"

He leaned back, clearly satisfied. "I've considered that."

"Have you?"

"Ever since I read your thesis's first draft. Your work is outstanding, Asha. What you need at this point is a means of showing the world just how good you are."

The evening coalesced into two words: "Luke Benoit."

"Your patient's situation has become unique. I've had a word with the editor of the *Journal.* She is so interested, she's offered a preliminary spot in their winter publication."

Asha would have said that the evening could not contain another astonishment. She struggled desperately to control her swirling thoughts. *The American Journal of Psychiatry* was one of the very top publications in the entire world. To have her name on an article, while still a graduate student, would be planting a flag at the top of Everest.

"This news was the opening I needed to speak with the dean of the medical school at my alma mater."

"I'm sorry . . . What?"

His words came at a rush. "I told him you were not aware of this discussion. But I felt . . . Asha, given the quality of your work, if this article is accepted for publication, the dean assures me your application would be viewed in a most positive light."

She found it necessary to turn away. The words bounced around her heart and mind, such that any number of responses seemed ready to explode from her.

Dino grew increasingly worried at her silence. "I know I've overstepped the boundaries. But I was concerned that they might not . . . Have I just destroyed the evening?"

She forced herself to focus on the man seated across the table. "Dino . . ."

"Yes? Talk to me. Please. I'm dying over here."

She reached for his hand. "You have just redefined the meaning of a wonderful first date."

CHAPTER 29

The instant Asha entered her apartment, she knew it was time to make the call.

Her mother was a late-night person. Glenda Meisel's most productive hours began around the time Asha's father went to bed. Asha's mother liked to say that the Internet had saved their marriage. She worked until after midnight most nights. She had retired from full-time hospital administration, but still served as consultant to a number of the regional health clinics. Glenda and Aiden Meisel lived within a true partnership, one strong enough to overcome the disparate natures of their lives and habits. Asha loved her parents dearly, but their relationship astonished her. Her father possessed the typical surgeon's autocratic nature. He ran the surgical wing like a personal fief. His standard way of addressing his team was a soft bark. Asha's mother was also highly opinionated and extremely stubborn. She was without question the only person who could keep her husband in check. Most of the time.

Asha had dreaded this call since watching Jeffrey's Ferrari roar away. As far as Glenda Meisel was concerned, Jeffrey made an almost-ideal match for her daughter. All right, yes, Jeffrey had succumbed to temptation in a moment of personal weakness. Which only heightened his need for a strong partner, as far as Glenda was concerned. She saw Jeffrey's wealth and potential rise within the turbulent Los Angeles waters as a sign that Asha had met her match. Asha hated to argue with her mother. But a drawn-out battle over Jeffrey was inevitable. Or so she had assumed.

The alternative struck her as Asha set her keys down on the front-hall table. She walked straight into the kitchen and dialed the number before she could come up with reasons to stop.

"Well, finally." Glenda had a clipped manner of speech when she was irritated. She was far too well-bred to shout. Instead, she carved each word from a block of iron-hard ice.

Normally, the first sign of her mother's chilled wrath was enough to have Asha frothing at the mouth. Their battles were few, but legendary. Tonight, however, Asha met her mother's ire with honeyed warmth. "Hello, Momma. How are you? How is Daddy?"

"Your father is working far too hard, as usual. Which you would already know, if you had returned any of my eleven calls."

"I am so sorry it's taken this long to come back to you. But something wonderful has been happening. And I wanted you to be the first to know."

Asha's tone did not completely disarm her mother. But it did manage to force Glenda to lower her weapons. "I thought . . . Well, what is it?"

"I have the most marvelous news." Asha pulled out a stool and seated herself. "I'm in love."

"You . . . What?"

"I've known him for two years. And I've liked him from the first moment we met. Sometimes it seems like even before then. But tonight . . ."

"Is he there now?"

"No, Momma. I wanted this to be just the two of us."

"But Jeffrey . . ."

"I know we need to discuss him. But could we set him aside for tonight? Please?"

"I . . . don't know what to say."

Which was a definite first. "I understand this must come as a surprise."

"A complete and utter shock."

"There's more, Momma."

"What . . . Don't tell me you're pregnant."

Asha laughed. "No, it's nothing like that. Actually, it's something I want you to tell Daddy."

"Darling, are you crying?"

She wiped her face and realized, "Maybe a little."

"Well, tell me!"

"I might be published in *The American Journal of Psychiatric Medicine.*"

This time Glenda did not respond.

"It's all very tentative. But my thesis adviser discussed a project I'm currently working on with the *Journal*'s senior editor. They think it's important enough to merit publication. They have given me a slot in the winter journal."

Glenda was married to a senior surgeon at a teaching hospital. She understood full well what the news meant. "Your father is going to be so proud."

"What about you?"

"Daughter . . . it's a shock. Yes, of course, I'm so happy for you. Thrilled, in fact."

"Thank you, Momma. There's more."

Glenda actually managed a fractured laugh. "All right. Tell me."

Asha had to clench the hand not holding the phone, and swallow very hard, before she could manage to say, "I've been invited to apply to medical school."

CHAPTER 30

Nine o'clock on Monday morning Lucius was seated in the outer office that served a number of the university's deans. Four secretaries and two summer interns worked behind the wainscoted counter. The room was octagonal and rimmed by six doors. Four were open. Lucius was there because the previous afternoon he had used his new phone to call Asha. He'd left a message with her answering service requesting an appointment. She had phoned back to say she had a cancellation on Tuesday, and reminded him that he had an appointment with the academic dean scheduled for nine today. For what reason, she had no idea, and having Lucius ask her did nothing to improve the tone of their conversation. Lucius pressed her because he had no choice. Asha finally conceded that he had been very worried about the meeting, and feared the university was going to kick him out.

Lucius had been up for almost four hours. The predawn start was his way of dealing with the fear of another attack. Lucius had always relied upon his mental strength and stability. It was the loss of this faculty, as much as the experience itself, that frightened him. For the first time Lucius knew a genuine sympathy for the traumatic state this young man must have endured.

Lucius had spent most of Sunday dreading the loss of mental control and the return of that dark bedlam. But he took Sonya's advice and tempered his activities and rested. He ate yogurt and fruit for breakfast and had a smoothie for lunch. For dinner he ate a bland but satisfying meal at a vegetarian restaurant. Returning to the guesthouse, he recalled how Winston Churchill had suffered from bouts of depression, and had referred to them as attacks by his black dog. For whatever reason the dark hound had left Lucius alone that day. Sunday night he slept and did not dream.

On Monday morning he was the restaurant's first client. He then dressed in his new training gear and walked the silent streets. There was a unique pleasure in the dark silence, the padding of his new shoes, the sound of his breath. An hour later, he returned to the guesthouse, showered and dressed, checked his list, and set out. First stop was his apartment. Lucius had the taxi wait while he started the six sleepy students on their tasks. Then it was off to the university.

The academic dean's secretary apologized that Lucius had to wait, but there had been an urgent situation regarding some exam. Lucius assured her he did not mind. He pulled a hard-backed chair slightly away from the others awaiting their appointments. His new laptop was in his new briefcase, leaning against the chair leg. He used his new phone to work down his list of calls.

His first was to the hospital. Jorge, the orderly who had helped Lucius make that crucial phone call and identified the attorney, was not on duty until eleven that morning. Lucius left a message and clicked off, only to discover that brief link to those first hours was enough to leave him perspiring.

Lucius then stepped into the hallway and called Sol Feinnes, the attorney who had helped him escape the hospital. The secretary's voice grew guarded when he identified himself, which only heightened his own sense of unease. Whatever trust he received from these people would clearly be hard-earned. He set up an appointment for that afternoon and was about to return to the office when a voice said, "Luke!"

An attractive young woman rushed toward him. She wore half a T-shirt that was cut off to show her midriff, and boots that laced almost to her knees. Her denim shorts were tight and frayed. Metal rimmed both ears and sprouted from her nose and her navel. The tattoo of a giant bird of prey wrapped around her right side. Her dark hair was streaked with purple. "Man, what *happened* to you?"

"I . . . had an episode."

"I called your place. Mannie said you had freaked out, they were probably gonna lock you up. I shoulda probably come by, but you know how it is with me and authority." She surveyed him from hairline to loafers. "What's with the threads, you got a court date?"

Lucius felt a rising sense of helpless dread. He pointed to the door beside him. "I . . . need to get back."

"First you gotta tell me what's going *on* with you. And why are you talking like that?"

He had no interest whatsoever in discovering what she meant. "I've forgotten everything. Including your name."

Her face hardened to a remarkable degree. "What is this, your idea of a brush-off?"

"It's the absolute truth."

"Yeah, right." When he said nothing further, she snapped, "When your memory decides to turn back on, don't bother calling."

Lucius watched her storm away, then retreated into the office. He seated himself and wiped his face. He had half expected something like this. But the reality had been far more unsettling.

Lucius liked to think of himself as a hardheaded businessman. Give him a problem and he would find a workable solution. But entering into this new realm meant confronting one uncontrollable event after another.

Women had always confounded him. Jessica Waverly had been no different in that regard, then or now. He had no idea how to go about contacting her. Everything he had learned suggested that she was completely beyond his reach. Her status and her wealth would form impenetrable barriers. He disliked how his mind shifted back and forth between Jessica and the strange woman who had accosted him in the hallway. Then he realized the receptionist was referring to him as "Mr. Benoit."

"Yes?"

She said, "The dean will see you now."

CHAPTER 31

Dean Rhea was an older Hispanic woman whose dark hair was streaked with a steel that matched her gaze. She was dressed in a stylish linen suit of gold-and-cream stripes. She greeted him with a stern expression and the words "Do sit down, Mr. Benoit."

Luke took the lone chair directly opposite her, and reflected that many students must have endured their most horrid hours while planted in this very same position.

"I asked for this meeting in order to determine the level of progress on your independent project," she said. "Or the lack thereof."

Lucius had no idea what she was talking about, so he remained silent.

"We agreed to give you the spring semester off. And to hold your place as a junior in the business department. But in return I wanted to see considerable advancement both in your work and in your ability to handle the responsibilities of your personal situation."

Lucius did not respond.

She slipped on a pair of reading glasses and tapped the keys on her computer. "Now, then. Your project was to make a detailed analysis of the trust your parents established."

Lucius breathed a silent sigh.

She mistook his response and her tone hardened. "I must warn you, Luke. Unless there has been substantial—"

"The lawyers responsible for the estate are stonewalling me," Lucius said.

"Explain."

"I have made repeated requests. The attorney of record is Graham Avery."

"I know him, of course, since he serves on the university's board of trustees." She inspected him over the rim of her spectacles. "Proceed."

"His tone could hardly have been more condescending. I have three letters from him directly, and half a dozen more from his junior partners." Lucius knew this because he had spent hours going through the packing crate Luke Benoit had used to store his business correspondence. "Store" was a generous term. The crate had as little order as a rubbish bin. He went on, "The attorneys' responses range from patronizing to outright rejection. They state that the trust was established to protect my interests, and from this they claim the right to deny me information."

She took off her glasses and settled back. "Go on."

In fact, Lucius was grateful for the chance to run through his findings in advance of his meeting with Sol Feinnes. "I have made a preliminary assessment of property values in this neighborhood. A house of comparable size on the same street recently sold for seven hundred thousand dollars. But the Benoit property is three times as large, almost an acre and a half. I would estimate the value at somewhere approaching a million dollars."

Dean Rhea said, "The Benoit property."

"Correct. It was deeded to . . . me by . . . my aunt." Lucius found her gaze too penetrating. His only recourse was to rise and start pacing. "There is an initial base income derived from three tenants, whose rent is more than the trust's monthly outlay to . . . me. This monthly stipend has not altered since the accident that killed . . . my parents. There is also the matter of the inheritance, and any insurance they might have taken out. My concern is, the attorneys of record are abusing their position and draining away the reserves."

"What do you intend to do about it?"

"I have a meeting with another attorney this afternoon at three."

"Who is it?"

"Sol Feinnes."

She nodded. "The university has dealt with him on occasion. Come back and sit down, Luke." When he did so, she asked, "What happened to your accent?"

Lucius had no idea what she meant, which left him only able to say, "I've endured a . . . shock."

She examined him intently, but merely asked, "Are you still planning to take the remedial class in accounting this summer?"

"That won't be necessary."

"Excuse me?"

"I've been studying on my own. Quite a lot, actually." He was struck by a thought. "But summer school sounds like an excellent idea. Is there a higher-level finance class on offer?"

The dean slipped back on her spectacles, checked her screen, and observed, "Your records show an 'incomplete' on all your previous attempts at accounting, Luke. Which I imagine was the professor's way of being kind, given your . . . history."

"As I said, I have been studying. Extensively."

She tapped the keys. "There is a class in business and financial analysis. Open to graduates and undergraduates. I see space is available."

"That sounds perfect."

"The professor is the same one who gave you your incomplete in Intro to Accounting. She will insist upon interviewing you."

"That sounds more than reasonable. May I trouble you for her contact details?"

Dean Rhea regarded him over the top of her spectacles. "I must say, Luke, this is hardly the conversation I had expected to have with you today."

"I understand."

"We have, of course, received notification from the hospital of your recent . . ."

"That was a terrible mistake, and won't happen again," Lucius said. He could feel his face flame. Whatever she said next would only make matters worse. He pretended to inspect his watch. "I have time to speak with the professor before my next appointment. But only if I go now."

The meeting with the professor lasted all of twenty-six minutes. The professor was a slender black woman with an accountant's directness. "Well, you've certainly made improvements in your wardrobe, I'll give you that."

"Thank you."

"I have a meeting with prospective clients. I do consulting work on the side." She rose from her desk and pointed to the exit. "Let's walk."

The university campus was laid out in a series of incomplete circles, a gentle maze of buildings and parking areas and tree-lined walks. The professor said, "So you've been studying on your own."

"Quite a lot, actually."

"It would need to be a lot, given the level of work I saw in the past. Tell me, what would your response be to the issue of . . ."

The questions took them across an interior courtyard and into a newish building that flanked the university entrance. Lucius stumbled in several places, mostly over issues related to changes in financial codes. But his ability with numbers and balance sheets had transferred with him, a feat he was desperately relieved to have confirmed.

They stopped before a conference room bearing the professor's name and the current date and time. She inspected him once more, the same intent gaze he had endured from the dean. "Your choice of terms suggests a surprising use of out-of-date texts."

"I found them . . . accessible."

"Well, you need to bring your knowledge into the twenty-first century. Class begins Friday. In the meantime I want you to work your way through the *HBR* textbook entitled *Finance for Managers.* You'll find it in the college bookstore. Come to my office half an hour before class. I will want to check your progress."

"I can do that."

She offered him the tight glimmer of a smile. "Do you know, I actually think you can."

Lucius bought the managerial finance book at the university shop, then left the campus. He used his phone's remarkable mapping ability to chart his course and set off walking. He was not ready to drive just yet. Besides which, going on foot offered him an opportunity to reacquaint himself with the town he had once known so well. He stopped by a barber's for a haircut, then entered a branch of Luke's bank. He wrote out a check for cash and got in line. When the teller was free, he offered up the driver's license with that sullen man's photograph, and asked for his balance, and accepted his cash, and thanked the teller. And tried to stifle the feeling that his every act was a profound lie.

The hospital occupied its own cul-de-sac on the university's north side. He dreaded returning. But he owed the orderly money. He entered the main lobby and asked the receptionist to page Jorge. As he started toward the chairs by the front windows, a voice called, "Mr. Benoit?"

Lucius turned and faced a dark-skinned gentleman in a doctor's white coat. His gorge rose with the shock of recognition. "Yes?"

The doctor must have seen the revulsion in his gaze. He revealed a remarkable warmth. "Joseph Emeka. I was the ER doctor on duty when you arrived."

"I remember."

"Do you? How interesting. I had heard from Dr. Barbieri that you have suffered memory loss. I'm glad to learn it was only temporary."

Lucius saw no need to correct him. "Thank you."

"How are you?"

"Coping."

"You appear to be doing far more than that." He surveyed Lucius's appearance with evident approval. "I am glad to see you looking so well."

Lucius had always trusted his ability to assess people. And his gut told him that this was a man who genuinely cared. He ventured, "There have been some very hard moments."

"I can imagine. What brings you here?"

"I wanted to thank an orderly for assisting me."

Emeka gave him a knowing look. "This wouldn't be the orderly who supplied you with the phone call, by any chance."

"If it was," Lucius replied, "it would do neither of us any good to admit it."

Emeka revealed the most astonishing smile. His entire face became illuminated. "Certainly not. In that case I should probably depart before the gentleman arrives. Do let me know how things progress, will you?"

CHAPTER 32

As soon as Asha's ten o'clock patient departed on Tuesday morning, she set up her Minicam on its tripod. She positioned it behind her chair and to the right, opposite the window. When Luke knocked on her open door, she greeted him with, "Come in, Luke. How are you today?"

"Fine, thank you."

"Let me just go wash my hands." When she returned, she found he had pulled over one of the straight-back chairs and was seated directly opposite the desk. Establishing very clear boundaries. As she had expected. She settled in behind the table, opened the laptop, and keyed in the camera. "Would you be comfortable with my recording our sessions?"

"Is that necessary?"

"Absolutely not. If you dislike the idea, I will turn it off."

"Very well."

"Thank you. And one final bit of administrivia." She passed over a standard form supplied by the university. "I have one of these on record, but I thought given the recent, well . . ."

"Alterations we have discussed," Luke supplied.

"Right. This permits me to discuss your case with others." She forced herself to add, "I would also like to write it up for an article, but only if you agree."

"I see no reason to object."

"There is a copy for you as well." She watched him read and sign the form. "You look very nice today. Are those new clothes?"

He nodded. "One of the students introduced me to Target. And IKEA. I have been burning through money."

Today, Luke wore a white button-down shirt, pleated navy trousers, and dark loafers. He sat erect, watchful, reserved. She wrote down the word "aware."

Everything that Luke Benoit had not been in their previous consultations.

She asked, "How was your meeting with the dean yesterday?"

"Meetings. Plural. They went fine."

"Who else did you see?"

"A Professor Russell. She is teaching a summer class in advanced business finance. I needed to convince her that I could handle the work." He crossed his legs. "May I ask a question?"

"Of course. You can ask—"

"How is it that I am twenty-two years of age, and am still a junior at this university?"

"You still don't remember?"

"Virtually nothing."

"You are currently in your third administrative leave."

"You arranged these?"

"Just this one. Another was granted when your parents had their accident. The other was requested by one of your previous therapists."

"How many therapists has . . . have I had?"

"I am the fourth."

"Is that normal?"

"Is . . . Luke, I don't understand your question."

"Switching around like . . . Never mind." The exchange seemed to age him. He shook his head, said quietly, "That poor kid."

Asha made rapid notes. The responses formed almost a textbook DID, or dissociative identity disorder. Amnesia of his other existence. Complete disconnect between personalities. Except for . . .

Asha asked, "Do you mind if I call you Luke?"

He seemed surprised by the question. "It is my name."

Asha made another note. This was a serious breach of standard DID behavior. In virtually every case study she knew about, the patient became tense and angry when addressed by the name of one of their other personalities. "It's just, well, you claim that your previous name was . . ."

"I don't claim it. My name was Lucius. Then. Not now."

"Then, as in, before you died."

"Correct." He glanced at the camera. "Is that why you wanted to record this session? Should I repeat my story for the world?"

"Would you mind doing so?"

"No. Not really." He proceeded to give a shortened version of the story he had last told her on Dino's porch. Asha studied him as he spoke. The calmness, the self-possession, the intensity, were all utterly at odds with other case studies. This change in personality went far beyond anything she had found in her research.

The most recent conversation with her grandmother rose unbidden. The thought that Luke Benoit might actually be telling the truth was utterly unwelcome. And yet . . . Asha experienced a split of her own. For one brief instant she faced the prospect of rejecting her entire professional training. And seeing Luke as Lucius. As a man, a *new individual,* seated there before her.

Then she realized what Luke had just said, and the world snapped back into focus. "Say that again."

"I've spoken with your grandmother by phone. The night before last I had an attack. I needed a friend."

The news was not as jarring as Asha might have expected. Her grandmother had always been as irritating as she was wise. Sonya did what Sonya thought best, and paid no attention to what others desired or the world expected. Asha responded as calmly as she could. "If you needed help, why didn't you call me?"

His expression hardened. "Why are you recording this session? Why are we not discussing the incredible nature of my return? Because you don't believe me."

To that, she had no response except, "Tell me about the attack."

Even here she found a distinct separation between the patient she had been treating previously and the man seated before her. Luke's description was . . .

The word she sought was "clinical." Luke Benoit talked like he was describing physical symptoms to a doctor.

Asha said, "You need to go back on your meds."

"Sonya said the same thing. You cannot possibly understand how hard it is for me to accept that. Even so . . ." He opened his briefcase, pulled out a Target bag, and upended it on the desk. He showed genuine distaste at the fourteen containers that rolled about. "These are all the medicines I found in his . . . that is, my bathroom cabinet. I would ask that you please show me which I should take, and what the minimum dose might be."

"Luke . . . you need to understand, all of these are impacted by whatever other substances you swallow or smoke or whatever."

The grimness aged him once more. "My student workers located his . . . What was the word they used?"

"I'm sorry, I don't . . ."

" 'Stash.' I threw it all out. I told you. I will not be using any such things ever again." He waved an angry hand at the plastic bottles. "Just give me one. Please. In case of another attack."

She began sorting through the bottles, aware of the camera, aware also that Dino would insist upon using this as an opportunity to get him back on a daily regimen. "All of these work better if you use them regularly."

"I would rather deal with the next attack on my own than take daily doses." He crossed his arms. "I have begun eating vegetarian. And something else, vegan. Yes. Perhaps that will be enough."

She accepted defeat, and pushed one container toward him. "Two of these at the first sign of distress. And if that is not enough, take one of these."

"Thank you."

"Will you at least keep these others, just in case you change your mind?"

He started to argue, then shifted. Asha actually saw it happen. Luke said, "On one condition."

"Yes?"

"Your grandmother has invited me to church."

"She *what*?"

"Next Sunday. But only if you grant me permission. Asha, I thought your grandmother was Muslim."

Asha reached over and cut off the recorder. "Sonya is . . ."

"Unique," Luke offered. "A very special lady."

Kooky was what Asha had been thinking. Her actions from time to time were nothing less than bizarre. Asha knew she would call her grandmother as soon as Luke left. Just as she knew Sonya would do whatever she thought best, regardless of what Asha thought or said.

Luke drew her back by saying, "I would very much like to do this." He swept a hand over the cluster of containers. "Give me your okay, and I will hold on to all these."

"Will you take them?"

"I'm sorry. No."

"Luke, these were prescribed for your own good. They form a daily regimen that stabilizes your mood swings—"

"And obliterates my mental capacities. Again, no."

"Then I am afraid I cannot agree."

"Very well." He smiled. "The first lesson of a good negotiator is to enter into any new deal with a clear knowledge of how far you will go."

"Is that what we are doing?"

"Absolutely." He swept the other twelve bottles back into the plastic bag and handed them over. "Throw these away for me, will you?"

Asha stared at the bag, but what she really saw was the coming argument with her grandmother. No matter what she said, no matter how powerful the reasons Asha had to forbid this meeting, her grandmother would go ahead and do precisely what she wanted.

Asha sighed defeat. "I agree to your visit. On one condition."

CHAPTER 33

The idea came to Lucius while he was seated in the attorney's waiting room. Sol Feinnes and his associates occupied a suite of offices in a new building meant to look old. The exterior resembled an oversized Spanish mission, and was located between the Old Town and the courthouse. Lucius gave his name to the guard by the entry and was directed to the fourth floor, where the receptionist apologized with professional smoothness that the attorney was running behind schedule.

The waiting area was a fine-enough place for reflection, done in the pastel colors of an early sunrise, with comfortable chairs and nice prints and a collection of interesting magazines and fresh coffee in a corner alcove. The receptionist was busy with her work, and people came and went, and nobody seemed overly interested in just another young man there to take the lawyer's time. So Lucius poured himself a mug and seated himself and extracted the Sunday newspaper advertisement from his briefcase. He marveled at the power and wealth this four-page spread represented. The list of dealerships ran down the entire side of the first page, twenty-three in all. Lucius recognized several, of course, but the majority of them were in locations he had never even visited.

Lucius traced his way down the list to the final name. As had happened the previous day, just reading the address caused his breath to lock in his throat.

When he had recovered somewhat, Lucius took a careful look around the reception area. Four men and two women were hunched over spreadsheets. The receptionist was talking quietly into her headset. Lucius did not want to stand up just then. He was uncertain whether his legs could support him.

He took his phone from the briefcase and punched in the number below the address. He could feel his hand tremble as he listened to the rings.

"Quarterfield Classics."

"Yes. I'd like to speak to someone about a restoration."

"Hold, please. I'll put you through to our service department."

As he waited, Lucius tried to tell himself that he was just another client. Just another caller. Just another . . .

"Service."

"Hi. I have a Jaguar Mark Ten that needs, well, quite a lot."

"Do you, now?" The man's voice brightened considerably. "Which year?"

"Sixty-nine."

"What's the mileage?"

"Three thousand seven hundred."

"Say again."

"Thirty-seven hundred. It's been under wraps for decades by the looks of things."

"You don't know?"

"I . . . inherited it. Yesterday was the first time I ever saw the car. It hasn't been driven in so long the tires have frayed."

"So you can't drive the car to us. Is that what you're saying?"

"Right. The battery's dead. And all the rubber fittings will need replacing."

"But otherwise . . ."

"The car is in absolutely pristine condition."

"Where are you located . . . I'm sorry, I didn't catch your name."

He caught himself in the act of saying *"Lucius Quarterfield."* The realization should not have hurt like it did. "Luke Benoit."

"I'm Mike Alderson, assistant chief of this madhouse. Where are you located, Mr. Benoit?"

"San Luis Obispo." Luke gave his address.

"Let me have a look at our book. Okay, we could have a truck down your way tomorrow, say around eleven? Matter of fact, I might drive the rig myself."

Lucius imagined some people would find the private office of Sol Feinnes to be a severe and forbidding place. But for him it had the opposite effect. Unlike the reception area, here everything was very functional. A few plaques and degrees on the walls, a credenza with a couple of potted plants, a desk, a sideboard, shelves. A spartan sofa set and coffee table in the corner. And boxes of legal documents and pending cases. Lucius felt very much at home. Sol Feinnes had no time for trifles. And neither did Lucius.

Feinnes listened to Lucius run through the same overview as he had given the dean. How Graham Avery had deflected Benoit's feeble attempts to learn what his firm was doing with the family's estate. Sol Feinnes then asked, "You have the correspondence with you?"

"Seven months and counting," Lucius confirmed, and passed over the file he had prepared the previous evening. "I have also made a time line of the exchanges."

"You've tried phoning?"

"Several times." At least he hoped that was true. "It changed nothing."

Feinnes swiftly scanned the letters. "The written documentation is revealing enough. Avery and three junior partners have all responded at one point or another." He shut the file and set it on his desk. "They are stonewalling."

"I agree."

"What is it you want?"

"To withdraw the trust from their firm," Lucius replied.

"No court on earth would grant you the right to take over these finances yourself." Feinnes was equally firm. "Let's not forget the circumstances under which you and I met. If I were to present your request to the court, the attorneys of record would put the hospital doctors on the stand and draw out every last sordid detail. The court would have no choice but to deny your request. And you could run the risk of being declared mentally incompetent."

Lucius felt his face go fiery red with shame. "Do I strike you as incompetent?"

"No, you do not. Which is the only reason we are having this conversation."

"Someday I hope to tell you the complete story of what I have been through since . . . our last meeting," Lucius said. "For the moment let's simply say that I have had a complete and total change of direction."

Sol Feinnes was intelligent, aware, and clearly comfortable withholding judgment. "Noted."

"One of the doctors does, in fact, want to lock me up. He hasn't said as much, but I'm certain . . . Can you write a letter stating that I'm no longer a patient under their care?"

"You wish to terminate all therapy?" The gaze became harder, more assessing. But all the attorney said was "Are you certain that is a good idea?"

Lucius felt his face grow hotter still. "I intend to continue seeing Ms. Meisel. But I want to be the one in control of my outcome."

Sol Feinnes nodded slowly. "I can write Ms. Meisel a letter to that effect, certainly."

"Thank you. Now back to the trust. My end goal stays the same. I want those attorneys removed from control. So tell me how far we can go in the short term."

Feinnes pondered this, then decided, "We should file a motion for an external audit of your trust. Until this is complete, we also request that all funds be frozen. Given this history of correspondence, I would assume the court would grant our request without delay."

Lucius wished there were some way to erase the shadow he saw there in the lawyer's gaze. With time, perhaps, but not today. He said, "Do it."

CHAPTER 34

On Tuesday afternoon Lucius returned to the guesthouse and watched as the new carpet was fitted. Then the students helped carry up his new IKEA furniture. All the while, he wrestled with the thought of residing here. Lucius knew the point was coming. But the prospect still filled him with dread.

He then worked with the students on the downstairs apartment. It was far easier than upstairs, especially once the rear bedroom ceiling was repainted. When he began to tire, he retreated to the rusting picnic table under the backyard eucalyptus trees and read the finance text. The terminology was completely new, as were many of the regulations. He chafed at the prospect of doing business under so many new state and federal laws. The tax code had certainly not improved. Even so, the task helped to ground him more firmly in the here and now. He had lived and breathed these elements through his entire short career. This was work he could firmly get his teeth into.

The second attack came while he was reading that night. Lucius could almost feel the black dog circling his bed. As though it resented the pleasure he found in study. This time he did not hesitate. He took the two capsules and then went out on the guesthouse front veranda and waited. The fountain sang its soft melody, the stars glimmered overhead, and the dismal cloud gradually slipped away. The pills did not entirely erase the gloom. But eventually they did make it possible for him to return inside, cut off the light, and sleep.

The drug was still with him Wednesday morning. Lucius did not rise until after nine. He took a briefer walk than the previous two days. Then he ate what had become his customary breakfast of yogurt and fruit and tea. He gazed longingly at the serving trays of bacon and eggs and sausage and French toast. If the attacks were going to continue, what was the point of his diet? But he turned away in the end.

He returned to his room, packed his belongings, and checked out. A taxi deposited him at the house a little after ten. The upstairs apartment smelled of fresh paint and carpet dust. The living room contained the oversized television and stereo and a new sofa set from IKEA. The bedroom was bare, save for a new pallet and shopping bags of sheets and towels. In the kitchen the new fridge only accented the other implements' battered states. Lucius returned downstairs, supposedly to check the students' progress, but mostly to escape. As he accepted the tenants' gratitude over the transformation of their living spaces, Lucius wondered if he would ever feel able to claim the upstairs apartment as his own. If he could free himself from the dark hound. If he could not be reminded at every turn of the impossibility of his existence.

He wondered if perhaps taking the drug had caused the dog to hang about longer this time. He took his textbook out back and seated himself at the picnic table, struggling to find his equilibrium in this unsettling day. This new life and realm certainly carried their share of burdens.

Then as now, Lucius was coping. It was what he did. Cope.

When the tow truck pulled into his drive, Lucius rose from the table as the driver called. "Mr. Benoit?"

"That's me."

A burly man eased himself down from the cab. "Mike Alderson. Where's the lady?"

"In the backyard."

Alderson had the easy manner of many senior mechanics, assured in his hard-earned knowledge, dedicated to work he clearly loved. "I sure hope you weren't fooling, what you said on the phone."

"Give me a hand with this tarp, then you tell me." Together they hauled off the filthy cover. Then Lucius took a step back.

Alderson whistled. "Oh, my sweet word."

If anything, the car looked even finer than before. For the first time that day the gray blanket lifted entirely from Lucius's mind and heart. "Isn't she a beauty?"

"That, she is." Alderson patted the hood, as he might in calming a nervous filly. "Mr. Benoit, I took the liberty of phoning one of my favorite collectors."

"This car is not for sale," Lucius replied.

"Now hold on, just hear me out. The man is willing to offer you top dollar—"

"I've wanted to own one of these for as long as I can remember."

Alderson nodded reluctant acceptance. "Mind if I have a look inside?"

The Quarterfield tow truck was almost as long as a semi. The bed had more than enough room for a second vehicle. Which was how Lucius had the idea of asking Mike Alderson if he'd take the Kia as part payment for the repairs. Alderson seemed embarrassed to even be around the battered car, which endeared him to Lucius even more than before. He accepted Lucius's claim that it was another inherited vehicle, and cranked the Kia up behind the Jag. Then he covered the Kia with the filthy tarp and tied it down tight.

Mike Alderson was not much of a talker, which suited Lucius just fine. This was his first journey out of San Luis Obispo, and the trip north was familiar enough to fill him with conflicting emotions. The road was certainly better than he recalled. The Pacific Coast Highway was a divided four-lane highway for much of the trip. Then it went to a three-lane for a while, the asphalt ribbed and crumbling down both edges. The last time Lucius had driven this stretch, the PCH had been a gleaming new promise leading California's coastline into a bright tomorrow. Now it was in desperate need of repair, the traffic far too heavy for its present condition.

When Mike took the turn signposted for Miramar Bay, Lucius thought for a moment he was going to be sick to his stomach. His heart hammered, his skin felt clammy. The sun glared harsher than he remembered, the hills were brown as tinder. Here and there were scarred shadows of what he assumed were recent fires. He started to ask Mike, but then decided it did not matter. Not nearly so much as the sudden impression that captured him.

Lucius felt as though the pressure on his fragile state heightened with each passing mile. The black dog seemed to race alongside the tow truck, almost but not quite able to leap on board and attack him once more. He knew it was absurd. He knew the drugs disagreed with him at some visceral level. He knew, he knew . . .

He leaned his head against the seat rest and sighed.

Mike glanced over. "You all right there, bub?"

"I haven't been on this road in . . . a while."

Mike's eyes were covered by dark Wayfarers. But the expression he showed was gentle and concerned. "Last trip didn't go so well?"

Lucius did his best to push away all the tumult and all the questions for which he had no answers. "The love of my life lived up here."

"She dumped you." It was not a question.

"Something like that."

"You been back since?"

"No."

"Man. That's tough." Mike jerked a thumb at the load behind them. "'Course some would say bringing that lady back to life is worth a few bad memories."

Lucius felt his face stretch into the parody of a smile. "Maybe so."

"How'd you hear about us, anyway? Not that I'm complaining. It's just, Quarterfield Classics mostly deals with the serious collectors. There's plenty of garages nearer to San Luis that could handle this job."

Lucius had no idea what to say, except, "I wanted the best."

When they came around the bend, and the dealership appeared, Lucius groaned.

"What is it?"

"Stop here for a minute, will you?"

"Sure thing." Mike pulled over. "You don't look so good."

Lucius had no choice but to say, "I met her here."

"Who, the heartbreaker? Here at my dealership?"

"In the front room." He swallowed hard. "It looks . . ."

It looked exactly the same. A trifle smaller, perhaps. But otherwise it was precisely as Lucius remembered. The showroom's glass wall bulged to his right. Directly in front were three cars. A red-and-white vintage Corvette gleamed between a Rolls-Royce Corniche convertible and a Packard. To his left a young saleswoman walked an elderly couple toward a slate-gray Bentley.

His internal state was certainly not helped by them halting on the roadside.

Mike had pulled over in the exact spot where Lucius had parked.

On that last dreadful day.

Lucius opened his door. Took a hard breath. "I think I'll walk from here."

CHAPTER 35

On Wednesday morning Asha visited with two patients housed in the hospital's mental ward. Afterward she took over a free table in the main cafeteria and began working through the final proof of her master's thesis. The paper was officially not due until December, but the previous evening Dino had sent over his final revision notes, and then urged her to complete the work and submit.

An hour later, he had called to say, "Give me the green light and I'll inform the university that you are also ready to sit your exams this summer."

Asha idly ran a finger along a groove in the table's surface.

Dino said, "I believe this is the point at which you thank me for what is an incredible step forward. This frees you up to focus on your *Journal* article."

"I'm thinking."

"Asha, there is nothing to think about."

Actually, there was. "I've never had a relationship like this."

"Like what?"

"One where we are both open to change. And willing to accept the need to grow beyond our comfort zones."

It was Dino's turn to go silent.

"My relationships to this point have all followed a sort of circular pattern. I observe. I analyze. I push. They resist. We argue," Asha went on. "Sooner or later, something happens and it becomes necessary to break things off. Then the blame begins. I say they're deflecting, they're being absurdly childish . . ."

Dino remained silent.

"In Jeffrey's case the breaking point was named Tiffany. Several of them, probably. And, of course, I blamed him. But I'm at least partly at fault. I see that now for the first time. I chose Jeffrey. Nobody forced me into that relationship. And part of what appealed to me about him was the fact that he had this evident flaw. He needed to grow beyond where he was, if he were to ever become a fully-functioning individual. And I assumed that was what he wanted. So I pushed him. Hard. Until he finally . . ."

Dino's voice was a soft burr. No longer the distant analyst. There. With her. Caring. Deeply. "Don't you think you're being a little hard on yourself?"

"No." Asha cut off her computer. "What I think is, talking to you is like looking into a mirror I've run from all my adult life."

"Asha . . ."

"What?"

"Are we in a relationship?"

"I certainly hope so." Her laugh was shaky. "I'd hate to think I'm making these confessions to a boss."

"Then it's time for a confession of my own." Dino took a long breath, then, "When I got home from our date, I walked out on my deck and thought I was finally waking up from a long hibernation."

"I understand," Asha said softly. "Can I ask you something?"

"Anything."

"What did you like to do? I mean, something you've given up from the time before you . . ."

"I know exactly what you mean." He thought a long moment. Asha found that very moving, how he considered her question important enough to give it time. "I loved to hike. She never much cared for it, so, well . . . I haven't been in years."

"Thursday is your day off, right? I can take the afternoon. Let's go."

"Really, you'd do that?"

"I've never been what you'd call an outdoors sort of gal. But I'd love to try. Just go easy on me, okay?"

"Do you even have a set of hiking boots?"

"Let's see. They're lace-up footwear with no heels, right?"

"Now you're playing with me."

"I'm seeing my last patient at noon. I'll meet you at one thirty."

He was smiling now, she could hear it in his voice. "Come prepared to get all hot and sweaty."

Asha was drawn from her reverie by a voice saying, "Ah, Ms. Meisel, just who I was hoping to run into. May I join you?"

Asha recognized the emergency room doctor who had met them after Luke's attempted suicide. "Of course, Dr. . . ."

"Emeka."

She shut her laptop and slipped it to one side. "By all means. Do sit down."

"I hope I'm not interrupting something important."

"I'm reviewing my master's thesis. But my mind's not on it. And to tell you the truth, I wanted to speak with you."

"About Benoit."

"Right. Dino, that is, Dr. Barbieri, has suggested I write this up as a journal article."

"I personally think that's an excellent idea."

The slender ER doctor's meal consisted of two yogurts, an herbal tea, an apple, and a packet of crackers. Asha asked, "That's all you're eating?"

"I've been on duty all night. Anything else sits like a concrete lump in my gut." His face was fine-boned and almost gaunt. The smile rearranged his features from neck to forehead. "Hardly the correct medical terminology, but true just the same."

"The morning we met, you struck me as utterly unflappable. Calm, poised, the perfect ER doctor."

"On the surface, at least, I suppose that's true enough." He patted his middle. "But down here it is another story."

"Maybe so, but if I ever need urgent care, I hope you're the attending doctor."

"Charming, as well as lovely." He spooned up the yogurt. "I saw your patient yesterday."

"Luke Benoit was here?"

"Briefly. He said he needed to thank one of the orderlies."

"The phone call to that attorney," Asha guessed.

"That is my assumption as well. I would imagine money exchanged hands." He scooped out the last spoonful, then said, "The alterations I observed in Benoit were, well . . ."

"Extreme," Asha suggested.

"Virtually overnight he has become what appears to be an individual in complete control of himself. Stable, calm, alert." He opened the second yogurt. "Quite astonishing, really."

Asha heard the unspoken question and decided there was no reason not to tell the ER doctor what had happened. She recounted the claims Luke made over dinner, and his previous day's statements regarding Dino's grandfather. She finished with, "That transformation will be the basis of my article."

"You are thinking it represents a split personality?"

She leaned back. "These days the correct term is 'dissociative identity disorder.' DID for short."

"I believe I recall reading that somewhere. Thankfully, it is not something we ER doctors must concern ourselves with."

"To answer your question, yes, that is probably the correct assessment," Asha replied. "But it's important not to cloud the early stages of analysis with assumptions. The result can be that I look for evidence to support my belief, rather than seeing what truly affects the patient."

"A lesson I must continually stress to my young residents," Emeka confirmed. He began peeling his apple. "I have no real idea what this DID actually represents."

"There is very little agreement on *anything* related to DID," Asha replied. "Which makes it so interesting."

Health professionals even argued over the definition of DID, or what could be classed as its root cause. A growing number of diverse events were now grouped under the general heading of DID. But the core issue, the one component all clinicians agreed upon, was the emergence of a different-personality state. This was usually combined with partial amnesia and patients' refusals to accept any evidence contradicting the new personalities. In other words, patients *disassociated* from all aspects of reality that did not conform to who they now saw themselves as.

Asha described how Luke Benoit also followed the standard pattern on an emotional level. This was referred to as "reduced emotional reactivity," which went a long way to explaining how he appeared so, well . . .

"Normal," Emeka supplied.

"Not a very clinical description, but yes," Asha agreed. "Normal in dress and mannerisms. Very reserved and controlled in speech."

"You are saying this is different from how the patient was prior to his episode?"

"Night and day," Asha agreed.

Emeka ate a slice of apple, then half a cracker, followed by a sip of tepid tea. Thoughtful. Intent. "Has there been a case where the clinician has actually observed the moment when the individual's personality fashioned the split?"

"Never," Asha replied. "Not once in the history of psychological research."

"Which means this article could launch your career into the stratosphere. Congratulations, Ms. Meisel."

But Asha thought his response held little real enthusiasm. "What is it?"

He shrugged. "Probably nothing."

"No. Please. I want to hear what you're thinking."

His motions became very slow, almost formal. He laid down his knife. He arranged the items on his tray. He turned the handle of his cup. Then, "Have you considered the alternative?"

"You mean, that Luke Benoit is telling the truth? That he actually died, and this other person just somehow popped into his physical form?" Asha gave the doctor a chance to deny it, then said, "Are you seriously considering this?"

"I have been an urgent-care physician for eleven years. Head of the ER wing here for five. And in this time I have seen some things that would make Benoit's case appear, well, utterly pedestrian."

Asha had no idea how to respond.

Emeka nodded, as though agreeing with her silence. "My name comes from the Igbo language, spoken mostly in the northwestern provinces of Nigeria. The literal translation is 'God does great things.'"

Emeka continued to nod slowly, a gentle rocking, only a few inches in each direction, almost a trancelike motion. His gaze, however, remained piercing. Brilliant as a dark-rimmed fire. "When I came to the United States to do my medical training, I discovered a distinct division among doctors regarding my religion. Many within the medical community tend to discourage, even scorn, the very concept. As though a Christian doctor risks returning to the dark ages of medicine. But for others, attending church is considered part of a normal existence. Perhaps a bit outside the mainstream these days. But a churchgoer is still an accepted member of society, which is the same in my home country. And yet, within this American religious culture, there is a distinct difference from what I knew at home."

Asha opened her mouth, searched for some proper response, but came up blank.

"'Confining.' Yes, that is the word I am looking for. Americans see themselves as a powerful people. And rightly so. But they carry this sense of power and control into their churches, and the result is, the room for miracles becomes very small. But in some ways I remain a product of my native land. And in Nigeria there are very many aspects of daily life that cannot be understood, much less controlled. So my name, the pronouncement that God still abounds and manages to surprise and astonish, that miracles do still exist in this modern era, has validity."

"So you're saying that Benoit . . ."

"What I am saying, Ms. Meisel, is that your study of this patient holds a very real interest to me personally. There is a great deal of discussion these days over near-death experiences, and yet the medical community treats it as a passing fad. They would prefer for it to simply go away. Incredible as that may seem." Emeka stood and gathered up his tray. "Would you be so kind as to keep me informed of this patient's progress? I would appreciate that more than I can say."

CHAPTER 36

The sun spilled through the Quarterfield Classics' west-facing showroom windows. It turned the car positioned at its center into a burnished reflector, hearkening back to a world that had no place in this day and age. The vehicle was a defiant note against the whirling dervish of constant change.

It was the same model Buick that had stood in that very same position the day Lucius had first met Jessica.

Lucius could not remember what the color of the original car had been. But he knew the model. He set his hand upon the front fender, marveling at its presence.

A saleslady said, "Sorry, sir. That car isn't for sale."

Lucius did not turn around because he did not want to reveal his tears. "I'm actually here to have a car serviced."

"Is that your Jaguar that Mike's been going on about?"

"Yes." He cleared his eyes. "This is one beautiful machine."

"Certainly is." She offered him a card. "Mike says you're not interested in selling your Jag. But I'd be glad to help in case you change your mind."

Lucius accepted the card without actually focusing on the

young lady. "Would it be all right if I stayed in here for a while?"

If she found anything wrong with his fractured demeanor, the saleslady gave no sign. "Sure thing. You're not allowed to bring drinks in here, but there's coffee and cold beverages in the service waiting area."

"Thank you." Lucius pretended to inspect the car while she walked away. There were a couple of prospective customers loitering at the showroom's other side. Their voices echoed a refrain of money and softly-spoken passion around the chamber. But here by the Buick, Lucius was left alone.

He pulled over a chair from an empty sales desk and seated himself. Precisely where he had been on that fateful morning. So very, very long ago.

Lucius was so utterly captured by memories and loss that he did not notice a thing until the cane tapped his leg. "Young man, this establishment has failed to lay out a welcome mat for loiterers."

He should have risen to his feet. He should have done a hundred things. Instead, he was unable to do more than gape at the woman who towered over him.

She was narrow-framed and her features were pinched by far more than age. She leaned on a cane and her hand trembled from the effort required to keep herself upright. "Well? Are you incapable of offering some faint hint of an apology?" Then she glanced at the car, and her eyes went round in horror. "Is that your handprint on my machine?"

The saleslady rushed over. "This gentleman has brought in a vintage car for restoration, Ms. Wright."

"That does not give him the right to paw my Buick!" She glared furiously as Lucius struggled to rise. "Do you have any idea what you were leaning against?"

"Yes."

"Yes, what?"

"Yes, I know the machine."

"I doubt that very much." She joined her hands together on the cane. "Well, go on then."

"This is a sixty-eight Riviera. The car was redesigned in sixty-six and now shared its platform with the Olds Toronado and the Caddy Eldorado. This is the Gran Sport model, with a four-hundred-thirty cubic-inch V-eight, which replaced the old 425 Nailhead—"

"All right, that's enough." His answer only seemed to heighten her peevishness. "What possible reason could a young man like yourself have for being obsessed by old machines?"

"This particular Riviera changed the way cars were seen in America," Lucius replied.

"And you have failed to answer . . ." She noticed the service chief hovering nearby. "Yes, what is it now?"

"Sorry, Ms. Wright. I just wanted to let the gentleman know about his car."

"Well, go on, then. Though why that couldn't wait is beyond me."

"Sorry, ma'am." But not even his boss's perpetual bad mood could completely erase Mike's grin. "The lady is fairly close to being ready to roll."

"Are you sure?"

"Young man," Jessica snapped. "Mike Alderson happens to be the best in the business. Not to mention as fixated on outdated machinery as you appear to be."

"I put in a new battery and turned her over. She purrs, man. As lovely a sound as anything you're likely to hear," Mike went on. "Of course she needs new points and plugs and hoses and tires and brushes. But I can have that done by tomorrow."

Lucius was grateful for the chance to focus on something beyond the woman glaring at him. "So do it."

Jessica demanded, "What manner of vehicle has this young man brought in?"

"A Jaguar Mark Ten, Ms. Wright."

She faltered slightly. "A Jaguar, did you say?"

"One of the sweetest ladies I've seen in a long while. Barely broken in. Been kept under wraps for how long?"

"Years," Lucius replied softly. "Decades."

"Just waiting for today," Mike said cheerfully. "You should hear that lady sing."

Jessica waited until Mike stepped away, then said, "Young man, you may walk me out."

CHAPTER 37

The only thing that kept Lucius tied firmly to the here and the now was his hold on Jessica's arm.

He did not actually support her at all. He merely touched the back of her left elbow, the arm that did not hold the cane. She stumped across the showroom, ignoring the nervous looks cast by everyone within sight. Lucius perceived everything with absolute clarity. But the only things that mattered were his three fingers that touched this lady's arm.

She waved an impatient thanks at the salesman who held open the showroom door. Jessica did not speak again until they were crossing the sunlit forecourt. "I suppose you know all about my car as well."

Lucius saw the uniformed woman standing beside the open passenger door, and realized she was headed toward . . .

His car.

The last he had ever owned.

She barked, "I do not care to be kept waiting, young man."

He had to swallow hard. "I know it."

"Well?"

"It's a sixty-eight Impala."

"Right so far."

His voice sounded strangled. "The four-door version was known as a Caprice, but this one has many of the features designed for the SS. Three-ninety-six V-eight, full-coil suspension, Powerglide transmission—"

"Very well, that's enough." She offered grudging approval. "I suppose you could go on for hours if I allowed."

Lucius did not reply.

"Are you this knowledgeable about all vehicles?"

"Mostly American models," he replied. "Fifties and sixties, mainly."

"How remarkable. May I ask why?"

He had no idea how to respond, except, "It used to be my work."

"I would have assumed a handsome young man such as yourself would have preferred to lose himself in electronic gizmos and the like." Jessica allowed the woman to help lower her into the passenger seat. Then she raised one arthritic hand and halted her aide from shutting her door. She looked back toward the showroom. "Clunkers, they're called nowadays. Gas-guzzling dinosaurs that should all be sold for scrap."

Lucius followed her gaze. The showroom windows formed a series of sunlit mirrors. The car on display was invisible. But he knew they could both see it clearly. He turned back. And drank in the sight of her. "I think they're beautiful."

The afternoon light was not kind to Jessica. Every line was visible, every scar of age. But her features still bore the stamp of determination and her gaze still held a fiercely brilliant light. Lucius thought she was regal as a queen.

Jessica said, "This place never made financial sense."

"It doesn't need to," Lucius replied.

"Is that so?" She glared up at him. "And what, may I ask, do you do with your time when you're not idling away the hours in my front room?"

"I study finance at Cal Poly."

She tightened her gaze. Lucius wondered if this was perhaps as close to a smile as she could manage these days. "This particular way station on the highway to nowhere costs me a small fortune to keep open. I claim it brings in the sort of high-value clients that also acquire our more expensive new models. But we both know I am, what is it they say these days? Blowing smoke."

"You don't need to justify a passion," Lucius replied. "This place and these cars bring you pleasure. Not to mention how you come here and meet others who share your enthusiasm."

"Is that so?"

"Yes. And the Miramar Highway is most certainly not leading nowhere."

"You know my town, do you?"

"I did. Once."

She nodded. "As you must return to collect your vehicle tomorrow, you may stop by my residence for tea. Three o'clock. Be on time."

Lucius thanked her, then shut her door and watched as Jessica Wright departed. She did not look back.

He was still standing there long after his car had vanished into the afternoon heat. Struggling to breathe around a broken heart.

CHAPTER 38

No one at the dealership found it strange when Lucius asked for help booking a room in Miramar Bay. After all, he had a pristine vintage Jaguar in the shop, due for its rollout the next afternoon.

Of course it could have also been how the entire business came to a standstill at the news that Jessica Wright had invited him to tea.

Even the patrons found it necessary to come in and inspect this odd duck who managed to charm the dealership's owner. Lucius pretended not to notice the stares, but there was little he could do about the young saleslady's chatter as she drove him into town. "That woman scares me to death. How on earth did you get on her good side?"

Lucius was still recovering from the meeting. His voice sounded distant to his own ears. "We talked cars."

The saleslady's name was Clarissa, and she drove a restored convertible MGB very fast. "Humph. I know cars. Why do you think I work there? For my health? That lady gives me a heart attack every time she walks in the front door."

"Heart attack" was how Lucius described this lady's driving habits. "Watch out for the truck."

"I see the truck. I didn't even know Ms. Wright *had* a good side." She downshifted and gunned the engine. "What did you *say* to her?"

"Vintage American vehicles are beautiful. You can't pass over a double yellow."

"Don't say 'can't.' Never say 'can't.' 'Shouldn't' sounds bad enough." She glared at him. "Why are you smiling?"

"You sound like Jessica."

"'Jessica'? You call her *Jessica*?" She red-lined the engine and did a controlled four-wheel slid around a corner.

Lucius gripped the door with one hand and the windshield's metal rim with the other. "Maybe I should walk from here."

"Don't be silly. It's another three miles." She looked over once more, and this time was defeated by his grin. She slowed considerably. "Sorry. I drive crazy when I'm mad."

They did not speak again until Clarissa pulled into the parking area of a fifties-era motel, a low-slung structure once known as a motor court. She cut the motor and said, "Ms. Wright keeps threatening to shut our place down. Twice now, she's ordered me to move someplace else, last time it was Ojai, become assistant sales manager. Pretend I love new cars. Make something of myself. Build a proper future. But I don't want to leave Miramar. And I don't want to leave Quarterfield Classics." She turned in her seat. "Did you actually call her Jessica?"

"Not to her face."

"Oh. I thought maybe that was the secret. Speak her first name, and Ms. Wright goes from angry lioness to house kitty."

"I doubt very much anything would ever make Jessica become a kitten."

"There you go again. Jessica. Maybe it's because you *think* her name." When he didn't respond, she said, "She really asked you to tea?"

"Yes. That reminds me. I don't know where she lives."

Clarissa pointed in a vaguely eastern direction. "Head back over the first ridgeline, and look for the clouds of sulphur."

CHAPTER 39

A blustery wind blew off the Pacific as Lucius left the Miramar Bay guesthouse and strolled down the town's main avenue. The motel was a nice enough place. Lucius was fairly certain he recalled it from before. It had been spruced up, of course, and the rooms had been redone as efficiency apartments. He found the sense of familiarity to be most reassuring.

Lucius walked down to a men's shop the guesthouse proprietor had suggested. The wind was strong enough to toss the trees around and cause the few pedestrians to scurry. He watched two incoming rainsqualls slowly draw toward the coast. Miramar had changed, but not nearly as much as he had feared. Everywhere he looked were signs of new wealth. Even so, the town somehow maintained the same low-key charm that had so appealed to him.

Lucius was the shop's last customer of the day. He purchased a pair of hemmed slacks and a dress shirt, underwear, and socks. He had not planned on staying the night when he'd left San Luis Obispo, and had no intention of arriving for tea in the same clothes as today.

The rain arrived as he was climbing back up the central road. He slipped into a restaurant several blocks from the guesthouse, thankfully one he did not recall. A strikingly beautiful woman said, "Welcome to Castaways. Are you escaping the downpour or looking for a place to eat?"

Lucius thought he had never heard a more appropriate greeting. "A little of both."

"Table service hasn't started yet. And in any case we're all booked up. But you're welcome to take a seat by the bar."

"The bar," Lucius replied, "will do me just fine."

Lucius had sea bass cooked in a sauce as delicate and light as anything he had ever tasted. He tried to do the meal justice, but his mind remained locked on the events of that afternoon. Being with Jessica again had left an indelible mark upon his soul. Just as Lucius had known it would.

What he had not expected was the aftermath.

The rain passed and the wind calmed and the sunset sparkled through the restaurant's rain-dappled windows. The interior wood paneling glowed a honeyed welcome. Castaways filled up with people determined to have a good time. Lucius held to his customary solitude, and reveled in his sense of peace.

The emotional storm he had known ever since his return was gone now. He had no idea when it might resume, or if the black dog would assault him once more. Nor did he much care. There was no longer any need to fight the tumult or tear apart the mysteries. His presence now held a purpose.

Jessica needed him.

Lucius recognized another lonely soul when he saw one.

The bartender was a striking Latina with flashing dark eyes and a face that seemed to look for a reason to smile. "How was your meal?"

"One of the finest I've ever eaten."

"That's what we like to hear. Another sparkling water?"

"Not right now, thank you."

"How about dessert?"

"Just coffee, please."

"No problem." She left and swiftly returned. "Cream or sugar?"

"Black is fine."

She was joined by the lovely owner, who asked, "Everything good here?"

"Everything," Lucius replied, "is just fine."

"You wouldn't happen to be the young man who charmed Jessica Wright today."

Lucius felt as though his perch on the bar stool had suddenly turned precarious. "I'm sorry, what did you say?"

She clearly enjoyed his shock. "You must be new to Miramar Bay."

"I've been here before. But not in years."

The bartender said, "So you're seeing it for the first time as an adult."

The manager cut off his response by extending her hand across the bar. "I'm Sylvie Cassick."

"Lucius . . . Luke Benoit. How did you hear?"

She showed him a lovely smile. "When my fiancé first arrived, somebody told him that gossip was a small town's version of reality TV."

"There are no secrets in Miramar Bay," the bartender said. "I'm Marcela Reyes."

"Marcela usually waits tables, but my bartender is dealing with a sick mother," Sylvie said.

"I'm thinking we should make this permanent," Marcela said. "The tips are better and I get more chances to flirt."

"I'll tell your husband you said that," Sylvie said, then asked Lucius, "So how did you tame the fire-breathing dragon?"

Lucius shrugged. "I have no idea."

Marcela asked, "Did Jessica Wright really invite you to tea?"

Lucius nodded. "I can't get over how the whole town knows my business."

"Not, like, every single person," Marcela said. "There's bound to be some poor housebound grandpa who hides behind his drapes with a loaded shotgun, waiting for the kids to trample his awful flowers."

"Marcela."

"I'm just saying."

Lucius asked, "So what is Jessica's story?"

The two women looked at each other. Marcela asked, "Did I just hear him call the dragon lady Jessica?"

Sylvie said, "I have actually had a waiter offer an entire night's tips just to have her seated somewhere else."

Marcela said, "I hear she wasn't always like this. Such a . . ."

"The words you are looking for are 'difficult client,'" Sylvie offered.

"Whatever. But then her husband ran away with that model . . ."

"Who is five years younger than their daughter," Sylvie said.

"Actually, it's her ex's daughter by some LA weathergirl."

Sylvie waved that aside. "Ms. Wright adopted her. Now her only child lives in Hawaii and has made a profession of spending her mother's millions. Ms. Wright has been alone for, how long?"

"Years," Marcela said. "And now she's sick."

"Really," Lucius said. "Jessica is ill?"

"Very, from what I've heard." Sylvie pointed down the bar. "Marcela, your patrons are waving at you."

"Oh. Right." She flashed him a smile. "Nice to meet you, dragon tamer."

Sylvie said, "If you'll come in tomorrow and tell us what her house is like, I'll let you eat for free."

CHAPTER 40

It wasn't raining when the taxi pulled up to the massive stone gates, but it would be soon. The sky was dark and the air was close and utterly still, as though the world held its breath. Aghast at what Lucius was about to do.

The driver asked again, "You're sure you have an invitation?"

"Yes."

"Ms. Wright don't see nobody these days."

"You've told me. Three times." He counted out the fare and added a tip. "Thank you."

"I'll hang around," the driver offered. "Just in case. Long walk back to town, and there ain't but three cabs in Miramar Bay."

"Suit yourself." Lucius rose from the cab and walked over to the left-hand pillar and pushed the button set beneath the camera and speaker.

"Yes?"

"Luke Benoit. I . . . Ms. Wright invited me."

"Step to your right. Are you alone?"

"I am, yes."

"I was told to turn you away if you came with anybody else. I see a face there in the car behind you."

"I had to come by taxi. My car won't be ready until tomorrow."

The speaker clicked off. Lucius waited through four long minutes, and then the gates groaned and creaked and opened.

"Well, now I've seen everything," the driver said, and drove off.

The house was simply gargantuan. His footsteps scrunched along the graveled drive, making unsteady imprints in the perfectly groomed stones. With every step he took, more of the white monstrosity came into view. It seemed to go on forever. The curved front steps were a full sixty feet wide, and the portico was rimmed by a dozen pillars big as redwoods. The portal was so vast it turned the woman waiting for Lucius into a solemn miniature.

As he climbed the stairs, she greeted him with, "You might have made the trip for nothing."

Lucius recognized her as the same lady who had driven his car the previous day. He knew she was mistaken, but saw no need to correct her.

The woman led him inside, shut and locked the door, and punched numbers into a box by the door frame. "Don't try leaving unless I'm here to let you out. Security would just go crazy."

"I understand."

"This way." She led him through the cavernous front hall, beneath a crystal chandelier as big as a car. They walked down a long corridor and into a vast sitting room of white furniture and walls, white silk carpets over a white marble floor. "You can wait here."

"Do I have to?"

The woman huffed softly. Lucius could not tell if it was a

laugh. "I suppose you can go sit in the garden room if you'd rather."

"Yes, please."

"Come on, then." She led him down yet another endless corridor. Her voice echoed off the distant ceiling. "You came out here from Miramar by taxi?"

"It was either that or walk."

"Shame you spent all that money for nothing. The night nurse says Ms. Wright had herself a bad spell. She most likely won't come down." She pushed open the double glass doors. "I'll bring you a tea. Then I'll have one of the gardeners drive you back to town."

"I'd rather wait."

"Didn't you hear what I said? Ms. Wright don't see nobody these days."

"Just the same. I don't have anywhere else I need to be."

The woman seemed ready to argue, but in the end merely shrugged. "Let me know when you're ready to head out."

The conservatory was large enough to house so many fruit trees Lucius could not count them. Some grew from stone-lined wells set in the terra-cotta floor. Others stood in great wooden vats. There were flowers everywhere. Gilded cages held a variety of colorful birds. Their song competed with the three fountains. It was a lovely place, for a prison. Lucius thought the stormy afternoon suited it perfectly.

The woman returned with a silver tea service that she sat by the central fountain. She glanced at him, offering a silent invitation for him to give up and depart. When Lucius merely thanked her for the tea, she departed without speaking a word.

An hour passed. Lucius did not mind the wait. His life had a purpose now. The last time he had felt so certain, and so saddened, was the day he had left Jessica weeping in her mother's arms.

Rain started drumming on the glass roof high overhead. Lucius looked up, but what he really saw, in truth, was the day he had sat in his attorney's office, signing the new will, the one that had left Jessica all his dealerships. Thunder rumbled in the distance, a deep punctuation to his sense that all this was his fault.

Another forty-five minutes passed, then the glass doors opened and Jessica said, "You're still here, are you?"

Lucius rose to his feet. "I am. Yes."

The aide pushed in a wheelchair holding Jessica. She cast Lucius a doubtful glance, as though she was uncertain whether this was a good idea, or perhaps wondering if it was happening at all. "Where shall—"

"Leave me here and go fetch the young man a fresh pot of tea. He can wheel me about, can't you?"

"Of course."

She gave a three-finger gesture. "There's a table over in the far corner."

The woman continued to hover as Lucius pushed the chair, which meant she heard Jessica ask, "What do you think of my house?"

"It's absolutely horrid." Lucius heard the aide's soft gasp, but he didn't care. "How can you bear to live here?"

Jessica did not respond until he had positioned her so that she overlooked the rain-speckled glass wall and the emerald lawn beyond. She pointed with the same three fingers at a chair that was positioned some distance away. As he carried it over, she said, "My ex-husband convinced me we needed this place. Or wanted it. I forget which. It took three years to build. All the while, he was fooling around with that model. I realized he had always intended to make this their home. She probably would have loved it. Which is why I insisted on taking it in the settlement."

"Spite is not enough of a reason for you to stay here."

"It was at first. But now . . ."

"Move. Today."

She watched rain streak the glass. "Everything has become such an effort."

"Let me help."

When Jessica turned to look at him, she realized the aide still stood by the exit. "Why aren't you bringing this young man's tea?"

"Right away, ma'am." But she lingered a moment longer, her confusion clouding the look she gave Lucius.

Jessica waited until the doors closed to say, "Luke, that's your name?"

"Luke Benoit."

"Tell me about yourself."

"It is all rather repugnant," he warned. "What's more, it seems as though it all happened to another person."

"Nonetheless I want to hear everything."

"I actually don't recall much. I have managed to uncover some things, and more elements have been supplied by other people."

"Look here. I made a perfectly reasonable request. It's uncouth to refuse. Are you an uncouth young man?"

"I was. Apparently. Very uncouth."

"Well, now is as good a time as any to stop." She planted her elbows on the chair's leather armrests. Her hands formed an arthritic bundle by her chin. "You say it seems to have happened to another individual. So tell it as though it did."

CHAPTER 41

Lucius found it easier to talk while on his feet. He stood with his back to the table and spoke to his reflection. Rain fell and painted translucent designs in the glass. He began his story with the present. Any mention of the past would have to come later, or not at all. He described waking up under the shroud, then waking again inside the hospital room and meeting the doctors. He left out the shock at his own reflection, for the same reasons he did not relate anything about his past. He told her about calling the attorney on the orderly's phone. He described Asha Meisel's response, the drive to the apartment, the ghastly place he found there, the guesthouse . . .

Lucius stopped talking when he heard the doors open. He remained silent and stared out over the rear lawn as the tea tray was set down and the aide retreated. He wondered if perhaps the room was bugged. He supposed there had to be some sort of listening devices, in order to keep track of Jessica's needs. Especially in a house this massive. Lucius decided he didn't care whether the aide heard him or not.

When the door clicked shut, Jessica said, "Go on."

Lucius described learning about the previous suicide attempts. He related the meeting with the dean and the professor and the woman in the university corridor. He described the Kia and finding the Jaguar. He knew his story was disjointed. He also knew it sounded as though he spoke about events that occurred to someone else. When he was done, he remained standing there by the glass until she said, "Come sit down." When he did so, she said, "You remind me of a man I once knew."

Lucius found his breath had become trapped inside his throat.

"He was very special to me . . ." She turned her face to the rain-streaked glass. "Well. It was all very long ago."

Lucius fought down the desperate urge to confess. He dared not risk her labeling him insane. And that is exactly how it would no doubt sound. A rich woman confronted by a stranger who claimed to have loved her fifty years ago, then died in her arms. She would have every reason to eject him and, worse, bar him from ever seeing her again. What was more, it might hurt her terribly. Even so, the desire to tell her threatened to choke off his air.

Jessica interrupted his struggle. "Young man, you may pour me a cup."

Actually, he had the only cup. Before Jessica stood a mug with an oversized handle. When he had filled it halfway, she said, "That's enough. Now one spoonful of sugar and a smidgen of milk. How do you take yours?"

"Black." He watched her fit the arthritic fingers through the handle. "Do they hurt, your hands?"

"These days pain is relative. I am usually forced to choose between the dim-witted effects of drugs or discomfort." She slurped noisily. "What was it like, waking up under the sheet?"

"Horrible." He set down his cup, the tea untasted. "What I remember most is the cold. The room was frigid. And the arms holding me down. And the doctor's needle . . . It was a terrible moment."

They sat in silence after that. Rain drummed softly against the glass roof and walls. The birds chirped, defiant of the day and their caged existence.

Finally, then, Jessica pressed a button on the arm of her chair. Within seconds the doors opened and the stocky woman entered. "Sarah, this is Mr. Benoit."

"How do you do, sir." Her voice held the same confused wonder as her gaze.

Jessica said, "I understand your car won't be ready today. Where did you intend to stay the night?"

"Where I was last night. The guesthouse on Front Street."

"Nonsense. This mausoleum possesses sixteen bedrooms. You will stay here."

He watched the aide's eyes go completely round. "Thank you very much."

"Sarah, have the housekeeper make up the pool house." She gestured for the woman to take up position. As the chair was pulled away from the table, she said, "I fear I must retire. Make yourself comfortable, young man. We'll speak again tomorrow."

CHAPTER 42

On Thursday morning Asha woke to the realization that she was in love.

She was, after all, a highly skilled clinician. She was trained to detect the unseen emotions people thought they could hide from the world. And there was no other way to explain the giddy feeling she felt upon awakening. Not to mention the way she leapt from her bed and rushed around the apartment, all before coffee. Nor the smile she saw in the mirror. Like she was a teenager again, and she had a date to the prom with the high-school star. Instead of going for an afternoon hike with her thesis supervisor.

Only Dino was not just her boss anymore. And in many ways she now knew he never had been. Theirs had been a relationship that had perched for a year and a half on the precipice of love.

That was how it felt as she prepared her coffee and did her makeup and packed her gear for later. She would change before leaving the office. She found an old backpack from her undergrad days, stuffed behind the shoe boxes holding five pairs of overpriced pumps from Ferragamo and Tod's. These were stacked under matching outfits, all purchased by Jeffrey, and all crammed into the closet's right-hand corner. She had learned to navigate in stiletto heels because Jeffrey had claimed to love the way they reshaped her figure. She pushed aside the memories as she hunted for her hiking boots.

One reason why Asha had decided to take this apartment was because it came with a walk-in closet. Every time her grandmother visited, all the items that did not have a proper place were dumped here. Added to this was the fact that Asha hated to throw anything away. There was one clean furrow of carpet down the middle where she could maneuver, lined on either side by a jumble that had grown over time. Asha found one boot at the back of her sweater shelf and the other hiding under a dozen or so neatly folded Rodeo Drive shopping bags. Jeffrey again, naturally. As she stuffed her change of clothes in the backpack, she decided what she really needed was to ask her grandmother's help in clearing the closet. Sonya was almost savage in her rejection of elements that did not suit her concept of a life well-lived. They would spend the weekend arguing, open a bottle of wine and make peace, and depart as friends.

Thoughts of her grandmother brought Asha back to Lucius. When she was in her car and headed for work, she phoned Sonya and greeted her with, "I need to talk about Lucius driving down to LA this weekend."

"Good morning, dearest one."

"This could be a seriously bad idea, you two meeting up. I don't feel right about it."

"Say the word and I will cancel. I can only proceed with this if you agree."

Her grandmother's unwillingness to argue left her defenseless. "I'll discuss this with Dino."

"I think that is an excellent idea." When Asha did not speak, she asked, "Is that why you called?"

"Not really, no."

"Then what—"

"It's the age thing."

Sonya asked, "What age thing would that be?"

"You know perfectly well what I'm talking about."

"Dino is what, eight years older? Nine?"

She wailed the word. "*Twelve!*"

"Well, that is just terrible. Twelve years. Dino might as well be embalmed and stuffed in a glass display cabinet."

"Now you're making fun of me."

"Maybe just a little."

"So . . . you think it's all right?"

"What I think, my darling child, is that you have met your match."

Asha's morning sailed by. Her patients all had manageable crises. Their meetings all ended a few minutes early. She wrote out the required session notes with blinding ease. A few minutes before noon, she locked her office door and unzipped her backpack. Asha hummed as she laid out her change of clothes.

She had selected a pair of purple track shorts that had vees cut on the side, exposing rather a lot of thigh. She wore two top layers, a lavender tank top covered by an oversized sweatshirt from a late-night café she had frequented as an undergraduate. Across the front was a slice of their famous dessert, with the description BANANA CREAM PIE. Her boots were oversized and required two pairs of thick cotton socks. Last was a hooded Windbreaker she could tie around her middle. Asha checked her reflection in the bathroom mirror and declared, "A good time was had by all."

Dino called as she was starting her car. "Where are you?"

"Coming to meet you, if you'll just tell me where."

"Do you know Highland Drive?"

"No, but that's why they invented GPS."

"There's a cul-de-sac at the end. Parking's no problem." He sounded slightly breathless, as if he had accepted it was his job to be nervous for them both. "I'm at the sandwich shop on Hidalgo. Do you want anything in particular?"

"Hummus and sprouts on wheat, hot mustard, hold the mayo."

"Okay . . . So you're saying you're not interested in pastrami on white with extra butter."

"A joke. That's good." When he didn't come back, she said, "Dino."

"Yes, what?"

"This has just become a wonderful afternoon."

The nervousness was gone almost instantly. A very different voice asked, "Do you always know the perfect thing to say?"

"Hardly ever," she assured him. "Enjoy it while you can."

CHAPTER 43

Asha was standing beside her car, staring at the massive hill, when Dino pulled up and parked. She had seen Bishop Peak almost every day since her arrival in San Luis Obispo. She might even have thought, now and then, that it would be nice to climb up and enjoy the view. But there was a huge difference between idle reflection and seeing it as the day's challenge. Now she stood at the base and stared at the footpath that meandered through the adjacent pasture, through the grove of trees, then up and up and up . . .

"It's not too late," Dino said. "We can go for a stroll around the mission park."

She shook her head, still tracking the path that gleamed yellow in the sunlight. Up and up and up . . .

"Say something, Asha, please." When she still did not respond, he asked, "Are you afraid of heights?"

She was tempted to reply, Not until this very moment. Instead, Asha showed him her number one smile and said, "Let's get started."

* * *

"Bishop Peak is the tallest of the Nine Sisters, those are the old volcanic hills you see stretching across San Luis Obispo County. This used to be my favorite hike. When you asked me, you know, what I hadn't done in a while, this was what I thought of."

"I'm glad." Two words were about all she could manage, and they had not even started climbing. They had passed through the welcome shade of oak and bay trees, and were now traversing a grassy slope. The angle was so gentle it had almost appeared flat. Until, that is, they had started across. Now her breath sawed in her own ears. And up ahead was the climb. But she wouldn't think about that. She would try and focus on the next step, and walking with Dino, who was doing astonishingly well for a guy who hadn't hiked in years. Asha actually chuckled at what her grandmother would have to say right about then.

"Something funny?"

"I thought I was in good shape," she said, spacing her words around tight breaths. "I go to the gym, I jog . . ."

"The only thing that gets you fit for hiking is a hike," Dino said.

"Somehow that doesn't sound original."

He laughed easily. His breathing was calm. His long strides seemed to glide over the terrain. "About ready to stop?"

"I was ready ten minutes after we started out." Then she decided, "Maybe just a little farther."

Then the climb started in earnest. Dino led her up a trio of switchbacks, assuring her at each turn that there was a very nice halting place just up ahead. And when they arrived, Asha actually agreed with him. Stones formed a pair of smooth saddles, almost like prehistoric chairs, overlooking the hill to the east.

Dino handed her a bottle of coconut water. "That hill directly in front of us is Cerro San Luis."

Asha wanted to drink the entire container in one huge gulp. But she held herself to small sips between breaths. "Let's leave that one for tomorrow."

Dino unwrapped her sandwich and set it in her lap. She was not hungry until she took her first bite. Then the sandwich seemed to disappear all by itself. When she was done, and Dino asked if she was ready to continue, she found herself responding, "Absolutely."

The switchback trail climbed nine hundred feet over three-quarters of a mile. At least that was what Dino said. When the summit finally came into view, Asha felt as though she had managed the California equivalent of reaching Everest base camp.

She sank down on the bench shaded by the rocky peak and declared, "I may never move from this place. Not ever again."

Dino pulled another bottle of coconut water from his pack. As she drank, he named various points to the vista stretched out before them—Cal Poly, San Luis Old Town, Laguna Lake, and in the distance the Santa Lucia Mountains.

Her heart finally slowed, her breath eased. She sat and felt the heat radiating off his body. As comfortable and as weary as she had ever been.

Dino finally asked, "Are you sorry you came?"

"No, Dino. Not at all."

"It's just, you're so quiet."

"I was thinking . . ."

"What?" When she remained silent, he pressed, "Talk to me, Asha."

"I was thinking how this is what a real relationship should be. Where we press each other to grow in unaccustomed directions. Challenge each other to do what doesn't come natural."

It was his turn to go silent. He took the bottle from her, drank, handed it back. Finally he rose to his feet and asked, "Ready to start down?"

She tried to tell her legs it was time to stand up, start putting one foot in front of the other. But she did not find the strength to rise. "Can I just wait here for the next bus?"

He looked down at her, his face silhouetted by the sun. "Asha . . ."

"What?"

"Do you think it would be all right if I kissed you?"

Suddenly rising to her feet was the easiest thing in the world. "Absolutely."

CHAPTER 44

On Thursday night Lucius dined alone in the palatial pool house. The cook offered to prepare him whatever he liked. When Lucius replied that he would prefer a plate of whatever fresh vegetables they had on hand. He felt uncomfortable being waited on. But the cook and Jessica's aide both seemed intent on keeping him in this role as guest. Sarah arrived while he was eating, bearing his meager belongings from the Miramar Bay guesthouse. But instead of carrying them in his shopping bag, everything had been transferred to a valise made from Italian leather so soft he could have rolled it up and stuffed it in his pocket. Inside he also found a brand-new razor, toothbrush, shaving cream, lotion, shampoo, conditioner, deodorant, even a silver-backed hairbrush.

All the comforts of home.

Upon returning home Thursday evening, Asha fell asleep in the bath. When she woke up, her muscles had stiffened to the point that getting out of the tepid water required a number of serious groans. She made a fruit salad for dinner and tasted nothing. She was asleep before her head hit the pillow.

She awoke at a quarter to five on Friday morning. Half an hour later, she finally accepted that she was not going to go back to sleep. She rose and put on an extra-large pot of coffee, then took her time stretching. She carried the first mug as she made a circular orbit of her apartment, reflecting that the previous day's hike had given her a fresh new perspective on many things. Over her second mug she reviewed her notes and watched segments of the video of her latest session with Luke Benoit.

She then poured herself another mug and reviewed her very first session with Luke, which she had also videotaped. Three and a half months earlier, he had reluctantly agreed to the camera. Luke had repeatedly glared at it, as though suspicious of its motives.

Asha then went back to the latest session, and froze upon the moment she had agreed that he would join her grandmother for church. Luke smiled at the camera, the satisfied look of a professional negotiator who had gained what he wanted. He was going to see Sonya that weekend. He was pleased with himself, and what was more, he showed a genuine affection every time he glanced at Asha. She switched back to the first session from three months ago.

She studied the young man with his scruffy appearance and unshaven cheeks and red-rimmed eyes and slouched position. The differences between them were so great, they might as well have been images of two different patients.

The idea came to her while she was making notes over the extreme contrast between the two sessions. Up to then, writing a journal article had seemed like she had been invited to build a lunar rocket. And the reason was, she had not known how to begin. There was simply so much to say, so many changes, such an extreme shift, really night and day . . .

Now it seemed so simple, really. She would begin with Dino's predawn phone call.

She set down her coffee and drew up a new page file. The words flew from her fingertips. She had never typed so fast, for so long. The ideas took shape an instant before she wrote them down.

Six and a half pages later, Asha typed the words "In conclusion," and then stopped. Her fingers remained poised over the keyboard. The screen shone on her face, illuminating all her uncertainties. She knew what she was going to say. She felt now as though she had known it before she sat down. The act of writing had merely solidified everything she had already come to know at some deeper level.

Her grandmother was right.

It did not matter whether this young man, who called himself Lucius had indeed died and returned forty-nine years later. That was not the issue. At least, not to her. As therapist to this patient, Asha had been wrong to focus upon it. It had blinded her to the vital concern.

Luke Benoit now lived a different life.

Her fingers would still not type the words. She saw there on the empty screen all the rejections and derision her words were bound to unleash. But it changed nothing. She was bound to the truth.

Asha forced herself to begin writing. She was as careful and professional as she knew how. She wanted others to understand the conclusion she had reached, and why. Even if they utterly disagreed. Even if they thought her to be deluded. Even if they threatened her career.

The patient who returned was not the patient who had departed.

When she next looked up, Asha was astounded to discover she was due for her ten o'clock meeting with Luke Benoit in forty minutes. She had been at this for four and a half hours.

Swiftly she scanned her writing once more, and was filled with a conviction that it was not just good.

It was *ready.*

Lucius woke twice in the night, fearful that he had been overtaken by the black dog. But the attack did not come, and both times he eventually returned to sleep. He awoke soon after dawn, slid open the glass doors, and stepped outside to discover a pair of swimming trunks and fluffy robe on the chair next to his door. He held them up to his waist, wondering if they and the valise and silver hairbrush had once belonged to the former lord of the manor.

The swimming pool was rimmed on two sides by a veranda, which joined to the L-shaped apartment. The guest chambers were twice the size of Luke Benoit's apartment. Everything about this place was gargantuan. Lucius changed into the trunks and went for a swim. The pool was overheated, but he did not mind. He thought he shared the morning with only a few birds and a passing squirrel, but as he toweled off, the cook came down the path leading to the main house. She carried a tray that held coffee and breakfast. "Good morning, senor."

"And to you, ma'am."

"Last night I forget to ask what kind of fruit you like. There are peaches and blackberries here in the bowl." She unfolded a starched linen cloth and covered a poolside table. "The yogurt, it is plain but I can bring you other flavors. And here a banana."

Lucius wondered if someone had run into town this morning, just so he could have his requested breakfast. "This is perfect. May I ask your name?"

"Consuela. You are certain, you no wish for toast or eggs?"

"No, thank you, Ms. Consuela."

"The senora, she had another bad night."

"I'm sorry to hear that."

"This morning she tell me she is not coming down today."

Lucius was disappointed, but all he said was "I understand."

Consuela hesitated, then added, "Senora Wright, she is too much alone. It is good you are here."

"Thank you, ma'am. That means a lot."

"When you are ready, come speak with me, and the gardener will take you to the car place."

He watched the woman return down the long path, then ate his breakfast in thoughtful silence.

An hour later, the gardener drove him away in a late-model Mercedes. The man did not speak once the entire journey, which suited Lucius just fine.

The dealership came to a complete standstill when Lucius rose from the car. He pretended that nothing was out of the ordinary, though that required a bit of a stretch when the lady handling the service counter informed him that there was no charge for his repairs. Lucius was tempted to argue. Paying his own way was an ingrained habit. But the woman was already nervous enough, dealing with a man who had spent the night in the forbidden kingdom. So he thanked her solemnly, and asked, "Is Mike around?"

His question only heightened her anxiousness. "He had to run into town, Mr. Benoit, sir."

"No problem. Would you please thank him for me?"

"Absolutely, sir. Soon as he's back I'll tell him."

Lucius accepted the keys and followed her directions out back.

The Jaguar gleamed in the sunlight. They had polished the exterior and, from the fragrances that greeted him, saddle-washed the leather interior and even waxed the burl. Lucius slipped behind the wheel, rolled down the windows, and started the car. The only reason he didn't shout with joy was because of all the eyes watching him.

Lucius was just pulling from the dealership when his phone rang. He could have ignored the incessant chime. Perhaps he should have. But then with a start he realized that he had missed an appointment with Asha. He pulled over to the side of the road and rummaged through the leather valise, which Sarah and the cook had both insisted he take. Naturally, the phone was on the bottom. "Hello?"

Asha sounded almost as anxious as the woman at the service counter had looked. "Are you all right?"

"Yes, yes, I'm fine. But I got sidetracked by events. I'm sorry."

"So sidetracked you couldn't be bothered to check your messages?"

"My . . . messages."

"On your phone, Luke."

"You must show me how—"

"I'm in no mood for that. Do you realize if I had told Dino that you'd missed your appointment he would have wanted to alert the police?"

"I . . . No."

"I want you to come by now."

"That's not possible."

"Why not?"

Lucius hated how this conversation made him feel guilty. He disliked even more the sense that he owed that pair of doctors an explanation. "I'm not in town."

"Where are you?"

He took a breath. Knowing it was all going to come out now. "I'm in Miramar."

CHAPTER 45

When Luke did not arrive for his ten o'clock session, and then did not respond to her phone calls, Asha grew increasingly alarmed. Her apprehension only deepened when she learned where he was, and why.

Calling Dino did not help at all. He responded to the news with an alarm all his own. He grilled her like a cop, demanding every shred of information she had, which was very little. Then he said he had to alert the school's administration, and asked her not to leave her office until she heard back from him.

It was a shame, Asha reflected, that the harmony between them could not have lasted a little longer.

Dino called back at four thirty, while she was with the day's last patient. He left a message that they had a meeting with the university president at a quarter past five. Asha completed the day's paperwork, then crossed the campus through dry desert heat. The admin building's air-conditioned foyer greeted her with a frigid blast. Asha thought of Luke describing the moment he woke up in the morgue, the biting cold, the astringent odors, the sheet covering his face. She decided she could not bear to seal herself inside the elevator and took the stairs.

Asha had never been in the president's office before. She was surprised at how grand it all looked. The outer office was vast, the waiting area large enough for three different groups to sit in relative privacy. Dino was waiting for her there, seated in a leather sofa by the side window. "You're on time. Excellent."

"Why are we here?"

Dino managed to talk and type at the same time. "Events have reached the point where the administration needs to be alerted to the Benoit situation."

Asha repeated, "The Benoit situation."

"Right." He cut off the phone and slipped it into his pocket. "Do you want a coffee or something?"

"A water would be nice."

Dino rose and crossed to a kitchen alcove. He pulled a bottle from the small fridge and returned. "I think you should be the one to speak here."

She nodded. "I was afraid you were going to say that."

"It's not just because you're Luke's therapist. You handle the entire situation better than I ever could. Something about Luke sets me off."

"Really? I hadn't noticed."

"Liar." He smiled and leaned in closer. "Changing the subject. You know my family owns the Barbieri Vineyard."

"Of course."

"They're having a family gathering this weekend. My older brother's daughter has gotten engaged. They want you to come."

"You told your family about me?"

"I told my sister you were taking me for a hike. Word spread through the family system. You might have heard the drums."

"I didn't take you anywhere. You dragged me up and carried

me back down." She felt the rest of the room recede. "Your family wants to meet me?"

"It will probably be awful," Dino warned. "They'll crowd around you and ask every imaginable question, all of them far too personal and extremely embarrassing."

"They sound lovely," Asha replied. "Of course I'll come."

Dino started to reach for her hand, then pulled back. "Saturday I'm speaking at a medical convention in LA. I'll overnight at some hotel near the conference and drive straight to the family place Sunday morning. Can you meet me there?"

The idea took shape before Dino had even finished speaking. "What time is your conference over?"

"I should be done by six." Dino's handsome features tightened with very real concern. "Asha, I have to warn you, my family will show you all the polite decorum of an invading horde."

"I'm certain I will love every minute. And I'm already excited about the chance to know this aspect of your world."

He studied her for a long moment, then said softly, "I wish I could kiss you."

"Funny, I was thinking the exact same thing," Asha replied. "If I can arrange things with my folks, would you like to have dinner Saturday at my home?"

Dino's response was cut off by the secretary. "Dr. Barbieri, the president will see you now."

CHAPTER 46

Patrick Roland, the president of Cal Poly, had formerly been CEO of a bank based in San Francisco. Roland was as polished as a flesh-colored gemstone. His silver hair was razor cut, his suit tailored, his tie woven with the school colors. Even his frown seemed to gleam. "Perhaps it would be best if you gave it to us from the top, Dr. Barbieri."

"I will allow my associate to respond," Dino replied. "Asha Meisel has served as Benoit's therapist for the past several months."

Ron James, head of the alumni department, demanded, "You had no idea your patient was going to blow up in our faces like this?"

"Ron, please. Let's hear what they have to say."

"Jessica Wright is the university's largest donor. We've spent *years* working our way into her good graces. Now Dr. Barbieri informs us that everything we've done is being threatened—"

"Ron."

"—by some *nut*? Will somebody please tell me how this happened without anybody knowing?"

"That's enough." Roland turned to Asha. "Ms. . . ."

"Meisel."

"Summarize for us what is going on here."

The meeting held a different tone than the peer review, but in many respects they were very much the same. Asha and Dino were isolated on one side of an oval conference table meant to hold twenty. Across from them, the university president was flanked by Dean Rhea and Ron James. These three, Asha knew, held the power to crush her professional ambitions.

Yet as she summarized Luke's third suicide attempt and the subsequent change in his character, Asha felt as though she listened to herself from a very great distance. It was impossible that she could sound so, well, *professional.* Her delivery was precise, calm, swift. She did not *defend.* Which, of course, was how she would have expected to handle this situation. She completed the overview in less than ten minutes. Then she waited.

Naturally, Ron James exploded the instant she finished. "Let me get this straight."

"Ron, please . . ."

"Look. I have the right to know—"

"Actually, you don't. Not yet anyway. I invited you here for information purposes only. If you insist upon continuing with these outbursts, I will be forced to ask you to leave."

The warning had the effect of stifling the alumni chief. But the effort of staying silent turned his face beet red. Which Dean Rhea found mildly amusing, or so it seemed to Asha. Only then did she realize her calm delivery and the alumni director's outburst had changed, well, everything.

Rhea and Roland were on her side.

Roland seemed to confirm this impression by asking, "So you think your patient has, what, a split personality?"

Dean Rhea surprised them all by saying, "Actually, that would explain a lot. The Luke Benoit I've recently dealt with was not the same student as before."

Roland said, "Elaborate, please."

Rhea hesitated. "Off the record?"

"Nothing we discuss will leave this room." Roland turned to his left. "Is that completely clear, Ron?"

The alumni chief must have detected the same trace of steel as Asha, for he merely said, "Clear."

Rhea said, "I have long felt that Benoit used the accident that cost him his parents as just another in a long line of excuses. He played the perpetual victim better than any student I've had contact with."

Roland said, "You didn't force his hand."

"I didn't feel that I could. He was utterly alone in the world. I responded to his latest request and gave him another semester off. But I also warned him that if he didn't make substantial progress on an independent project, I would be reviewing his situation. We met earlier this week."

"And?"

"Like I said, I confronted an entirely different individual." Rhea seemed to wrestle with herself for a moment, then added, "He astonished me."

Roland leaned back. "'Astonished'?"

"He was precise in his comments. He had hired an attorney to assist him in the project. What was more, he had studied accounting on his own. He's now enrolled in a graduate-level finance class for the summer term. The professor checked him out and confirmed he was ready. This, after almost flunking him last year."

Roland cast his gaze at the ceiling. Pondering.

Then the alumni chief took the silence as his chance. "I don't get any of this." He stabbed the air between himself and Asha. "You've watched him go through three suicide attempts and we're only talking about this *now*?"

Dino said, "Actually, Ms. Meisel has only been his therapist for six sessions."

"Eight," Asha quietly corrected.

"Luke Benoit has changed therapists four times in the past two years," Dino finished. "If Ms. Meisel had not established this level of trust, we would not know anything about his recent actions."

"Well, we know now," James barked. "The guy is a menace. Lock him up!"

Roland lowered his gaze. "Can that be arranged?"

Asha gave Dino a chance to respond. When he remained silent, she addressed the dean seated directly opposite her. "You've seen how he acts. Say we took him to court and sought an injunction to have him placed in the mental ward."

"We wouldn't stand a chance," Rhea declared.

Roland asked, "Did you say he'd hired an attorney?"

"Sol Feinnes," Asha replied.

"Oh, man." Ron James rubbed his face. "Could this get any worse?"

Roland went back to studying the ceiling. This time the room waited with him. Finally he said, "All right. Ms. Meisel, what would you suggest as our course of action?"

"Call Jessica Wright. Explain the situation. There isn't really much else we *can* do at this stage."

Roland dropped his gaze. "'At this stage.'"

"Right. There is considerable disagreement over many elements of DID, as split personality is known nowadays. But most professionals agree on this one issue. Sooner or later, the patient will be confronted with some external event that challenges the lie he has constructed to support this new version of reality. And when that happens . . ."

Ron James demanded, "What?"

"They fall apart," Dino said. "A complete and utter meltdown."

Meyer rapped his knuckles on the table. "In that case, we have every reason to contact Mrs. Wright and alert her to this risk."

"I'll handle this," Ron James said.

Roland appeared ready to argue, but after a moment's hesitation he merely said, "Urge Mrs. Wright for her own safety to avoid any further contact with Benoit."

Rhea said, "What about all the time when he's not with you? He sees you, what, once a week?"

"Twice."

"So what happens if this meltdown occurs when he's off on his own? We need someone to help us monitor this guy."

"Difficult," Dino said. "Luke Benoit is a loner. He feeds on isolation."

Asha said, "Actually, I do have one person who could help."

Ron James slapped the table. "And I'm telling you that's not enough! We've got two ongoing projects costing us thirty-five million dollars, and they're both dependent on Jessica Wright's participation!"

Roland nodded reluctantly. "What do you suggest?"

"I'm not suggesting, I'm demanding! You put a harness on that kid and you rein him in!" Another stab across the table. "You order him to stay away from Ms. Wright. And if he won't obey, you corral him in a padded room."

This time it was Dean Rhea. "Ron."

He took aim at the dean. "You say he's enrolled for the summer? Fine. If he won't obey, you kick him out."

Roland asked, "Is that even possible?"

Rhea replied slowly, "A case could be made for his not having fulfilled his obligations as a student. He could be expelled."

"Do it," Ron said. "Now. Today. Unless he agrees to stay away from Ms. Wright. Permanently. Not even a postcard."

Roland gave the ceiling another careful inspection. Then, "I need to alert our attorney."

"And the board of trustees," Ron added. "They'll be ready to hire a paid assassin, if that's what it takes to keep our five-year building plan intact."

Roland sighed. "I will handle the board."

Ron redirected his ire at Asha. "And find somebody with more experience to handle this guy."

Dino's tone hardened. "There is no one more capable than Ms. Meisel. I know that for a fact."

Ron James started to object, but Roland halted his next outburst with a single look. He then turned back to Asha and asked, "Now tell us about this outsider who might help us keep an eye on Benoit."

CHAPTER 47

There was nothing in the therapist's rule book, Asha reflected that Saturday afternoon, which came anywhere close to covering her present situation.

Seated in a patient's car, which happened to be a vintage Jaguar in pristine condition. A car she had not known even existed until the patient had pulled up in front of her door.

The door in question being that to her private apartment.

Driving to Los Angeles. With a GoCam positioned on the dash so as to monitor the patient while he drove.

Discussing his contact with the university's largest private donor.

A contact which, from everything Asha had learned about the donor, was simply impossible. Because the recluse had not just *seen* Asha's patient.

Jessica Wright had invited the patient into her home.

The home into which no one from the university had entered. *Ever.*

What was more, the patient *had spent the night.*

As Asha listened to Luke recount his meeting with Jessica

Wright, and the home he described as a gargantuan monstrosity, she kept adding to the list.

And there certainly was more to this inventory of impossibilities.

Because they were not simply out for a Saturday drive. *Oh, no.*

They were going to Los Angeles, because . . .

Wait for it.

Luke Benoit was going to church with Asha's own grandmother.

And Asha could not attend with them, because . . .

Drumroll, maestro.

Asha was having dinner with her parents tonight. And Dino. Who was already in LA for his conference. And then early Sunday they were turning around and driving back north because they were going to a family gathering at the Barbieri Vineyard.

Asha resisted the urge to laugh out loud.

It was a very good thing that she had the camera perched there on the dashboard, in order to catch everything she was probably missing.

It was then that Luke Benoit uttered what were quite possibly the only words that could have brought the moment fully into focus.

He said, "I'm worried about you."

The car was not in any way modern. The leather seats did not form-fit her body like she was accustomed to. There was burl everywhere, so much wood the car's interior resembled a rich man's study. The steering wheel was large and an odd mix of wood and leather. The tires hummed over the freeway's uneven surface. The engine gave off a soft growl.

When Asha did not respond, he went on, "They are coming after me."

"Who, Luke?"

"The university. Surely, you must have heard. Their attorney has been in touch with Sol Feinnes. The dean has called and threatened me with expulsion. Not to mention the professor saying she had to receive permission from the president before I can start the summer term." He did not glance over once. His attention remained focused upon the road ahead. He kept his speed right at sixty. His grip on the steering wheel was far too tight. "Sooner or later, they are bound to view you as someone to blame."

Asha looked down at the notebook in her lap. She had not written one word since they had started off two hours ago. "Would you like me to drive?"

"Why, am I doing something wrong?"

"Not at all. It's just, you seem very tense."

"Did you hear what I just said? I am worried that you might become caught up in the university's maneuverings."

"Luke . . . Jessica Wright is Cal Poly's largest individual donor. Of course they're concerned."

"This goes far beyond being concerned. But that's not the point."

"What is the point, then?"

"They are doing this to stop me from seeing Jessica. That is not going to happen. Which means your own future could become threatened simply by being associated with me."

"Luke, can being in touch with this old woman really mean so much that you would risk your future?"

He shot her a single glance. "I know you don't believe me. I know all this is a charade of one form or another, as far as you and Barbieri are concerned."

"Luke—"

"Hear me out." He released one hand long enough to tap the steering wheel in time to his words. "Jessica Wright is the only aspect of my entire existence that holds any meaning whatsoever. If we are going to continue at all, you must accept this."

Asha was silenced as much by his manner of speech as the words, which in themselves were a shock. Luke spoke with an authority and stonelike resolve that simply did not fit with anything she knew about him.

"I have always been a hardheaded businessman. I identify a problem. I study it. I find a solution. I put it in place," he went on. "I work with allies who know and trust me. But all this is different now."

She managed to ask, "Different how?"

"I have lost my business record. I am seen as a suicide risk. I have no one who trusts me. I am . . ."

She finished, "You feel isolated."

"This is not about *feelings.* This is *fact.*"

"What do you intend—"

"I don't *know* what to do. Jessica is sealed behind this fortress of money and power. She is isolated by choice and by past hurts. She is ill. She *needs* me. And I have no idea how to proceed. How to . . ."

He was halted by the ringing of his phone. Luke fumbled it from his shirt pocket and handed it over. "Answer that, please."

"Are you sure?"

"There are only a handful of people who know my number. It could be important."

She touched the tab. "Luke Benoit's phone."

A woman demanded, "Who is this?"

"My name is Asha Meisel. I am Mr. Benoit's associate. Who am I speaking with, please?"

"Hold a moment." The phone was cupped or muted. Asha waited.

Luke asked, "Who is it?"

"I have no . . ."

The woman came back on. "Can you put Mr. Benoit on the phone?"

"He's driving. Can I take a message?"

"This is Sarah, Ms. Wright's aide. Ms. Wright asks if Mr. Benoit can join her . . . Where are you now?"

"On our way to Los Angeles."

"Just a moment, please."

When the phone went silent again, Asha said, "Her name is Sarah . . ."

She was halted by the transformation to Luke's face.

For a moment Asha feared he was going to burst into tears. The expression was so intense, she could not have named it as fear or pain or agony or . . .

Joy.

The woman came back on. "Can Mr. Benoit be here Monday morning?"

"Yes," Luke said, almost a groan. "Tell her yes."

"Nine o'clock," the woman continued. "Ms. Wright says, 'Be on time.' "

CHAPTER 48

When Asha was six, her father had accepted a position with the UCLA School of Medicine. Later that year they had moved from their home in Santa Monica to the top floor of a new condominium building in Brentwood. Asha had been very unhappy there at first. She had missed their garden and being able to walk or bike along the streets filled with other children. She had disliked the elevator with the buttons almost too high for her to reach. The building's dark-jacketed security had made her feel very uncomfortable. Their new home's broad expanse of pale coral carpet had seemed to invite little hands to spill things. In a child's mind Brentwood was an odd sort of place, filled with big buildings and broad streets and people in suits. But as Asha had grown into her teenage years, she had found herself enjoying the proximity of the Montana Avenue shops and cafés. And now she could see how the home was ideal for her parents.

They were seated on the broad balcony watching the sunset when Dino called for the fourth time since her arrival. "Asha, I can't tell you how sorry—"

"It's fine," she replied. And, actually, it was. "They understand. Really. Don't worry."

He sighed. "I'm done. May I come in my suit?"

"Of course."

"It's just, if I go back to the hotel, it'll mean another forty-five minutes at least."

"No, just come. And don't rush."

Asha cut the connection and said, "Dino apologizes for being late. Again. The conference switched the time of his lecture, and there was nothing he could do about it."

"It happens," her father said.

Asha liked having this chance to talk with her parents alone. Her father had been late as well, kept at the hospital by an unscheduled surgery. He had come in, kissed his wife, and headed straight into the shower. This had been his habit for as long as Asha could remember.

Now he sat in between his wife and daughter, dressed in an open-neck shirt and cotton slacks and boat shoes with no socks. As relaxed as a man on holiday.

Asha asked, "How do you do it? You've just shown up from an emergency, and here you are, not a care in the world."

There was something in his gaze that made her wonder if perhaps he had anticipated such a question. "You have to learn to turn it off. Find some way to step out of one world and into another. Either that or you make a mess of both."

"If it was only that easy," Asha replied.

"I didn't say it was easy. Only that it was necessary." He waited a moment, then asked, "Do you want to tell us what is the matter?"

"I honestly don't know what I want."

Her mother asked, "Did you and Dino have a fight?"

"No, Mom. It isn't Dino. Well, I suppose in a way . . ."

Her father asked, "Is it the patient your grandmother mentioned?"

Asha could almost see the gears working inside her mother's head. It was a thoroughly unprofessional way to describe the mental process, but true nonetheless. Glenda Meisel was every inch the lady, polished and immaculate and in control. The fact that she and Sonya were so very similar, and yet so extremely different, had been a point of confusion for Asha since childhood.

Glenda asked her husband, "How is it you're speaking with your mother about one of Asha's patients?"

"Because Sonya is meeting him tomorrow," Aiden replied. "Is that what has you so troubled?"

"In a way. I'm sorry. I wanted this evening to be all about Dino. But I just can't seem to set this case aside."

"It happens," Aiden replied. "Can you talk about it?"

"Of course she can," her mother said. "If Sonya knows, why shouldn't we?"

Which, of course, was the real reason why Glenda had any interest in Luke Benoit. It was not the patient or how he troubled her daughter. It was the fact that her mother-in-law knew something she didn't. Under any other circumstances Asha would have found that mildly hilarious. As it was, she was simply grateful for the chance to talk it through. Again.

Dino arrived then, and what might have been a formal time of greetings and apologies was cut short by Asha's parents wanting to hear the rest. If Dino was troubled by her discussing Luke Benoit with yet more of her family, he gave no sign. Instead, Asha had the impression he actually approved.

When Aiden asked about confidentiality, Dino replied, "Asha has received written consent from the patient to divulge whatever she wishes of this case. We intend to take this public, and the legal disclosure is vital."

Asha added, "And the patient insists that he is not, in fact, a patient at all. He remains involved in therapy only as a way to stop any further discussions about hospitalized care."

The only way they could understand, of course, was if Asha

started from that momentous day. She had related the points often enough that she could discuss them and still have mental space to reflect on what it all meant. From this strange mix of distance and proximity, Asha felt as though the day had changed everything. It had been the start of so much, *The American Journal of Psychiatry* article and the relationship with Dino . . . So much began at that moment when her patient had woken up beneath the frigid white shroud.

The case dominated the dinner conversation. There was, in fact, little room for nervousness or reserve on anyone's part. Asha's case study captured them all. Between courses Dino shed his tie and jacket. Asha's mother draped it over the back of the sofa, something she would normally never have allowed. But she was too involved in the telling to leave the room.

It was only when she reached the drive down to LA that Asha realized she had somehow talked her way through the entire dinner. She looked at her empty plate and tried to recall actually taking a bite of anything.

Dino, however, rose to the occasion. "This has been a lovely meal."

"Thank you." But, for once, Glenda's attention was elsewhere. "Let me start the coffee. Don't say another word until I get back." When she returned, it was to say, "I can't imagine anything much worse than nearly dying and coming back to find myself in the morgue under a sheet."

Her father nodded. "No doubt it was a tremendous shock on every level."

Glenda asked, "How does anyone recover from such a thing?"

Dino replied, "In Luke Benoit's case, you develop a second personality. One for whom the suicide attempt did not actually occur."

Asha said quietly, "Sonya does not believe that's what happened."

Her father said, "Mother believes the young man's story is real?"

"Not exactly. What she said was, she has no reason to disbelieve him." Asha turned to Dino. "Dr. Emeka agrees."

Her father said, "I'm sorry, who?"

Dino replied without taking his eyes off Asha. "The chief of urgent care at Cal Poly's hospital. An extremely capable doctor."

"Who actually believes your patient died . . . and somehow comes back to life as a man who died five decades ago?" Her father looked from one to the other. "Is that what you are telling me?"

Asha told Dino, "I recorded the drive down today."

He nodded approval. "And?"

"There is something I want you to see."

"Will you tell me what it is?"

"If you insist," Asha replied. "But I'd rather have you observe this without my opinions clouding your judgment."

Dino actually smiled. "You have reached a conclusion?"

"No. It's not that. But I am beginning to detect a trend. A series of events that when they're taken alone don't mean much. But when grouped together, they reveal something very, well . . ."

Dino liked that a lot. "Show me."

Glenda said, "Can we watch, too?"

CHAPTER 49

For the evening's entertainment, on the night Asha introduced her parents to the man she truly loved, they watched the video of a patient talking into a camera perched on the dash of a vintage Jaguar.

It was only later, when she lay in her bed and reflected on a most astonishing evening, that she wondered how she had come to think of this as natural. Which was exactly how it felt. Natural that Dino would shift the coffee table over to the balcony's flower boxes and open her laptop. Natural that her father would compress four chairs into a tight semicircle facing the table and the LA night. Natural that they would make mugs of coffee in the kitchen, carry them back outdoors, and stand at the railing for a time while Dino described the medical convention where he had spoken earlier that day. Her father knew of the conference, of course. Interestingly enough, the two men did not sweep off into a discussion filled with medical jargon. Instead, they touched on a few of the luminaries whom they all knew. They spoke of the hotel. They spent a few moments discussing San Luis Obispo as a place to live and work. Then they set down the mugs and together they sat down and her father said, "Let's have a look at this young man."

The car's motor sounded louder than Asha recalled. And it was rather disconcerting at first to see other automobiles rushing past Luke's window. He held to a moderate speed, his gaze focused tightly upon the road. After a while, though, Asha ignored these distractions and allowed herself to be swept along by this retelling. She had her notebook opened in her lap, her chair positioned so that she could see the pages in the light spilling through the sliding doors behind her. She had jotted down the time positions where particular issues were raised. But she did not need to refer to them. She found herself recalling the entire conversation with vivid clarity.

Asha played the tape in segments. She kept each long enough for the others to capture images of the topics as they arose. Then she moved on before the viewing became tedious. Asha knew she and Dino would go through the entire session together. And that was how she thought of the drive now. One elongated session. The fact that Luke Benoit insisted he was no longer a patient changed nothing.

Asha introduced each segment by stating the topic Luke discussed. The longest segment, by far, was the one following the phone call from Sarah, Ms. Wright's assistant. Asha played that in its entirety. She froze the image of Luke's rapturous response to the woman's invitation. And waited.

Her mother was the first to speak. "Are we talking about *the* Jessica Wright?"

Aiden asked his wife, "You know her?"

"Yes, Aiden, and so do you. We met at the fund-raiser in Santa Barbara for mobile medical centers."

"Of course."

Glenda asked her daughter, "So this young man claims to be the founder of Quarterfield Motors?"

"Incredible," Aiden murmured. "Mother actually believes him?"

"No, Dad. Again, that's not what I said or what Nana meant."

"Explain this to me."

Asha loved her father very much. But she also knew he was limited in his perspective by his job. Every time he entered the surgical ward, every time he lifted the knife, he held a patient's future in his hands. Life or death. There was no room for mistakes or subtle half measures. Asha said, "Nana hasn't said. But I think she has set the entire issue aside. She sees a lonely young man who is in need . . ."

"Of what?" Aiden demanded.

"A friend. One who does not judge."

He frowned at the screen and did not respond.

Dino was seated between her parents. Asha leaned forward slightly so as to study him more clearly. She was very gratified to see him frowning intently at the frozen image. She said, "You see it, don't you?"

Glenda asked, "See what?"

"In our profession, there is a lot more argument than agreement when it comes to split personalities. Even what to call them. But there are a couple of issues that everyone agrees on. The first is, the shifts in character are temporary. Something happens, some emotional upheaval, and the patient switches." Asha pointed to the screen. "We are looking at a huge emotional jolt. But what do we observe? A singularly intense response. Since the hospital we have witnessed no reversion to the original Luke Benoit."

Dino's entire face tightened. She knew he was locked in a silent argument with her. And she did not mind. She was not looking to convince him. She was simply laying out the evidence. "This has troubled me ever since our first session following his release. Luke told me he had experienced a very deep wave of depression. He described it as a vicious assault. And yet he did not shift back to the original personality. He simply described the incident, and asked for medicine that he might take the next time it happened."

Dino said reluctantly, "He then changed his diet."

"Luke Benoit has been addicted to fast food for years," Asha confirmed. "Overnight he replaced this with a vegetarian regime. Which he has maintained ever since. Again, we are talking about a consistency that defies what we know about DID."

Glenda looked from one face to the other. "What does this mean?"

There followed an altogether strange sort of ending to their dinner.

There was none of the formality that Asha might have expected for the first time her parents met Dino. She had not brought very many men home, only three as a matter of fact, including the pimply-faced young man who had taken Asha to her high-school senior prom. And, of course, the last had been Jeffrey. Asha had known her father did not think much of him. But Jeffrey had charmed her mother, as he did almost every woman who came within reach. Aiden had not wanted to taint that evening with disagreement, so he had kept his opinions to himself. But Asha had known what her father had thought of Jeffrey.

She could not help but compare that evening to this one.

Everyone had pretended not to listen in as Aiden had telephoned Sonya and spoken to her about Luke Benoit. He had then returned to the living room and confirmed what Asha had told them. No, Luke was not with her that evening. No, Sonya was not hosting him in any way. Luke was there to accompany Sonya to church, nothing more. Dino and her father had then insisted upon Asha and her mother letting them clear up. The two men were talking quietly now about some medical issue, working side by side in the kitchen, loading the dishwasher and wiping down the counters. Asha stood by the balcony railing, watching the men through the glass doors. And she waited.

Her mother was seated with her back to the living room, facing her daughter by the railing. Glenda was immaculate, as always. She tended toward the bright fashionable colors of the St. John line. There was no telling what Glenda was going to say, as she sat there tapping her pearls with one hand. Asha waited in silence, reflecting that her mother certainly had any number of topics to choose from. There was Jeffrey, of course. And the way Luke Benoit had dominated their evening. And how Asha had allowed her professional life to intrude. Not to mention Dino, and his age, and his role as her supervisor and boss.

Asha tried to keep her nerves from showing. She was determined to wait out her mother. Nor did she want her tension or defensiveness to emerge. She hoped the evening would end on as nice a note as possible.

But when Glenda did speak, it was to observe, "Dino does not agree with your assessment of that poor young man."

"I suppose I knew he wouldn't," Asha replied. "But I needed him to see the evidence."

"Of course you did." Glenda patted the chair next to hers. "Come sit down, dear. I promise I won't bite."

Asha did as her mother requested.

Glenda said, "I like him."

Asha took another long breath, and released another batch of tension.

"He is very dashing, in a rumpled and weary sort of way."

Asha said, "Sonya says Dino reminds her of Granddad."

"Interesting. I can see that too, now that you mention it." Glenda was quiet for a moment, then said, "You were five when he died."

"Six," Asha corrected. "Three days after my birthday."

"That's right. How could I have forgotten? You cried for days." Glenda smiled at the night. "You two remind me of Aiden and myself."

Asha lifted her chair and turned herself around, so as to face her mother. Glenda continued to stare out over the city's nighttime glow. Asha said, "Excuse me?"

"In so many ways. I waited all night for your father to mention it." Glenda lifted her gaze to the clouds turned golden with reflected light. "How long have you been seeing him?"

"If you mean dating, just this week. But I suppose I've been infatuated with him since we first met two years ago."

"Tell me about that."

Asha described going in for the graduate interview. How they had spent most of the time discussing Dino's latest publication, an introduction to crisis therapy that was already being adopted as a college textbook. But what Asha mostly thought about was that Glenda was not smiling at anything her daughter was saying.

When she went silent, Glenda said, "I fell head over heels in love with your father the first time I saw him."

"You never told me that."

"I never told *him.*" Glenda smiled at her daughter. "I had to bide my time. Give Aiden the chance to realize we were meant to be together."

"How long did that take?"

"Almost two years."

"Wow," Asha breathed.

The two men chose that moment to step onto the balcony. Aiden asked, "Are you ladies having a nice chat?"

Asha replied, "Wonderful."

CHAPTER 50

Lucius was outside the Hilton Garden Inn when Sonya arrived early Sunday morning. She had sounded very formal the previous evening when he called to confirm his arrival. When he slipped into the car, her greeting was colder still. He waited until she was driving to ask, "Was I wrong to come?"

She did not pretend to misunderstand. "My son telephoned last night. He was most concerned about our spending this time together. I assured him it was church and nothing more. No meal, not even coffee."

"I understand."

"Yes, I see that you do." She glanced over. "Do you know, I would imagine that you could prove to be most relaxing company."

"But not today," Lucius replied, liking her very much. "Not with your son and granddaughter perched in the backseat, worrying over what might happen next."

She drove them along the empty Sunday streets and halted, facing across from a green expanse. "This is Bicknell Park," she said. "And the monument you see there is the Armenian Genocide Memorial."

Lucius stared through the windshield at a circular cluster of eight tall arches. The pillars supported a distant roof, white and very solemn. As they sat there, one car after another divulged families and couples of every age. Many of them were dressed entirely in black, the women's head covered in knitted kerchiefs. They climbed the stairs and laid flowers at the memorial's base. They stood there for a time. They greeted others with the somber formality that Lucius might have expected at a funeral. Then they returned to their cars and drove away.

"I wanted you to see this because it has an importance upon what we will next witness," Sonya went on. "The first Armenian immigrants arrived in the United States after the Hamidian massacres of the 1890s. Then another wave followed the Armenian Genocide of 1915. In the seventies there was yet another mass immigration as the Soviet Union began to collapse. Now there is a fourth wave of Armenian immigrants arriving from Lebanon, Iran, Syria, and Turkey. As a result there are more Armenians living in the Los Angeles area than anywhere else in the world outside their home country."

She reversed from the parking space and drove in silence. Lucius had no idea where Sonya was going with this, but felt no need to press her for an explanation. This was Sonya's story. Her tempo. Her morning.

She joined a long line of cars pulling into a vast parking area and waved to the young man signaling her into a space. She cut the motor, took a scarf from her purse, settled it over her hair, then opened her door. Lucius rose from the car and went around to accompany her. As they joined a long parade of families headed into a massive concrete cube of a building, Sonya went on, "Armenia was the first country to adopt Christianity as its official religion, in the year 301. The Armenian Church claims to have been originated by the missions of Apostles Bartholomew and Thaddeus in the first century. The country today is surrounded by Muslim nations. The entire region is in flux. There are constant border disputes and incursions by one army or another. Much of this conflict is financed and coordinated by my home country, Iran."

They entered the church's massive vestibule, where Sonya was greeted by one family after another. She did not introduce Lucius, and the parishioners did not press. Lucius observed a rainbow assortment of people and races and even manners of dress. Most of the women wore kerchiefs over their heads, but not all. Sonya guided him into the sanctuary, a vast chamber shaped like a shallow square bowl. She selected a pew toward the back, where they could sit and observe as the hall rapidly filled. A band played upon the dais, the music offering a pleasant isolation.

"Los Angeles is home to the largest Persian community outside Iran. What is more, it also contains the largest Kurdish population in the West," Sonya went on. "This church serves all three communities, which in itself is an astonishment, for the Kurds and the Persians and Armenians have been at war for over two and a half thousand years." She gestured out over the congregation. "Now here is what I want you to see. Look there."

"I don't . . ."

"In the midst of my own tragic undoing, I was approached by this community. Remember what I told you on our drive to Dino's home. I was a product of my nation, and my nation is held in the amber of its past. I was orphaned and I was alone." Sonya gazed out over the rapidly filling hall. "These people welcomed me. They taught me by example that I was free to choose. I could walk away from the elements that invited me to live in dreadful solitude. I could join them here in this island of refuge and peace."

As Lucius listened, he felt an image take shape behind his eyes. He saw himself seated not in a church, but rather a harbor. Surrounded by people who had all come for the same reason as himself. They sought an hour of calm. Here they were protected. Sheltered. Here they might know a brief instant of peace. And all the while, out beyond the harbor walls, the sea roared and the storm raged.

Sonya said, "Almost every family here carries its burden of calamity and woe. Each face you see, from the youngest to the old. They are immigrants, they are unwanted, they are unable to find the kin they left behind. They have loved ones trapped in the sea of refugee tents lining the Syrian borders. They have every reason to remain locked in solitude and sorrow."

Sonya turned to him and said, "I am Persian. It is my legacy. No matter that I am disowned by my family for marrying the love of my life. Or that I am banned from ever returning to my homeland. I speak of this because you need to understand that I am a woman of two worlds. I love the West and its constant push into tomorrow. The freedom this grants individuals to live their own lives, free of the chains of the past, you cannot imagine how liberating this is, especially for a woman. And yet I remain distinctly a part of my heritage."

"It is in your blood," Luke said.

Sonya leaned toward him. The church lighting carved her features into shadow and yellowed stone. Lucius thought she had never looked so much like a queen as now. Sonya said, "The West has liberated us, especially women. But in the process it has lost something."

"The past," Lucius murmured.

"The *mystery.* In my homeland the past is not some distant series of half-forgotten events. It is part of the here and now. It defines today. What does this mean? How could it possibly be important enough to discuss with you?" Sonya's accent was richer now. "Listen, then, and I will explain. The people of my land have learned to live with the impossible and the unexplained. The West seeks to define. To classify. To explain. The East says, some things cannot be clarified. Not now. Not ever. And that is why I found comfort in this haven. Because here, in this place, the Western culture is set aside, and the heritage of my homeland is embraced. In song. In prayer. In the company of good people living in two cultures."

"You believe me," Lucius realized. "The events that brought me here, they are real . . ."

Sonya tsk-tsked. "Why do you waste time with such comments?"

"But . . ."

"Pay careful attention. What I think of your story, that is not the issue." Sonya gave him time to object. When he remained silent, she said, "There is one question you must answer. Are you ready?"

"Yes," he replied, and he was.

"Here it is, then. The eternal quandary that every one of us either faces, or spends our entire life fleeing." She was close enough now for him to smell the gentle fragrance of lilacs. "What will you do with the gift of your next breath?"

CHAPTER 51

Dino arrived back the next morning at six. Asha's mother greeted him with a peck on the cheek and a hot breakfast no one said they wanted, but which everyone ate with gusto. Asha and Dino left promptly at six thirty. Her parents stood there on the sidewalk, waving them off. Asha rolled down her window and waved back, until Dino's SUV turned a corner and they disappeared from view. As he pulled up onto the freeway, Asha said, "That's a first."

Dino waited until she had rolled up her window to say, "Don't expect anything so pleasant from my family."

Asha liked everything about the morning. How they had the freeway almost entirely to themselves. How there was an easy sense of gentle harmony between them. How the sun was both brilliant and pleasant, not a cloud or hint of smog. How they were a couple, doing things that couples did.

Three hours later, they entered the Barbieri estate through stone gates shaped like two welcoming arms. A pair of tall signs stated that the vineyard was closed for the day. The drive rose along a gentle slope with acres of grapevines stretching out to either side. The leaves held a minty springtime color, fresh and new and in sharp contrast to the ancient twisted plants. When she commented on that, Dino said that many of the original vines had been brought over from Italy seventy years ago.

The family was huge and loud and greeted her with a great wave of people and noise. Asha had no choice but to allow herself to be swept along, back through the public tasting rooms and out to the rear courtyard, where a long table had been set beneath a grove of elms. Three barns and dozens of tall oak barrels framed the stone veranda. Birds flitted about overhead. Children ran and shrieked. Their elders laughed and argued and chattered. Asha was seated in the middle of the table and plied with questions and comments and antipasti and a deep red wine. She had no trouble in pretending to ignore any question or comment that she found inappropriate. The table was that loud.

Asha watched as Dino became the children's focal point. They refused to let him even sit down. He was pulled away by dozens of demanding little hands and voices. He smiled an apology back to where she was seated, clearly embarrassed and enjoying himself immensely.

To Asha's right sat the family matriarch, a wizened old woman named, of all things, Bernadette. She was brown and small and wore a shapeless knit dress with a mottled neck ringed by black glass beads. Asha could easily imagine her dressed head to toe in black, clustered together with other village women, screeching at something awful the grandchildren were doing.

Instead, when she spoke, it was to say, "Our Dino is a master at charming the little ones."

"He's the same with his younger patients," Asha said. "It was one of the first things I liked about him."

"Was it indeed?" She had a gaze dark and piercing. Asha felt as though she was being probed by a black scalpel. "What else attracted you?"

"I liked him before we ever met. He wrote the textbook that drew me into counseling."

She drew back a notch. "My grandson wrote a book?"

It was Asha's turn to be surprised. "You don't know?"

"Young lady, my grandson says almost nothing about himself. He is the most closed-up individual in my family. It has been a bone of contention since he was as young as those who pester him now."

Asha had no idea what to say.

"He brought his ex-wife . . . You know about her, I suppose."

"A little. Yes."

The old woman sniffed. "Then it's probably more than the rest of us. Dino brought her here once only. I saw her again at their wedding. After that, not at all. I have no idea what she did with her life, other than buy clothes none of us cared for. Too extreme and too aggressive. She looked like a fashionable shark, if you want my opinion." She made a brushing motion with her arthritic fingers. "I do not care to speak about that one anymore."

"Fine by me," Asha said, thinking how remarkably like Sonya this woman was. Not in any external fashion. But down deep. Where it mattered most. They could have been sisters. "Dino has authored four books, and I don't know how many articles."

"This is true, what you are telling me?"

"Your grandson has an international reputation. He is a master in his field."

The old woman watched Dino push a shrieking trio of young girls in the woven hammock hung between two elms. "You can explain to an old woman what these books are about?"

"It would be my pleasure," Asha replied, and meant it. "Can I ask you something?"

"In this family, my dear, you do not need to precede your questions with a request for permission."

An answer worthy of her own grandmother. "Bernadette is not an Italian name, is it?"

"Hardly. I was named after my grandfather's forbidden sweetheart." Her cheeks dimpled at Asha's surprise. "He was a porter in the grandest hotel in Rome, perhaps the finest in all Italy. He fell in love with the daughter of an Irish diplomat. There is much supposition about their affair, but all anyone can say for certain is, a ticket was purchased for him to travel to California by steamer. He had six children by my grandmother, all boys. I was the first female offspring in our family. He insisted upon naming me."

"Your grandmother must have loved that."

"I was sixteen months old before I was christened. That is how fierce the argument was. My naming has become part of the family's lore. Of course such fables grow richer with the years." The dimples grew deeper. "The last time someone shared my naming tale with the young ones there, I heard something about a witch and a tower and perhaps even a dragon or two."

Asha found herself liking the old woman enough to ask, "Are we to become friends?"

Ancient fingers curled around Asha's wrist. "Do you know, my dear, I believe we already are."

CHAPTER 52

Lucius drove straight from the Los Angeles church to Miramar. The journey took a little less than five hours. He held his speed to sixty miles per hour and let the other vehicles sweep past him. Traffic was very heavy, and several times the southbound lanes appeared to freeze up like a giant parking lot. The Pacific Ocean slipped in and out of view. The sunlight was strong. He noticed all these things but was impacted by nothing except his destination.

He arrived back at the guesthouse just after six. The manager was clearly surprised to see him again, but greeted Lucius with a severe formality and gave him the room he had used before. He let himself in, set his case on the narrow dining table, then crossed the town's main road and entered a very pleasant diner. By the time he finished eating, Lucius was almost nodding off in his booth. He returned to his little room, undressed, and was out for the count.

The next morning he walked down to the café and took his time over a smoothie and a black coffee. The jangle of the door's bell and the hissing steam and the chatter offered a sort of comforting normality. He got a refill on his coffee and drew out his pad and pen. But there was no list to work through this day. Everything began and ended with seeing Jessica again.

The Wright home was as utterly unappealing as the first visit, a great heaping monolith of white stone and ego. Sarah was there on the front portico, just as unwelcoming as before. Lucius offered a greeting, accepted her silent rebuke over his disturbing their peace, and followed her back down the long central corridor to the conservatory.

This time, however, Jessica did not keep him waiting. He was still standing by the glass wall when the door behind him opened once more. "Why does our guest not have tea?"

"Because your guest does not want anything," Lucius replied.

"Nonsense. Sarah, phone Consuela and ask her to fix a tray."

Lucius decided not to object. "Good morning, Jessica."

She waited while Sarah positioned her chair just so, close to the rear glass wall, but in the shadow of the striped canopy. When her aide phoned the kitchen and returned, Jessica said, "Sarah, you need to hear this. Sit down over there."

Sarah cast Lucius another of those glances, equal measure resentment and curiosity. The way she moved, like she swam through some viscous fluid, made Lucius fairly certain she had never been seated here before.

Jessica did not speak again until Lucius had settled into his own chair. "I wish to hire you as my secretary."

Lucius decided it was good that Sarah was seated. Otherwise he was fairly certain she would have keeled over from the shock.

"I suppose we can come up with some fancier name, if 'secretary' offends your male sensibilities."

"'Secretary' is fine," he replied.

"I would want you available day and night. Which means you must reside here on the premises."

"Not inside the main residence," Lucius replied. "The pool house will do me just fine."

She seemed to find that humorous. "Aren't you going to inquire over your pay?"

"No."

"For a student of finance you seem very cavalier in your attitude."

"I'm not agreeing to this job for the money," Lucius replied. "I'd just as soon you not pay me at all."

Sarah's shocked expression deepened even further. He knew she was suspicious of his motives, and rightly so.

But Jessica looked at him. Not in the sideways manner of a matron taking on a new hire. Really *looked.* For an instant the film of pain and age vanished and a trace of the old spark returned to those eyes. Lucius found himself staring into the gaze he had known and loved.

Then the moment passed. Jessica was once more an elderly woman clearly afflicted by more than the weight of years. "Very well, young man. I accept your terms. Sarah, you may transport me back upstairs."

But as she was wheeled from the room, Jessica glanced back. Just a fleeting look, but long enough for Lucius to see that same glimmer of the past. Only filtered by everything that had separated them, and still did so today.

Sarah, Jessica's aide or servant or whatever she was, avoided Lucius for the rest of the day. He would never have found Jessica's office, had it not been for Consuela. The cook was beside herself with joy over his arrival. "I pray and I pray for you to come. Okay, maybe not *you.* But somebody who is *alive.* Somebody who will open up these windows and bring *life* into this place."

"You don't like the house?"

Consuela sniffed. "What is there to like in this place? It is so big, I walk through rooms and I think ghosts follow me, the sound my feet make. But then I know it is only the echo. What ghost would want to live here?"

As he ate his lunch in the kitchen, a solid-looking woman in a white nurse's uniform entered and greeted him with an unflappable calm. She accepted his name but did not give hers in return, which Lucius found only mildly odder than him being here at all. She collected a tray with food for two and departed. Consuela said, "That is the day Ruth."

"I don't follow."

"The day nurse and the night one, they are both named Ruth. And the housekeeper. She, too, is a Ruth." Consuela revealed a lovely smile. "Ms. Jessica, she calls this 'being efficient.'"

"The nurse is very quiet," Lucius said.

"Ms. Jessica, she tells the service, 'Don't send me talkers. If you send me somebody who jabbers, I send them right back.' The night Ruth reads all the time. She has the tablet, the computer without keys. It shines like a night-light. She sits and she reads." Consuela looked at him. "Ms. Sarah, she is almost this quiet. I go days and days and don't speak. When I go home, my husband, he catches all the words I store up in the days. Sometimes when he goes to bed early, he says it is because his ears are hurting him."

"You can talk with me all you like," Lucius assured her.

She flashed another smile. "My husband, he will thank you so very much."

The office had apparently not been touched in months. The pile of unopened correspondence blanketed the in-box and collected in four cardboard boxes hidden behind the desk. There were 147 messages on the phone. Consuela had no idea what the password was to Jessica's computer, so Lucius could not access her e-mails. When Lucius asked, the day Ruth told him that Jessica was sleeping and could not be disturbed. He returned to the office and said to the empty room, "What a mess."

In truth, though, he was actually very glad. There was work

that needed doing. He had a task, a role to play. She *needed* him. At four that afternoon Sarah appeared in the doorway and must have seen something that agreed with her, as she spoke to him for the first time that day. "She always told me not to bother."

"I understand."

She stood there and watched him sort the correspondence for a time, then said, "I imagine you'll be wanting to go through her e-mails."

"I do, yes."

"Her password is 'Lucius.' Do I need to spell that for you?"

His voice sounded strangled to his own ears. "No, thank you. I can manage."

CHAPTER 53

Asha's Monday morning began with a phone call from the university president's secretary, who instructed her to attend a meeting at three. She called Dino to make sure he had received the same marching orders. Dino told her, "They obviously know something about our patient's current status that we don't."

"He is no longer our patient," Asha replied. "I have received a letter from Luke's attorney to that effect."

"When?"

"It arrived this morning."

"Well, that should extract us from whatever mess Benoit is making for himself."

"That does nothing to help him through his current situation," Asha replied.

But Dino was having none of it. "Just as you said, Luke Benoit is officially someone else's problem."

Asha was leaving the office that afternoon when Luke Benoit phoned. Asha told him, "It's not good timing, I'm afraid. I'm due at the president's office in twenty minutes."

"Because of me, I suppose." He sounded very matter-of-fact.

"What have you done now?"

He laughed. The sound stopped Asha in her tracks. Standing there outside her own door, the keys in her hand, unable to move. She tried to recall if she had ever heard him even chuckle before just then.

Luke replied, "Jessica has appointed me her secretary."

"Say that again, please."

"The office is a complete and utter mess. No one has been in here for months, except to dump another load of correspondence."

"Luke . . . where are you now?"

"In the pool house. Or cabana. It's more like a hotel suite. I worked through lunch. Her unanswered e-mails contain five quarterly reports on her corporate accounts. Apparently, she's not even glanced at them. Consuela just came in and ordered me to stop and grab a bite. Which is when I realized I hadn't called you."

"Wait, you're *living* there?"

"For the moment. We'll see how things develop. Actually, that's not why I called. I wanted to thank you for allowing me to visit with your grandmother."

"You're welcome. Luke . . ."

But he was not done. "She challenged me in a way that's hard to describe."

Asha realized she had to move if she did not want to be late. She forced her legs to carry her down the corridor and out the front door. "Please try and tell me."

Luke repeated Sonya's words about living in the moment. "There was something else, she didn't actually say it, but I heard the message as clearly as if she did. I need to accept that I am alone out of habit. But some of the issues I face can't be dealt with on my own. I need . . ."

"Help," Asha offered.

"Friends," Luke corrected. "People I can trust. And who trust me."

Asha had an uneasy sense of missing a very important message. She knew this conversation contained a crucial ingredient, some elemental charge that would alter everything. She had no idea what it was. But for the moment it was enough to sense its presence.

"Asha?"

She thought on the letter she had received from his attorney, and asked, "Is there anything else you feel I should know?"

It was his turn to hesitate. When he responded, it was to say, "There is. Yes." Another hesitation, then, "I think Jessica suspects."

CHAPTER 54

Dino was already seated in the boardroom when she arrived. He pulled out the chair next to his as President Roland looked pointedly at his watch and said, "We're all present now? Yes? Good. Ms. Meisel, I believe you know everyone except Graham Avery, vice chair of our board of trustees. Very well. I've asked you all here because of news that just came in this morning. One of Ron's staff has developed a close personal relationship with Ms. Wright's aide. She called this morning to inform us that this Benoit individual has apparently inserted himself into the Wright household as the woman's personal secretary." Roland let that sink in for a moment, then said, "Ron, why don't you start."

Ron James rose from his position and walked to the front of the room, where a large screen was sliding down from the ceiling. He showed artist's renditions of two new university buildings currently in the planning stages. He moved through the cost structures with a nervous but practiced manner. The numbers appeared and flowed and vanished. The meaning was very clear. Without Jessica Wright's normal level of investment, both of these projects would be halted.

Asha listened with far less than full attention. She found herself recalling the hospital peer review with vivid clarity. There was the unmistakable sense that the two events were tied together. If only she could identify the missing element. If only . . .

"Ms. Meisel?"

"I'm sorry, yes?"

"Do you have anything to add to these proceedings?"

"About what?"

"Did you really say that?" Ron James stomped back around to his position. "Your patient threatens the future of this university!"

Dino replied, "Point of clarification. Luke Benoit removed himself from therapy. This morning Ms. Meisel received official confirmation from his attorney."

The president asked, "May I see?"

Asha extracted the letter from her purse and handed it over. Roland read, then passed it down to the trustee. Avery was sleekly overweight and carried himself with a glossy self-important air. His cuff links flashed as he adjusted his spectacles. "Sol Feinnes has been in touch with us as well."

The president asked, "About what?"

"A minor matter related to his ill-advised representation of this Benoit individual. A question about our handling of his trust. Not really germane to our discussion. But another bit of evidence."

Asha nodded slowly. She remembered where she had heard Avery's name before. Luke Benoit had directed some of his most acerbic comments at the attorney responsible for his family's trust.

Roland asked, "Evidence of what?"

"Clearly, the young man in question has serious and troubling issues," Avery replied. "Wouldn't you agree, Dr. Barbieri?"

"Perhaps," Dino replied.

Avery showed surprise. "I would say this has moved into the realm of certainty. Luke Benoit releases himself from the hospital after a third suicide attempt, and now threatens the university's position with its largest individual donor. There is no 'perhaps' about it, Dr. Barbieri. In fact, it alarms me that you would even refer to this situation with such a response."

Ron James bounced up and down in his seat. "Now we're talking."

Roland asked the trustee, "What would you suggest?"

"Quite simple, really. We ask for the court to intervene. Luke Benoit is a menace to himself and others. He must be removed from Jessica Wright's proximity. He should be placed under strict supervision." Avery lifted his head far enough to erase the multiple folds along his neck. Even so, the gesture was weakened by the fat little dimple of a chin. "And if he objects in any way, we must ensure that Luke Benoit is locked up. Permanently."

CHAPTER 55

Asha remained immersed in her internal dialogue until the others had said their farewells. Dino then asked, "Do you have time for a coffee?"

"Actually, I need to talk with you."

"Great minds think alike. Where shall we go?"

"Nowhere, Dino. We need to do this *now.*"

"What, here?"

"Here is perfect." She waited until he resumed his seat to say, "I can not be party to what is taking place."

Dino appeared genuinely shocked, which disappointed her terribly. But not nearly as much as his words. "Do you have any idea what you are saying?"

"I know precisely what this means. May I tell you why?"

"Asha, you can't possibly suggest we side with Benoit." Dino waved at the empty seats. "These people are deadly serious."

"And they are wrong."

Her calm surprised them both. Dino opened and shut his mouth twice. Confusion and anger and fear worked through his features and his gaze. Finally he declared, "Luke Benoit has been a menace since the moment he returned to consciousness."

She knew what was happening, at least internally. She was reverting to the professional calm that had inflamed virtually every one of her previous relationships. Her response to friction had always been to distance herself, and that had infuriated every boyfriend she had ever had. Even so, she knew it was what made her a good clinician, this ability to retreat within an icy clarity. The problem was, her ability had no ON/OFF switch.

Now she heard the tragic lament of her soon-to-be broken heart, and knew she was helpless to close the distance, or show him her love and concern and desire for a different outcome. Instead, she heard herself say, "You've listened to me twice before, when you were about to make a serious error in regard to Luke. Will you give me that courtesy again?"

He crossed his arms, bracing himself for what he did not want to hear. "Go ahead."

"Let's start with the video I made of the drive. Do you remember what I said at my parents'?"

"Asha, a diversion from the expected pattern, especially with patients suffering from DID, does not hold any significance. *Everyone* disagrees over signal traits related to multiple personalities."

"Luke Benoit is not experiencing a split personality. He exhibits not one of the expected symptoms. He has changed. He is not the person he was before. We need to accept that and help him adjust to this new beginning."

There. She had said it. The declaration should probably have been softened. Couched in more professional language. Drawn out slowly. But at some level Asha knew that it would have made no difference.

She could see his response. It was etched in his features. Dino was siding with the board. Against her. And against Luke.

"Asha, even if you were right, which you are *not,* even if you were, you don't go against the university board."

"I have no choice."

"You have *every* choice. You have *every* reason to *make* that choice." He stabbed the air between them and the exit. "Those people can make or break your career!"

She knew then that it was over. He stood on one side of the chasm, she on the other. She felt her heart crack with the distress and the loss. But she couldn't change what she knew to be right. "I have to do what is best for my patient."

"Even if he does not consider himself in your care? You're going to throw everything away? The *Journal* article, medical school, your professional chances . . ."

As swiftly as she could, Asha related her latest conversation with Lucius. "It was the confirmation I needed. There in the voice and the words both. What do we always say about all personality disorders, the one issue we can always count on? The one trait they all have in common?"

Dino was silent, his jaw muscles rigid as he glared at her.

"They *deflect.* They *do not accept change.* Everything in their environment is twisted so as to *reinforce.*" She wiped her face. If only knowing she was right did not hurt so bad. "Luke *thanked* me. He accepted my grandmother's challenge to *grow.* What was more, he realized another personal issue all on his own. And accepted the need for further change."

"So you're telling me this guy has died and popped up—"

"No, Dino. I am just saying the near-death experience has created *something else.*" She laid her hands upon the polished table, palms up. "Near-death experiences can create huge and unexpected transformations. Many of them result in extremely positive outcomes. We have hundreds of case studies to draw upon. All I'm saying at this point is, Luke Benoit is not the same man he was before. We need to accept this and *help* him. That is our *job.*"

Dino remained as he was. Clenched and angry and shut away from her. "If you insist upon taking this course, it may well cost you your professional future."

Asha closed her hands, drew back, rose from her chair, and took the long way around the boardroom so she did not have to go near Dino. As she opened the door and entered the corridor, she thought she heard him call her name. Or perhaps it was merely the lament of an empty heart.

CHAPTER 56

Lucius was deep in the corporate accounts when Sarah stopped by to say she was leaving for the day. He ignored her hostile tone and pointed stare, and wished her a good evening.

Twenty minutes later, the day nurse pushed Jessica's wheelchair into view. She was dressed in a sky-blue frock that sparkled as it caught the lights. Her hair had been coiffed and looked to Lucius like spun silver. She declared, "I have rested better than I have in years."

Lucius rose and stood by the desk. A proper secretary. "I'm glad to hear it."

"I have a hankering to escape from this . . ."

"Mausoleum," Lucius offered.

"Precisely. Would you do me the kindness of taking me for a drive?"

Lucius was already moving for the door. "Absolutely."

There was, of course, no question which car to take, not even when Consuela walked him over to the mock stables and introduced him to a warehouse holding nearly two-dozen vehicles. When Lucius asked for the keys to the Caprice, Consuela said, "That is Ms. Jessica's favorite."

"I know."

"How are you knowing this?"

"Intuition," Lucius replied. He slipped behind the wheel and backed it carefully from its place in line, then drove around the sweeping drive to where the day Ruth stood by Jessica's chair.

When she was settled in the passenger seat, he asked, "Did you have anyplace in mind?"

"Most certainly," Jessica replied, and pointed forward. "Beyond those prison gates."

Lucius was uncertain that he would be able to find his way. But there was only one road that wound along the valley floor, back to the Miramar Highway. He took the main street through town, when suddenly he was struck by a thought. He pulled into a parking space and said, "Would you excuse me a moment?"

Jessica gave the passersby a sour look. "You're not intending to leave me here and go run off for hours, I hope."

"Five minutes, tops."

"I suppose I can amuse myself that long."

He left the car and sprinted back to where a tattooed young man polished the brass handles to the restaurant's entrance. "Sorry, man. We're closed."

"I just want to make a reservation."

"Not for tonight," the young man warned. "The place is booked solid. Word got out that Connor Larkin's gonna play."

Lucius had no idea what the young man was talking about, nor did he care. He entered the restaurant and found the proprietor filling the bar coolers next to the lovely Latina. Sylvie Cassick greeted him with, "If half the rumors we've been hearing are true, you could keep us spellbound for hours. Only not today."

Lucius leaned over the bar, getting in close enough for them to see his desperation. "I need to ask a really, really big favor."

There was a reassuring sameness to so much of Miramar. The town had grown, certainly doubling in size and perhaps more. But the main layout was precisely as Lucius remembered. He took it very slow. Driving his car with Jessica by his side was almost more than this much-improved young heart could bear.

He took the cliffside drive past a clutch of California pines. A stiff wind off the Pacific tossed their limbs almost like they waved a frantic greeting. The turnoff for Bent Pine Park was where he recalled. The place was much improved, the parking area paved and the adjacent pasture now holding a soccer field and playground for young children. The lot was about half-full. Lucius drove around twice before a departing pickup granted him a spot from where they looked out over the beach.

He rolled down all the car's windows, then cut the motor and sat there. Staring at the spot where he had breathed his last. Remembering.

Jessica spoke to the world beyond the windshield. "I've always considered this a special place."

Lucius had no idea how to respond, except, "It's very lovely."

"I used to find fireflies here. This was, oh, years ago. I mentioned it to a few people and they all said I was imagining things. Fireflies don't live along the central coast. Or if they do, they don't light up. But I know differently."

Lucius found his view of the sea blurring somewhat. "I believe you."

"Do you, now? How remarkable." She was silent so long, Lucius thought that was all she had to say. Then, "I came here with my young man. He died far too soon. This place is all I have left now."

Lucius swallowed hard.

"He was a most remarkable gentleman. But his health was not good. Terrible, actually." She sighed. "What does it matter? It's all gone now. Perhaps it was only real in my imagination. Like the fireflies."

CHAPTER 57

Dino did not call.

Asha read through her would-be article, adding several final paragraphs about case studies that pointed toward unexplained and drastic personality shifts after near-death experiences. Then she sent it to Dino as an attachment. Her e-mail held to a begging tone, asking him to read, to think, to reconsider.

He did not respond.

The tension kept building all evening. Asha's lovely little apartment became a cage. She forced herself to eat, but after a few bites she feared she was going to be sick. She could not even bring herself to clear the remnants. Just looking at food left her queasy.

The phone remained silent.

By ten o'clock she knew she could not hold it all inside. She did not want to call her grandmother. Sonya was already too involved. Sooner or later, Asha was going to have to explain the whole mess, but not now.

She called home.

When her mother answered the phone, Asha broke down. She was weeping so hard, she could not even speak.

"Asha, honey, take a deep breath."

She did as her mother said, then asked, "How did you know it was me?"

"Oh, darling. Do you really think I have so many women who would call me after ten and cry so hard they can't speak?"

For once, her mother's tart manner actually helped. "I've made a terrible mess of everything."

"You mean, with Dino?"

Just hearing his name was enough to cause her insides to cramp. "Yes."

"Are you sure it's your fault?"

"No. Not at all."

"But you've spent all night sitting there alone and blaming yourself."

"How did you know?"

Glenda Meisel chuckled warmly. "I may not be a trained psychologist. But I am a woman. Now catch your breath and tell me what happened."

As she recounted the story, Asha filled her kettle and put it on the stove. Talking helped immensely. When the water boiled, she filled a mug and pulled out a packet of herbal tea. The floral scent filled the kitchen. She finished her account of the terrible, awful day, then just stood there, dipping the tea bag up and down. Content to wait. Breathing easier than she had since leaving the boardroom.

Glenda asked, "What are you doing?"

"Making tea."

"An excellent idea."

There was the sound of running water, then a pot being set on the stove. The act of sharing drew Asha closer than she had felt to her mother since . . .

Since before Jeffrey.

Finally Glenda said, "Would you like to know what I think?"

"Yes, Mother. I would."

"Dino is acting like a perfect Mr. Potato Head."

Asha laughed out loud.

"You remember?"

"Of course I do." When she had been very young, the very worst thing Asha could say about an adult was that they were acting like the cartoon character. Asha had not thought of Mr. Potato Head in years.

"Asha, I want you to listen to me very carefully. You have done nothing wrong."

She reached blindly for the box of Kleenex.

"You acted out of your highest principles. You remained the true professional. You seek what is best for your patient. Even when the patient does not wish to consider himself under your care. You have defied the authorities that hold your career in their grasp. You have done so because it was the right thing to do. The *only* thing." Glenda was silent for a moment, then added, "Your father and I are very proud of you."

"Oh, Mom."

"Now you're going to ask what you should do about Dino. Correct?"

"Yes."

"You already know the answer, don't you? You must do nothing at all."

"I miss him so much."

"Asha, my darling, we could both see how much you two are in love. And now you've had your first major fight as a couple. You are right and he is wrong. It is that simple. You have grown through the experience. You are growing into the woman your father and I always knew you would become. It is now up to Dino."

"What if he doesn't . . ."

"Then it is best that you discover this flaw in him early. Now. Before you involve yourself any more deeply in his life and world."

She sniffed and wiped her face and swallowed hard. "You're right. I know you're right."

"Now you're going to hang up and go pour yourself a hot bath and then you're going to go to bed and know that I am there, stroking your forehead and loving you with every shred of my being." Glenda was quiet, then softly added, "Thank you so very, very much, Asha."

"For what?"

"For letting me cry with you."

CHAPTER 58

When Lucius rolled Jessica into Castaways, the entire restaurant came to a complete and utter halt.

The place were so quiet, he could hear the chair's left wheel squeak softly as he followed Sylvie Cassick through the main room and around the bar. Jessica handled it with regal grace, ignoring them one and all. Lucius could have cared less. His day was far too perfect for such inconsequential elements as a little frozen attention.

Sylvie stopped at the far end of the restaurant's long overflow table, where two empty places awaited them. "As I explained to your associate, Ms. Wright, we've been booked solid for weeks. Connor is playing tonight, you see."

"And Connor is . . ."

"My fiancé."

"How nice for you both." She glanced up at Lucius. "Will this do?"

"It's perfect," he replied.

When Sylvie started to remove the chair at the head of the

table, Jessica said, "Would you be so kind as to allow me to face the sunset?"

"Of course." Sylvie waited as Lucius fitted Jessica in close to the table and seated himself, then said, "Marcela will be your waitress tonight. Can I get you something to start?"

Jessica took small bites of every dish, including everything on Lucius's plates. She asked for champagne. After each meager sip Lucius reached over and refilled her glass. Her fingers were knotted and the joints overlarge, but she made do by will and determination. Her movements were slow, but very refined.

They spoke very little. The restaurant's noise rose and fell in waves about them. They watched the sunset. They commented on the gulls. The food they both found to be artistically designed and exquisitely flavored. They said as much when Marcela asked, and then again when Sylvie came over. Jessica found great humor in their astonishment. She told Lucius, "I have not always been their favorite client."

"That was then and this is now," Lucius replied.

"Indeed. Take more champagne."

"I need to drive us home."

"Oh, nonsense. What's the reason to be wealthy, if you can't call for a ride when the moment requires?" She tapped his glass with one finger. "Drink."

Sylvie chose that moment to step on the stage. She reached for the mike and said, "I suppose it comes as no surprise that my Connor . . ."

She had to wait through the cheers and whistles. When the crowd went quiet once more, she continued speaking. "Connor has finished filming. I'm happy to confirm that he's managed to escape LA again. Which means he's back home and ready to take his place here on the stage. Connor?"

A strikingly handsome man stepped through the crowd, pausing now and then to shake hands. His smile was arresting. The restaurant's lights seemed to track him as he crossed in front of their long table and climbed up to where Sylvie waited.

The crowd's cheer carried into laughter as he embraced the restaurant owner, leaned her over backward, and kissed her soundly. Marcela fanned herself with somebody's napkin and pretended to need Lucius's chair back to keep from falling over. Then she realized where she stood, and glanced fearfully at Jessica. But tonight she found only a smile in response, and a request for more champagne.

Lucius found Connor's singing to be a wrenching experience. Lucius knew every melody. And yet they were all refashioned to suit both the man and this new age. When Connor began a soulful rendering of The Drifters' "Save the Last Dance for Me," Lucius felt the distance separating him from Jessica grow so vast he could never reach her. Their time was past. His chance for any dance was gone. The music became a dirge to all that life had refused him. When the applause started, he rose and excused himself and walked outside. The night was cool, the sidewalks filled with lovers and good times. Lucius stayed there until he was certain his emotions were back under control. He waited until the next round of applause, then forced himself to return to his seat. The next song was almost as hard to endure, the Shirelles' "Will You Still Love Me Tomorrow." But Lucius sat there and smiled and clapped with the others. He kept reminding himself that he had handled much worse.

CHAPTER 59

Lucius woke early the next morning, as was normal for him. He had never thought he would be able to apply that word to himself again. Normal. Yet here he was, tracking down the garden walk with some night animal for company, letting himself into a kitchen that was as oversized as the rest of the house, hunting through the cabinets for coffee. He took his mug out to the rear stoop, where a trio of chairs suggested the help used this same space from time to time. He watched the light gather and pondered on the challenge of reinserting himself into Jessica's life.

The woman's age cracked his heart. All the years he wished he had been there for her. All the breaths he wished they had been able to share. The sights and sounds of a lifetime of love, never to be theirs. Lucius had all the reasons in a splintered world to mourn. But he still had this. The soft emerald lawn, the chirp of birds, the hope of another day with his beloved.

He was back in the kitchen refilling his mug when his phone rang. So few people had this number, he felt obliged to answer. "Hello?"

"It's too early. I know that. I should have waited. But I couldn't."

"Asha?"

"We need to talk. I've been up for hours. Are you awake?"

The words seemed disjointed, as though the thoughts behind them were scarcely strong enough to hold them together. "What's the matter?"

"So much." She sniffed noisily. "You told me you were an early riser. I hoped . . ."

"Asha, take a deep breath and steady yourself. I'm here and I'm awake. Now tell me what's wrong."

"They're coming after you."

"Who is?"

"Dino." Speaking the name was enough to threaten her ability to breathe. Then she managed, "Everybody."

When the day staff arrived at nine, Lucius sent word upstairs that they needed to speak. Another thirty minutes passed before Sarah came downstairs and said Jessica would meet him in the conservatory. Twenty minutes later, she wheeled Jessica into the garden room. Sarah hovered by the table until Jessica waved her away. Lucius stood by the rear glass wall until the door clicked shut, then said, "Something is about to happen. I'm sorry. But this can't wait."

"All the rooms in this house have microphones that feed into the pantry. Sarah and the night nurse also carry portable monitors." She gestured back behind them. "There is a switch beneath the light and temperature controls."

When he returned, Jessica went on, "I met my ex-husband through work. For a time that is all I did. The company was capable of swallowing every hour I had to give, and still remain hungry for more. My accountant introduced me to John Wright. Wright Motors was the largest automotive dealership in Los Angeles and was growing into San Diego. Of course I learned later that John had put my accountant up to the task of playing matchmaker. At the time I saw in John an opportunity to forge a much-needed alliance. He knew everything I didn't about the automotive business. My one condition, the one item on which I would not budge . . ." She watched him settle back into his chair. "But, of course, you know."

"Quarterfield Motors," Lucius said.

"The young man I told you about yesterday left me the company in his will. It was, and remains, a complete astonishment, both that he did so and that I managed to keep things running."

"You've done far more than that," Lucius replied.

Jessica waved away the compliment. "He had two reasons for doing so. He wanted me taken care of. And he wanted to stay close in the only way he could manage."

Her matter-of-fact tone again made Lucius wonder if she knew, or at least suspected. All he said was "Was he wrong to do so?"

"Who knows? It was all so long ago. I won't say learning the necessary lessons was easy. All this money and power reshaped me. At times it was all rather fun. But there were also some rather unpleasant elements, needless to say. My ex-husband assumed wealth granted him the right to do whatever he wanted, with whomever was within reach. John's dalliances grew to the point that I could no longer pretend at a marriage. Thankfully, a drawn-out court battle was avoided because he had developed a cocaine habit. When I threatened him with the documented evidence my private investigators had uncovered, he caved like the wretch he had become. I let him keep the San Diego dealerships, so long as he vowed never to set foot north of LA ever again."

Lucius asked, because his heart compelled him, "Did you ever regret loving your young man?"

"What a remarkable question. Life certainly dealt him a lousy hand. He did as well as he possibly could have." Jessica used her thumb and forefinger to wipe the edges of her mouth. "Shall I tell you what I do regret?"

"Please."

"When it came to love, he allowed himself to be fashioned by his circumstances."

Lucius felt his chest compress to where he could scarcely breathe.

Jessica continued to stare through the window. Whatever she saw twisted her features into haggard lines. "He was shaped by isolation. He fed upon his solitude. It suited his nature. I wanted to stay with him, nurse him, be his companion through the few days we might have known together. But he pushed me away. Oh, I'm certain he dressed his actions in some valiant intent to protect me. But he was wrong. Do you hear me? As wrong as wrong could be."

Lucius opened his mouth, but no sound came.

Jessica pulled herself back from the dark arena with a visible effort. "Never mind all that. What was it you wanted to speak with me about?"

Lucius fumbled his way through the early conversation with Asha. Long before he was done, he sensed Jessica's discomfort had become transformed into something far more severe. She appeared to have aged ten years since entering the conservatory. Lucius finished, "It's not that urgent. I can see her the next time I travel down—"

Her arthritic hand scrabbled across the tabletop. "You must call her. This very instant. Tell her to come up."

"Jessica, really, you're troubled. Let me ask Sarah—"

"'Troubled'? *Troubled?* Did you actually use that word?"

Lucius was pushed back in his seat by her wrath.

Her eyes flashed with an emerald fire. "In case it has missed your limited powers of observation, you are here to *do my bidding.* You should be fired for the felonious crime of male blindness! You control *nothing.* You understand *nothing.*"

"I'll call her, Jessica. Don't let yourself become—"

"Don't you *dare* tell me what I can or can't do."

He stopped. Took a long breath. And waited. Finally he said, "You're right."

"Am I?"

"Yes. I was treating you like an invalid. Which you are not."

She glared at him. "How am I supposed to argue with you if you insist upon agreeing?"

Lucius said it because he wanted to be certain he had it straight. "You want to see Asha Meisel. Yourself. Not for me."

She leaned back in her seat, clearly exhausted by her ire. "Be a good lad and go make the call."

CHAPTER 60

Sarah and the day nurse were stationed in the corridor just outside the conservatory doors. The day Ruth gave him a cursory head-to-toe inspection and declared, "I don't see anything more serious than a few second-degree burns. You'll survive."

Sarah asked, "Does she want anything?"

The day nurse said, "More ammunition, I expect."

Lucius said, "I think I just discovered why Jessica's employees all look like frightened rabbits."

Ruth snorted. "That was nothing. When your wounds are still smoking an hour after she's done, then you've had the full treatment."

Sarah asked, "Should I go in now?"

Lucius slipped around them. "I need to make a phone call."

The day nurse said, "I have always found a double brandy helps to reduce the calamity."

Asha arrived at the Wright home's main gates at four fifteen that afternoon. She had been delayed by the need to reschedule a number of appointments. Each phone call had been forced against the fear that she might never be permitted to see her patients again. That ending the romantic liaison with Dino, before it even had a chance to begin, was neither the worst nor the hardest step she would soon be taking. And yet not once in that horrid day did she worry over doing the wrong thing. Not even when she took time out for a call to her mother, and then another with Sonya, and wept her way through both. Not even when she packed her bag and said farewell to her beloved apartment. Not even when she started north, fearful that everything in her rearview mirror was lost to her forever. Not even then.

Luke answered when she buzzed the gate. He was standing on the bottom step when she approached what was quite possibly the biggest and whitest house she had ever seen. He opened her door and said, "Thank you so much for coming."

"What's wrong?"

"I have no idea." He appeared to dance in place even when he stood utterly still. "Jessica wants to speak with you. Urgently. She's said nothing more."

But as they started up the massive front steps, she said, "Wait."

"We really need—"

"Give me just one minute, please." Asha inspected him carefully. She had no idea what she was looking for, but she knew precisely what she had found.

The man standing between her and the house was moving further from the patient he had once been with each passing day. To deny this was to lie to herself. Worse still, it was to ignore all the evidence that pointed toward . . .

She might as well say it.

Asha took a long breath, then spoke the words that had echoed through her mind the entire journey north. "Should I call you Luke or Lucius?"

His features crumpled slightly, and for an instant Asha thought he might weep. Which granted her a remarkable sense of joining with him on this, the hardest of days.

"Whichever you prefer," he replied quietly. "And thank you so much for asking."

The bedroom was as vastly oversized as everything Asha had seen of this strange pale house. She crossed an acre of white carpet, beneath a white ceiling that curved twenty feet above her, perhaps more. The woman seated in the white silk chaise longue wore a cream-colored robe, as though she intended to allow the room to frame her.

Asha said, "Good afternoon, Ms. Wright."

"Call me Jessica, dear. Thank you for coming." She shifted her attention to where Lucius hovered in the doorway. "I owe you an apology."

"You owe me nothing," he replied. "Not now, not ever."

"As we were talking this morning, I realized I had convicted myself with everything that had confounded me about my young man."

Asha waited for Lucius to say something, but he remained mute, intensely focused upon Jessica Wright.

"I accused him of retreating from me because solitude suited him. But the fact is, I have done the exact same thing. I took the power of my money and built for myself precisely the same sort of solitary life." She held him with a brilliant gaze that defied her years. "I confess I never really got over losing my young man. Not a day has passed that I haven't thought of him."

Lucius opened his mouth, but no sound emerged. Asha thought she had never seen a more tragic expression, filled with impossible longing.

But Jessica seemed to find what she sought in his countenance, for she smiled and said, "Be a dear and grant me a moment of privacy with this young lady." She then turned to the two women standing by the nearest window and said, "I would like to speak with Ms. Meisel in private."

When the door clicked shut, Jessica said, "Forgive me for

coming straight to the point, my dear. But time is not my friend these days."

"Of course."

"This may be the only chance you and I have to speak without observers, you see. From this point forward it will be important that there are witnesses to everything I do and say with you. These others must confirm that I am in my right mind, in control of what faculties I have left, and am very clear in my purpose." Jessica stared thoughtfully at the door. "It would probably be best for them to observe this exchange as well. But I need to ask you something that might easily be misconstrued."

Asha pointed to her briefcase. "I brought a video recorder with me. If you like, I can set it up before we talk."

"Splendid." Jessica observed everything with a keen eye, but did not speak again until the video camera was set on its tripod and hooked up to Asha's laptop. Then she announced, "I am dying."

Asha did not respond. To say she was sorry was just too feeble. The woman was unlike anyone she had ever met before. Jessica Wright looked fragile as spun glass, and yet she was also fiercely alive. She gave the impression of an ancient bird of prey, perched upon her chair, fierce even to the last dip of her wings, the final flight through her last sunset.

"The doctors change their minds every time I allow them near," Jessica went on. "Some say it's a matter of days. Others, weeks. But none of them speak in terms of months anymore. My day nurse claims she's just hanging around to catch me when I keel over."

Asha asked, "How can I help?"

"It's not about my impending departure, if that's what you're thinking. Oh, I admit the prospect of facing that final portal terrifies me." Jessica's eyes tracked over to the closed door. "But having this young man enter my life has changed everything."

Asha found the breath catch in her throat.

Jessica's smile carried the weight of illness and age. "You've noticed it, too, then."

Asha had to work through several breaths before she managed, "I have. Yes."

"I am so very glad to hear it. I thought, well, I'm on so much medication these days, it would be easy to blame it on an addled mental state."

"You strike me as many things," Asha said. "Addled is not one of them."

"I am certain of very little these days. But I entered the Miramar showroom several days back and there he was—the loneliest man on earth. That was what I called him, you know, before. It applies even more now."

Asha found it necessary to wipe her eyes. "I've spent years training as a professional observer. And everything I see about this man tells me . . ."

"That either the young man out there has succeeded in deluding himself and us, or we are confronting the impossible."

Asha breathed more easily now. "Everything about the near-death experiences is under fierce debate. If these are indeed real events, it may force the entire medical profession to reshape their boundaries. That young man is the embodiment of everything they most fear."

"He simply can't be left to cope with this on his own. If indeed we are right in our suspicions." This time when she dabbed at her mouth, her fingers trembled. "They are bound to come after him."

"Whoever he is," Asha finished for her. Understanding now. "They are already on their way."

"Precisely. I don't need to see them to know the vultures are hovering just beyond the horizon."

"The university views his presence as a threat to their intentions."

"What utter nonsense. I have supported them ever since they took care of my parents in their final days."

"Whoever he is, he's a threat to the status quo," Asha said. "A complete and total unknown factor suddenly thrown into the mix."

"Then we understand each other." Her gaze drifted back to the closed door. "It would be so much easier not to believe him."

"And safer," Asha agreed.

Asha knew what she had to do long before she disconnected her equipment and carried it back downstairs. Luke wanted to speak with her, of course. But she put him off. When he tried to object, she had to grow firmer than she wanted. She could see he was still wounded by whatever had transpired between him and Jessica, whatever argument they had had prior to her arrival. But there was no time for that now. Any delay, and she would lose her nerve.

She carried her phone outside. She paced up and down the forecourt, her footsteps marking small craters in the otherwise perfectly groomed white stones. She wished there were some way to know what was going to happen. She wished she could stop her heart from hammering so hard it was difficult to draw breath. She wished she could know the right words to say. But her mind remained frantically blank.

Asha forced her trembling fingers to press in the number.

When Dino answered, she had to swallow hard. Twice.

"Asha?"

Just hearing him speak her name gave her the strength to say, "I need your help."

CHAPTER 61

Dino could not get away until late because of a hospitalized patient and yet another meeting with the university president and trustees. Then Dino called from the road, and again an hour later from the front gate. Asha descended the steps and turned to inspect the house. It looked even more imposing at night. Emblazoned by the countless spotlights, the residence shone like a pearl-white fortress.

Dino rose hesitantly from the car. He gave the house a brief inspection, then asked, "Why am I here?"

"Thank you for coming," she replied, glad for the calm note to her voice.

He followed her up the front steps like an old man. "Why are *you* here?"

"This way." She led him across the foyer and up the sweeping central staircase.

The upstairs corridor was thirty feet wide and carpeted in a white silk and wool blend that swallowed every sound. It seemed as though every light in the entire house was on. Asha reached the last door and knocked softly, then opened it and entered. She told the woman on the chaise longue, "He's here." Then she realized Dino was not following her. She turned back and said, "Either come in or leave, Dino. Those are your choices."

"Jessica, allow me to introduce Dr. Dino Barbieri. He is, or was, my graduate supervisor." Asha gave Dino an opportunity to correct her, to say the sun and planets still maintained their proper orbit. His silence tore another fragment from her heart.

Asha forced herself to walk over and seat herself in the high-backed chair. She turned on the equipment and ensured the video camera was feeding properly into the laptop's memory. She could do nothing about the tremor to her voice as she said, "Everything from this point on must be recorded."

Dino remained planted in the middle of the room. "Ms. Wright . . ."

"You may call me Jessica."

"It's just . . . I'm not certain I should be here."

Jessica merely turned to her and said, "Asha?"

"Come sit down, Dino." When he was seated in the chair drawn up next to her own, Asha went on, "I am going to show you two videos. The first will be of my most recent interview with Luke Benoit. It was shot two hours ago. In it he discusses his initial assessment of the Wright empire's current financial status. This extends far beyond Quarterfield Motors. Jessica has invested in a number of other ventures, but they are all held within the same financial structure as her dealerships. Something Luke is adamantly opposed to, as are her other advisers."

"I don't see—"

"The other video was shot of my initial conversation with Jessica Wright. Because of her health, I don't want to force her to go through what is clearly a distressing issue a second time." She sat there, studying this man from a very great distance. Wishing there were some way to reach across the divide separating them, and enfold him into an embrace strong enough to last, well, forever. Swallowing down the yearning regret was very hard indeed. When she was ready, she continued. "Jessica will then answer any questions you might have. Then you can decide."

"Decide what?"

Jessica addressed him for the very first time. "You know precisely what the issue is, young man. Asha claims you are highly intelligent and a trained professional. Don't prove her wrong with such inane queries. We want you to add your weight to what I intend." She waved a hand. "Show him."

When the two recordings were finished, it was well after midnight and Jessica was showing clear signs of fatigue. Dino stared at the laptop's cover and did not speak. Asha realized he was not going to ask for her assessment. Which hurt terribly.

"Jessica Wright is fully in charge of her faculties. She is no more certain of what has happened to Luke Benoit than you or I. But she has decided that she wants Luke to serve as adviser during the . . ."

When Asha could not say it, Jessica offered, "'Transition' works as well as anything else, I suppose."

She glanced over to the far corner, where Sarah sat with the night nurse. Neither had uttered a single word since all this began. Nor had there been any softening to Sarah's stony gaze.

Finally Dino sighed and said, "I need some time to think this through."

CHAPTER 62

A little after one, Lucius left the main residence and walked back to the pool house. He knew something was going on and he hated not being a part of it. He was exhausted and yet not the least bit sleepy. He sat by the pool and watched the lights deep inside the blue waters, and wished he knew why he was being excluded.

Then he heard a familiar voice. "Mind if I join you?"

Lucius wanted to send Dino away. He had never much cared for the man. He disliked intensely that Dino now knew something he did not. But there was a slim chance Lucius might gain much-needed information, so he said, "If you like."

"Thank you." Dino made a great show of selecting a chair and drawing it over. Then he said, "I suppose you know Asha asked me up here to gain my support."

"For what?"

Dino seated himself and watched the bugs flitter about the lights for a time. "Jessica wants to include you in the planning of her estate. For me to even consider backing this is ludicrous."

"So why are you here?"

Dino took his time answering. "Because of Asha."

Lucius nodded. "She is a remarkable woman."

"That, she is." Dino stared glumly at the night. "I'm supposed to be out here asking the sort of questions that would penetrate the fog and make me believe in what you've claimed. What I want to do is get in my car and drive as fast as I can back to, well, sanity. But I can't leave."

Lucius repeated, "Because of Asha."

"Because of her."

"Do you know, for the first time ever, you remind me a little of your grandfather." Lucius glanced over, expecting to see the same look of suspicion and hostility. Instead, the man merely looked sad. Lucius went on, "I miss him. Especially now."

From somewhere in the distance a night bird called. Then Dino asked, "What would you do in my position?"

That he had not expected. Lucius gave that the time it deserved. "I can't speak to you about my situation. A young man attempts suicide, wakes up in the morgue, and then claims to be somebody who died forty-nine years ago."

"It's ludicrous. Totally off-the-wall. It breaks every conceivable facet of medical protocol." He sighed again. "And yet Asha . . ."

"She challenges your position."

"She *threatens* me."

"Maybe that's what you need," Lucius said. "To be threatened."

Lucius half expected the man to rise and carry his secret tasks back up to the main house. Instead, Dino spoke with the tone of a man recently bereaved. "I lost my first wife to my job. I swore I would never let it happen again. So I shut myself away from all relationships for four years."

"Then you fell in love," Lucius offered. "With Asha."

"There's so much hanging in the balance," Dino said. "The risk I take even being up here . . ."

"I couldn't agree more," Lucius said. "You have a chance at love. Hope for a tomorrow shared with the one you care for with all your heart."

"No, I mean . . ."

When Lucius was certain Dino could not continue, he said quietly, "I know what you mean."

Dino's voice cracked. "What about my job? What about my professional standing? Even sitting here talking with you risks everything I've spent a lifetime building."

"That's not the question and you know it. If you were held by that dilemma, you wouldn't be here at all." Lucius gave him a moment to object. Then he spoke the words he wished somebody had said to him. Back when he had an opportunity for at least a few months of joy. Back before he had left the only woman he'd ever loved weeping in her mother's arms and driven away. "Asha is not asking you for perfection. She is asking that you trust her to know what she's doing. Even when it doesn't make sense. Especially then. She is asking you to give your love a chance."

Dino rose from his chair with the slow effort of a very old man. "Now you're the counselor and I'm the patient."

Lucius shook his head. "No. We're just two friends trying to find our way down an unmarked road."

Dino looked at him. In some respects Lucius felt as though it was the first time he saw Lucius at all. He started to speak, then turned and headed inside.

The word hung there in the dark after he was gone. Friends.

CHAPTER 63

Asha was making tea when Dino came in from the garden. "How did it go?"

"All right, I suppose." He rubbed his face. "What a day."

She was happy to see her hand remained steady as she lifted the brass kettle. "Like some?"

"I suppose it would be a good idea. Asha, come sit down."

But she felt too vulnerable, too afraid to accept whatever he had to say. "Let me fill the pot, then we can talk before we go back upstairs."

Dino pulled back a chair. "One moment. Please."

"Jessica is waiting."

"She'll just have to wait a little longer." When she was seated, he drew a chair up close to hers, and sat so their knees almost touched. "I am so very, very sorry."

It was ridiculous that a man could cause her to weep like this. She was forced to cradle her face with both hands and then settle down upon her thighs. She had told herself repeatedly that she was going to be strong. No matter what. And now here she was, sobbing so hard she feared she would not be able to hear what he said.

She would, in fact, probably have missed a very great deal. But Dino leaned over so that his face was in her hair, and his mouth very close to her ear. "You have entranced me since the moment you walked into my world. Sometimes late at night I find myself reliving that first hour together. You were so beautiful, so alive, so brilliant. And so uncertain of your potential. I listened to you talk and I knew, without a shred of doubt, that you would soon fly off to heights I could only dream of."

Stop, stop. Only she was not saying it to him. She was telling herself to stop crying and draw a decent breath and find the strength to raise herself back up so she was seated like an adult. Able to see him. And hold him.

"It's true. And what was more, I wanted to help you grow those wings. I thought there would be nothing finer than helping you leap into the sky, then be there to welcome you back to earth."

It was, of course, the most beautiful thing anyone had ever said to her. And spoken by the man she most wanted to hear say it. But she could not respond. She was still having trouble finding enough air to weep.

"For the past four years all I've had to live for is my work." He stroked her hair, with long, slow caresses down to where he could gently touch her neck and wet cheeks, then again. "When you told me of your findings, all I could see was how this threatened everything I had built up. I was terrified. I acted out of fear. When I watched you leave the boardroom, I was torn in two. My head said I was making the only logical move. My heart . . ."

Gradually her sobs eased. Tight little shudders ran through her body, then vanished. She sniffed and lifted her head far enough to wipe her nose. She wanted to tell him not to stop stroking her. But there was no need.

Dino went on talking. "The university did exactly as I expected, which is to bring together all their big guns and take aim at . . ."

His hesitation over the word was exactly what she needed. Asha forced her hands to press down on her knees, lifting her face up to the light. Only then did she realize that Dino's face was wet as well. She spoke the name softly. "Lucius."

He nodded. "Lucius."

Her vision threatened to dissolve once more. Impatiently she wiped her eyes. Determined to see him. To absorb everything about this moment.

"Lucius," he said again. "He asked me to be his friend. To earn his trust. By coming inside and telling you what I should have said there in the president's boardroom. That you were right and I was wrong. That either we are servants of the truth, or our profession has no meaning."

The distance between them was unbearable. She reached for him and said, "I love you."

CHAPTER 64

Lucius was woken at noon by a knock on the sliding glass doors. He had sat there for hours by the pool, watching the lights in the kitchen and Jessica's bedroom. Twice he had walked past the kitchen windows, observing Dino and Asha drinking tea at the vast kitchen table and strategizing and phoning around and waking up people. The only time they had spoken with him was to ask for the name of his attorney. Otherwise he had been politely but firmly shut out of everything. "Yes?"

"Sorry to disturb you, Mr. Lucius. But Ms. Asha, she says to tell you, 'The people are arriving in an hour.'" Consuela set his breakfast tray on the veranda table. "I am thanking you again for all you are doing. This place, it has come alive. Ms. Jessica, when I take her the tray an hour ago, she smiles and she says 'thank you'! Can you imagine? I spend two years in this place, chased by echoes and maybe ghosts. Now I am told, go and cook for all these people!"

Lucius watched her depart, poured himself a mug of coffee, and went inside for his pad and pen. Consuela's words had carried a message. Either that, or the knock on his door had served as his alarm.

He did not need to be a part of their conversation to know it was time to plan.

He stared at the pool's still waters, and forced his mind to walk down the lonely path. Beyond this lovely morning and the prospect of seeing Jessica again. Out past everything that made sense of his new existence. Into the shadows of tomorrow.

When he was ready, he started making his list.

An hour later, Lucius was standing on the top step as a helicopter shook the air over the house and descended onto the front lawn. Dino was still upstairs reviewing Jessica's medical records. Lucius saw Asha shiver as a tall, gaunt African American emerged from the rear door. "What's the matter?"

"That's Walter Douglas."

"I know that's Douglas. You were the one who said we needed him."

"You don't understand. He's the head of the UCLA Department of Psychiatry and the world's foremost Jungian psychoanalyst." Asha shivered again. "I don't believe this is happening."

"Believe it," Lucius grumbled. "I could buy a Bentley for what it's cost to get him here on such short notice. Don't you think I should know why he's here?"

"Jessica will tell you when she's good and ready," Asha replied, and descended the steps.

The man topped out at almost seven feet. His angular form and measured gait really did carry a birdlike quality. "Ms. Meisel?"

Asha's voice held a slight tremor. "Thank you so much for coming, sir. This is . . ."

"Lucius," he supplied.

The man's fingers were long enough to wrap around Lucius's hand. He examined Lucius for a long moment, then demanded, "Where is the patient?"

* * *

Dr. Douglas insisted upon interviewing Jessica alone, minus even the nurse. Asha set up the video camera, then retreated to the upstairs corridor.

Fifteen minutes later, Lucius stood alone on the graveled drive when Sol Feinnes emerged from the limo. "Thank you for coming."

"You didn't need to send a limo."

"I didn't. Dr. Barbieri and Asha did."

Sol halted in the process of climbing the front stairs. "The therapists who want to lock you up?"

"Not anymore."

"What is going on here?"

"I have no idea. They won't tell me."

Once inside the portal, Sol lowered his voice and said, "Yesterday afternoon the university officially requested a court order to have you locked up. They claim you are a severe risk to one of the most vulnerable members of our community. They have managed to obtain an immediate court hearing."

"When is it scheduled for?"

"In two days. And I must warn you, if word gets out that you are here, tomorrow could be your last day of freedom for some time." When Lucius did not respond, Sol added, "If the court rules against you, incarceration begins immediately. All my appeals will be lodged while you are residing in the hospital's secure wing."

"I can't think about that right now." Lucius pointed up the stairs. "See what they want. I'll be in the office. Come see me when you're done."

Half an hour later, the unusually tall man emerged from the bedroom and accepted their offer of coffee. He drank it standing in the corridor, idly smoothing down his tie with the hand not holding his mug. "Most remarkable. Ms. Meisel, during the journey north I studied your summary article on this young man. I also reviewed the videos you and Dr. Barbieri kindly forwarded. I must say, you appear quite young for the level of work I've seen here. You have been a therapist for how long?"

"Actually, sir, I have not yet received my master's."

"Is that so?" He turned to Dino. "You are her thesis supervisor, correct?"

"I am."

He glanced at how they held hands. "And more besides, I assume. Did you assist her in the preparation of this work?"

"On the contrary," Dino said. "I fought her every step of the way. To my shame."

Asha said, "He has been a positive influence on my training from day one."

"Most remarkable," Douglas repeated. He continued to flatten his tie. "It may interest you to know, Ms. Meisel, that I sit on the *Journal*'s review board. I was alerted to your possible article submission, as it falls within my area of interest. I intend to urge the board to publish your work. I would ask that you consider adding one final paragraph to your conclusion."

Asha felt almost giddy in her joy. "Of course."

"You may quote me as saying that the medical world has ignored the field of near-death experiences for far too long. Simply because these events probe the boundaries of our profession does not excuse this willful blindness. We are being confronted on an almost-daily basis with evidence for which we do not have answers. It is time for us to begin gathering and collating these events."

"I agree," Dino said. "I only wish I had reached this conclusion earlier."

Douglas tilted his head slightly, as though wishing to observe Asha from a different angle. "Have you ever considered applying to medical school?"

When Asha seemed incapable of responding, Dino replied for her. "She and I have recently been discussing this."

"As head of my department, I participate in the admissions review board."

"He's speaking of the UCLA School of Medicine," Dino reminded her. "Where your father works."

"Were you to decide to apply, I, for one, would view your application in the most positive light."

Asha became frozen in an amber of joy.

Walter Douglas surveyed the impact of his words with evident satisfaction, then said, "Now if you don't mind, I'd like to have a word with the young man in question."

CHAPTER 65

When Lucius was finally allowed to join the others in Jessica's bedroom, it was so this tall gentleman could interview him. Asha positively glowed as she set up her video recorder and then seated herself next to Dino. Walter Douglas was perhaps the most intense man Lucius had ever met. He leaned in close throughout, his gaunt frame folded like a caramel-colored stork. Lucius could see a light spray of freckles beneath his dark skin, see the tight silver curls woven into his hair, see the intensity that overlay his every word and gesture. But there was no hostility, nor distance, nor any apparent desire to doubt what Lucius said.

Douglas led him through a review of his first moments upon awakening inside the morgue, then the first days. Every time he obtained what he sought, Douglas nodded once and shifted Lucius forward with another precise question.

Lucius responded without hesitation. He found no need to deflect or defend. Without apology he spoke of his early animosity toward Dino. He described his experiences with Sonya the previous Sunday as a turning point. Jessica watched him with a thoughtful gaze. She lay in the bed, on top of the covers, propped up on four pillows. Her face had lost some of its burdens. She looked utterly calm. At peace. Even happy.

Douglas finished by asking, "What is it you intend to do now?"

That was, by far, the easiest question of all. "I'm waiting for you people to tell me."

"It's very simple, really," Jessica said. "Find whatever needs doing, and do it."

An hour later, Sol Feinnes found Lucius poring through Jessica's annual reports and sorting the stacks of unopened correspondence. When Lucius started to clear a stack of correspondence from one of the chairs, he said, "Leave it. I won't be staying that long."

"Will you tell me what's going on?"

"Jessica wants to do that herself." Sol smiled. "She is one amazing lady."

"At least we agree on that point."

"I retract what I said upon my arrival. Three recognized professionals have now stated for the record that they will stand in your corner, if the university is so unwise as to take the matter to open court."

Lucius stifled his desire for a more complete update. "I'm glad."

"You don't sound glad. You sound impatient."

"I hate being left out of everything." When Sol merely smiled once more, he added, "I'm the one who brought you people in on this!"

"Let Jessica explain." Sol glanced at his watch. "I'm due in court in two hours."

"How convenient."

"The lady will tell you when she's good and ready." Sol reached across the desk. "Thank you for allowing me to be a part of this. It's been a pleasure. And I mean that sincerely."

CHAPTER 66

For the remainder of that afternoon, the house hummed to a tune that Lucius could not quite hear. He joined the others for an early dinner and endured the quiet sense of repressed excitement that infected everyone else, even Sarah. He did not object, nor make demands. But it was hard, this waiting. He disliked having lost the sense of control, and knew it hearkened back to his previous state. And something more. Beneath the flow of plans and excitement lurked a darker current, one he suspected only he was aware of.

When the sunset began to stretch shadows across the rear lawn, Sarah emerged to say that Jessica had awoken and was asking for him. As he passed the closed office door, he heard Asha and Dino talking loudly on the speakerphone. It felt as though they had invaded even this fragment of his space.

When he entered the bedroom, Lucius intended to demand, to object, to complain. But he took one look at the figure seated on the chaise longue, and the whole wretched truth struck home.

Jessica was dying.

This was not some distant threat. It was happening now. Hours or days or weeks from now, she would be gone. Probably not weeks. Her hold on life was so tenuous every breath seemed an achievement. Neither the cream silk outfit nor the carefully coiffed hair nor the smile mattered. Lucius wondered how he had remained willfully blind to this fact, but he did not ask why it had come to him now. He knew. Jessica was the woman in control of everything. She had a purpose. His being allowed here, the work of these past two days, even the reason why she had excluded him until now. It was part of her plan.

Jessica said, "You've been sulking for all this time, now you won't join me?"

Lucius forced his leaden limbs to carry him across the room. "I don't sulk."

She merely smiled and gestured with arthritic fingers at a carefully wrapped gift on the table before her. "I have something for you."

He lowered himself onto the sofa beside her. "Jessica . . ."

"Hush, now. There will be time for all that. Open your gift."

The book was by Jane Austen and bound in ancient leather with raised gold lettering. Lucius had to assume he held a first edition of *Pride and Prejudice.* "I never read this."

"There is no better time than now to start your education. Read me the first passage."

He opened the book, swallowed hard against the burn, and began, "'It is a truth universally acknowledged, that a single man in possession of a good fortune, must be in want of a wife.'"

"Words you should take to heart." She reached over, closed the book, and said, "Don't you feel like a better man already?"

The words might as well have been drawn from their earliest times together. He looked into that brilliant emerald gaze, the fire unquenched by all she endured. The one portion of her that remained untouched by years or illness or loss.

Lucius asked, "How long have you known?"

"I suspected that first moment in the dealership. I've simply observed you and allowed the impossible truth to grow on me ever since." Jessica reached out those hands, the fingers twisted and swollen, and stroked his face. "Now I must rest."

CHAPTER 67

The dinner that followed was unlike anything Lucius had ever known, and almost more than he could bear.

Asha noticed his distress, and walked over to his end of the table. "A penny for your thoughts."

Because it was Asha who asked, and because her concern was genuine, Lucius replied, "It's very hard to smile through pain."

She drew out a chair and seated herself beside him. "How true."

"Don't you want to join the others?"

She smiled. "I am as joined as I could possibly be."

The kitchen was made for such a gathering as this. Consuela had room to move about freely, and she enlisted Sarah and the day Ruth as her assistants. The room echoed with multiple conversations and laughter. When the night Ruth showed up, the day Ruth showed no interest in departing. Even Sarah revealed a hesitant smile as Dino refilled her glass of wine.

Asha said, "How is Jessica?"

"Asleep. Thankfully. It's been a long day."

"Are you hungry?"

"Famished." Lucius saw a new and abiding connection within those lovely dark eyes. He added, "Everything about this evening leaves me feeling intensely guilty."

She sipped from her glass, and said, "I understand."

"I am hungry, and I'm looking forward to a wonderful meal." He stared at the glass he had held since entering the kitchen, and not yet tasted. "I have done everything I can to make Jessica's desires a reality. I have had a good day. I have prepared for what is to come. I am satisfied with my efforts."

"As you should be," Asha said.

"And yet all I feel is guilty. And sad. And . . ."

Asha smiled a welcome as Dino pulled out the chair on her other side. She took Dino's hand, entwined her fingers into his, and waited.

Lucius could read their gazes like a shared script. The reason why they were here. The message they knew he needed to receive while they were present and able to offer him the strength required to accept. He said, "Jessica is dying."

Their silent response served as well as a hundred volumes. The concern, the strength, the compassion.

Consuela chose that moment to announce, "Dinner is served."

Lucius kept to himself throughout the feast, a rainbow assortment of Mexican dishes. He observed the others and heard laughter to comments that mostly passed him by. And he struggled to breathe around a broken heart.

When they were all done, and Consuela beamed her acceptance of the gratitude and the compliments, Asha and Dino shooed the others away and cleaned up. They insisted Lucius stay where he was, which was good, because his eyesight kept filming over. As Consuela prepared to leave, she approached Lucius, murmured something in Spanish, and kissed his forehead. The warmth of her concern lingered long after the kitchen was rendered spotless and the two of them had resumed their places at the table.

Lucius waited until Dino had refilled their glasses, then said, "When Jessica and I first met, she declared I was the loneliest man that had ever drawn breath. And the neediest." He looked at the two of them seated there beside him, then quietly declared, "No longer.

"This evening, I am truly a man of sorrow and gratitude both. You have taught me. And counseled me. And come to my aid. Even when I told you I did not wish your assistance, still you came. Even when it meant risking all. I have almost no answers to the dilemmas, now and those still to come. In many cases I don't even know what questions to ask. But I have confidence that with your help I will find both."

He lifted his glass. "To friends."

CHAPTER 68

When Lucius pointed out that it was late for Asha and Dino to start back, Ruth took genuine pleasure in showing off the multitude of empty bedrooms. Once they were settled, Lucius walked back to the pool house. His bone-deep weariness served as the balm he needed. He slept until Consuela woke him at eight with a mug of coffee. After breakfast burritos and more conversation that he scarcely heard, Lucius escorted Asha and Dino down to their cars. He accepted embraces from them both, promised to phone regularly, and stood there long after the dust of their departure had settled.

Jessica slept through the next day. Lucius worked in his office, struggling to keep his mind and hands occupied. Sol Feinnes called midafternoon to announce that the university had quietly dropped their suit against him. Lucius did his best to sound sincere in his thanks.

Finally in the late afternoon Sarah came down and said Jessica was asking for him.

When he entered the bedroom, he found Jessica dressed and

seated in her chair. The night Ruth hovered just behind her. Jessica smiled a welcome and said, "That will be all, Sarah." When the door clicked shut, Jessica said, "I would like you to do something for me."

There was a wispy edge to her voice, a reedy quality that had not been present before. Or perhaps Lucius had simply not allowed himself to hear it until now. "Anything."

Of course they took his old car.

The night Ruth settled Jessica in the chair and accompanied them down in the elevator and along the side corridor and into the garage. She stood watching as they drove down the long graveled drive. Lucius disliked intensely how he had remained intentionally blind. But the moment had come to face the truth. That she needed him for something other than what he wanted, which was to live many long and happy years together. Instead, he would watch her die, as she had watched him. For a single solitary moment, as they passed through the tall stone gates, Lucius indulged in a bitter rage. The same futile pain that had engulfed him as he walked the beach and mourned a paltry life. Then it was gone. There was no room for such wasted breaths.

"My darling," she said softly. "There's something I want you to do for me."

"Anything."

"Careful. Agreeing to a contract before the terms are spelled out can be highly perilous."

"Now you sound like me."

"I should. I've been following in your footsteps now for almost fifty years." She angled herself so as to lean upon the side door and studied him. "You seem to be changing into your old self. Or is it just my fading eyesight?"

He drove the winding road through a gathering dusk. "Tell me what you want."

She shifted slightly.

"All of my holdings are being moved into a trust. One that you will head up."

Lucius nodded slowly. "I see why Douglas's presence was important."

"Vital," she agreed. "I wanted an outside specialist to confirm my lucidity. And be willing to address the matter of your own sanity, if those dolts at the university care to take things further."

"Did Douglas have any doubt of either?"

"He did not. None whatsoever. Though he confessed to being utterly flummoxed by much of what he'd heard. I told him there was nothing wrong with a bit of confusion. It aids one's digestion." Jessica gave that a moment, then asked, "Do you agree to my request?"

"I told you I would do whatever you asked."

She smiled approval. "Sol Feinnes will serve as the trust's public face. A place will be made for him on the university board. No doubt they'll object, since he's sued them twice in the past. But they'll either accept or not see another cent of my money."

Lucius disliked the topic, but he merely said, "I understand."

"You will be required to supervise all decisions regarding future investments and donations. And sign all checks. And serve as the company's chief overseer," Jessica went on.

"Jessica . . ."

"This is important, Lucius."

"And I said I will do it."

"I know you will. And that you will be excellent at it." She eased herself over to where she could rest a hand upon his shoulder. "I need to speak with you about my daughter. Carity was actually the product of one of my ex-husband's earlier dalliances. He claims the mother used Carity as a means of gaining funds. However that may be, the mother never showed any interest in raising her. Carity was not an easy child, and grew into an extremely difficult teenager. She was in and out of treatment centers for years. At least now she appears to be staying clean. Her official residence is in a trust-fund commune on Maui. She flitters about the planet, seeing the world through the lens of five-star luxury."

Lucius turned onto the main highway leading into Miramar. "I will see to her needs."

"Of course you will."

"I hate how this conversation is all about business."

She looked at him askance. "What on earth should it have been about?"

"Us."

"You silly young man. That has been the topic most precisely."

"You know perfectly well what I mean."

"Yes, Lucius. I know. You want to sit there and stare at me with those moony eyes."

"I do not have . . ." He saw her smile then. "You're laughing at me."

"Only a little," she replied. "And only because you deserve it."

"Jessica . . ."

She squeezed his arm with what strength she could manage. "I want you to set aside your sorrow for this one brief moment."

"I don't know if I can."

"Nonetheless, that is my request. Your ability to be matter-of-fact about life's calamities was a trait I always admired. I want us to share this sunset without histrionics."

"My heart is breaking," he whispered.

"And mine as well. But sorrow will not grant us a single extra hour. And giving into it will rob us of every possible joy."

He managed, "I'll try."

She settled her head upon his shoulder. "Thank you, dear one."

* * *

Jessica's breath seemed to catch in her throat as they pulled into the lot. Lucius turned off the car and watched helplessly as she struggled against some internal tempest. "What can I do?"

She held up one hand, the fingers gnarled as the pines lining the shore. *Wait.*

He was about to say they should go back, or perhaps straight to the hospital, anything except sit here and watch her suffer. Then it all eased, and she breathed once, twice, and said, "Help me down to the shore."

"I'm not sure . . ."

"Please, Lucius."

He could not deny her. His logical mind held no sway. He rose from the car, then opened the rear door to bring out her chair.

She said softly, "Be a dear and carry me."

Drawing her from the car was not easy, for she seemed incapable of helping in any way. But once she was in his arms, she felt not just light, but settled into the position he had waited a lifetime to experience. She nestled her head into the crook of his neck and said nothing as they approached the shore.

The sea was utterly calm, the beach empty save for a few gulls. The wind was silent, the air crystal clear. Dusk painted a rose-tinted froth across the western sky.

Then the fireflies joined them. A cloud of blinking lights swirled around his face. "Jessica, look."

She lifted her gaze and whispered, "Falling stars. Hurry, Lucius. Make a wish."

And she was gone.

A READING GROUP GUIDE

FIREFLY COVE

Davis Bunn

ABOUT THIS GUIDE

The suggested questions are included to enhance your group's reading of Davis Bunn's *Firefly Cove*!

DISCUSSION QUESTIONS

1. What do you think of the fact that Lucius was given a second chance? Was fate cruel or kind to Lucius, or both? How so?

2. Do you believe that true love transcends time and age? What do you think of the love between Lucius and Jessica?

3. Solitude was something that Lucius intensely disliked, and yet he also sought it out. He had grown up with it, he knew it, and when things became more difficult than they already were, Lucius retreated there. Can you identify with the struggle Lucius has over this issue?

4. Why does Lucius break up with Jessica? If you were in his shoes, would you have done the same?

5. What impact does Lucius have on Jessica throughout her life? How is her life changed by him—beginning, middle, and end?

6. Have you ever known someone who came close to death and returned, or read accounts of people who have experienced this? What do you think of this phenomenon?

7. There is a wide-ranging debate these days about NDE, as near-death experiences are known inside the medical profession. Some doctors and biochemists think that NDE does not occur at all. Instead, a new theory suggests that as the brain shuts down it emits strong electronic and chemical impulses that the conscious mind interprets as a new reality. What do you think of this more scientific explanation?

8. Who is Luke and who is Lucius? How are they different? If they had met, what would they have thought of

each other? They were each dealt a completely different hand by fate. Ultimately, who is the more fortunate?

9. In the Miramar Bay novels, the place itself is treated almost as a character in its own right. What do you think this says about the town? Do you believe such a place actually exists? If it does, would you want to go there?

10. Over time Lucius discovers the power of friendship, and does so with an eclectic assortment of people. At the end of the story, who do you think are Lucius's best friends? Have you ever faced such a situation where you found friends in the most unexpected of places?

11. Early in the story, Jessica describes Lucius as "the loneliest man on God's green earth." What makes her say this? Does Lucius change over the course of the story, and if so, how? Is he still the loneliest man on God's green earth at the end of the book?

12. What is the significance of the fireflies in this story, or do they have any significance? Do you believe in fireflies?